A Covenant With Life
Clifford Blair

magnificat press
Avon-by-the-Sea, New Jersey

A Covenant With Life
©1987 Clifford Blair
All rights reserved
Printed in the United States of America
ISBN 0-940543-04-4
Magnificat Press
Avon-by-the-Sea, NJ 07717

The characters and events in this story are fictional. Any resemblance to any persons, living or dead, is unintentional.

Dedication

To Alma—my editor, my friend, my love, my wife. The Lord has blessed.

About the Author

Clifford Blair is an attorney and bank trust officer residing in Norman, Oklahoma. He is married and has two grown children. He teaches an adult Sunday School class, and his hobbies include archery and martial arts. He and his wife have spent time as lay missionaries in Puerto Madero, Mexico, where much of *A Covenant With Life* is set. He is the author of a number of short stories and professional articles.

Prologue

The face frozen on the large TV screen in the darkened room was handsome, the gaze clear, direct, and engaging. Eric Braden recognized the man immediately—Senator Preston Gates. His attention quickened.

Braden, though he had been out of the country almost continually over the past few months, had heard reports of how Gates, keeping his campaign promises, had launched a comprehensive program to eliminate what the Senator called the two major sins of big government—immorality and illegality. It was an effort that had raised eyebrows in more than one center of entrenched governmental power, not the least of which were certain elements of the intelligence community, of which Braden was a member.

Gates was a relative newcomer to political office, although the qualifications were certainly there. An attorney with a masters in political science, he had held two major positions in the the Department of Defense prior to running for office.

His campaign had emphasized a certain hawkish bent toward the subject of national defense, as well as a tendency to appeal to the fundamentalist religious beliefs found among his supporters. All of this had made him quite appealing to voters of the Southwestern state he now represented in the Senate.

And that appeal was very much evident in the faces of the crowd surrounding Gates in the frozen frame of the video tape projected on the screen. But why was he, Braden, being shown this tape at all?

The sepulchral voice of Andruss answered the mental query out of the darkness, as if the man had somehow divined Braden's very thoughts. "This is the speech Senator Gates made earlier in the week. There is one segment that I—that is, the Operation, finds particularly disturbing."

The Operation, Braden thought, an innocuous, euphemistic name for the clandestine troubleshooting branch of American intelligence which acted as protector, bodyguard and nursemaid for the more highly profiled Central Intelligence Agency.

The agents of the Operation lived in a netherworld of lies and betrayal where sin was the foundation of life, and danger its very cornerstone. Over the years of Braden's association, he had not only learned to survive in this netherworld, but actually to thrive in it, living life on a razor edge like that of an assassin's dagger.

The Operation existed to take on the jobs and execute the missions which the CIA, crippled in past years by ruthless media and Congressional exposure, was unable or unwilling to handle. Agents of the Operation were assigned to bail their bigger sister out of trouble, to cover her tracks, to stand in for her in discouraging unwanted suitors, always avoiding any kind of exposure, always working behind the scenes. And as Director of the Operation, Andruss wielded an all but omnipotent power over its agents, Eric Braden among them.

The click of a remote control unit cut off Braden's reverie. The tape began to play, the sound track catching Gates in midsentence.

"...and during my years in the Defense Department, I began to realize that there exists a subversive web of covert intelligence organizations ostensibly operating under the auspices of the ...Federal government, but actually playing a free hand without Congressional and frequently without ...Presidential approval. The activities of these seemingly autonomous agencies are both domestic and international. They routinely engage in practices that are at best questionable, and at worst blatantly illegal, governed only by their own distorted views of what best serves the country.

"I hold our government agencies accountable. They need to work within our legal system, not outside it at the whim of their amoral 'end-justifies-the-means' mentalities. I am in the process of accumulating evidence of these illegal activities, documented proof of what can only be called atrocities committed in the name of our government both at home and abroad. Soon I will have a case strong enough to instigate a ...Congressional investigation into this matter, and to force ..."

Andruss again caught Gates in midsentence as he hit another button controlling the audio portion of the tape. Braden stood watching the fervent countenance of the Senator silently continue to deliver the remainder of his passionate speech as the tape rolled on.

After a moment, he turned toward the figure looming in the darkness. "So?" he said flatly. "Political rhetoric. Gates has just jumped on a popular bandwagon along with half the other politicians these days. Next week or year he'll go on to something else."

"We believe Gates is different," Andruss responded. "Granted, his is a popular theme. But our research on the man, our evaluation of him, indicates that this is somewhat of a cause to him. Remarkably, he appears to be making every effort to follow up on his campaign promises. He is already seeking to have a special committee, answerable directly to the President, seated to look into what he calls the 'insidious evil' of covert, extralegal intelligence operations."

Braden wished he could see the other man's face, although, admittedly, Andruss' austere features generally defied any effort at discerning his thoughts. Still, Braden wondered where Andruss was going with this. "So what?" he said aloud. "We've weathered Congressional inquiries before."

He might not have spoken for all the attention Andruss gave him. "The Defense people are listening to him. They'd like to see some of our activities curtailed to a certain extent, since there is always the risk of inadvertent adverse publicity causing a public backlash against further Defense spending. Gates has also gained bipartisan support for his efforts in both houses. He comes from a wealthy family and is very persuasive. He is still young enough to appeal to the baby-boom yuppies, but is also able to gain the support of the middle- and upper-age segments. One computer projection we ran showed him to be a likely choice for President in eight years."

The slight curl to Andruss' disembodied voice left no doubts as to his views on such a development. "Gates is a very popular man," he continued. "And very dangerous to us and to the Operation. We would not care to undergo any kind of probe spearheaded by him. He is too dedicated to 'his cause.'"

Braden seemed to feel an icy breath play chillingly over him. He did not want to confront the sudden intuitive realization growing inside him, but he now knew where this briefing was headed. On the screen Gates continued to harangue his crowd of followers.

The Senator looked strong and fit—probably worked out regularly. Braden looked away from the screen and stared into the darkness.

"Even in a relatively minor position in the Defense Department, Gates was getting uncomfortably close to uncovering some details of our particular branch of the intelligence system," Andruss resumed. "That is why I pulled a few strings and arranged to have him quietly reassigned and then dismissed. It was my sincere hope that he would avail himself of the opportunity to quit government work and go into private practice. Unfortunately, Gates was astute enough to perceive what had happened. He ran for the Senate, was elected, and appears to be pursuing that matter again with a vengeance. We simply cannot afford to have him serve out the rest of his term."

"So we kill him," Braden cut him off with cold deliberation, abruptly tired of Andruss' verbose rationalization of proposed murder.

"I really fail to see that we have any choice." Andruss was unperturbed. "It is regrettable that there is not another option available to us. But I have frankly exhausted all my indirect resources in attempting to alleviate this problem, to no avail. Direct action seems to be the only course open to us."

"Doesn't the man have any weaknesses, any vices?" Braden could hear the irritation in his own voice. "Something we could use as a lever against him? Some way to set him up?" My God, he thought, was he really sitting here discussing the relative merits of murdering a United States Senator as opposed to blackmailing him?

"Nothing." Andruss' voice carried a note of dismissal. "He appears to be happily married, is quite active in church, and has no personal vices to speak of. We have tried on more than one occasion to place him in — shall we say — compromising positions, twice with young girls and once with narcotics. None of it worked. The efforts only seemed to fuel his ardor."

Braden was glad Andruss had not gone into detail on the setup attempts. "There must be some other method short of killing him," he protested.

"No," Andruss cut him off with grim finality. "It is not like you to question my analysis of a situation, Eric."

Braden remained silent. He wondered if Andruss could see his face in the darkness.

"We will need this matter taken care of as soon as possible," Andruss went on after a moment. "The longer we wait, the more serious the consequences of Gate's probing may be. We also want it done outside of the country by terrorists or some similar organization so there will be no possible chance of it being traced back to us."

Andruss paused as if expecting some comment from Braden. Receiving none, he began to speak again. "These factors limit our opportunities, particularly within the time frame we are concerned with. However, Gates is scheduled to leave in two days with his wife and family on a junket to England. I have arranged for you to be attached to his party as a special security advisor. While in London, you will make contact with a group of Palestinians—a renegade faction of the PLO—who have been making overtures toward what remains of the IRA with some thought as to a union of their organizations."

As always, Braden strove to force his mind into a neutral mode, to concentrate solely on the technicalities of the situation Andruss described, without regard for its ramifications. Emotion, he had learned long ago, was a liability, a hindrance to his performance as an agent. But the implications of Andruss' words, like subtle scalpels, sliced unrelentingly at the layers of his dispassion.

The thought of the two terrorist organizations forming one unholy alliance spawned its own creeping horror. But the final madness was Andruss' calm directives for him to work with them as ally.

"The Palestinians have indicated a willingness to help us in this matter." Andruss' tone was detached, that of a lecturer addressing a rather dry topic. "It is they who will perform the actual — ah — assassination. Your job will be to coordinate matters, to see to it that they have the opportunity to carry it out."

Braden did not trust himself to speak. He felt a deadening numbness creep over him and realized he had been slowly shaking his head in a mute denial of what he heard. Had Andruss seen the movement?

"You are, of course, quite proficient in coordinating these matters and in carrying them out, so I wouldn't presume to intrude on your expertise, but I have studied the matter a bit."

Andruss paused as a prelude to his advice. "On the third day of his visit, Gates and his family will take part in a motorcade with the Crown Prince and his wife. The course they follow will take them through Piccadilly Circus, where a number of streets converge. These streets will, of course, be blocked off. However, if it could be arranged for one street to be left briefly unguarded, I believe a car loaded with explosives could slip through and intercept the motorcade. The driver would, in all likelihood, be killed, but the Palestinians seem to go in for such self-destructive methods of achieving their goals. Do you have any questions, Eric?"

Braden forced himself to reply. "No, sir." Was this what I fought in Viet Nam for? he asked himself bitterly.

"Very well. A file with further details will be provided for you. I might mention that if we do not succeed in our effort while the Senator is in London, we will not have another chance until he makes a brief trip to Central America some months from now. It would not be to our advantage to wait that long, given the current state of affairs."

Andruss plainly expected some kind of response. "Yes, sir." Braden said tonelessly.

"You will need to have a brief interview with Senator Gates upon joining his retinue," Andruss concluded. "For some reason he requires that of all those who are attached to him in any official capacity. It is regrettable that you cannot bring matters to a successful resolution then, when you're alone with the man."

Braden recalled Andruss' words the next day when he met Preston Gates in the Senator's Washington office for his private interview. If anything, Gates was more impressive in person than on the screen. A rugged vitality seemed to emanate from the man. And there was something more, what seemed almost an aura of presence, of purpose, that was not to be denied. Braden could sense the strength of the man's will and resolve.

Gates was inches taller than Braden—perhaps taller than Andruss, who topped Braden's six feet by a good three inches. When he came from behind his desk to shake Braden's hand, his grip was firm and hinted of latent power.

"Eric Braden. I understand you're to manage the security provisions for our trip." As he spoke, Gates ushered Braden to a seating arrangement of easy chairs and a couch in a corner of the office.

Actually I'm here to coordinate your assassination, Senator, Braden thought bitterly. He was careful to keep his face expressionless as he made polite response to the amenities.

"Which of our intelligence agencies are you with, Eric?" Gates asked once they were seated. "It wasn't too clear in the memorandum I received on you."

Braden gave his carefully constructed cover story of being an independent security advisor attached to the Central Intelligence Agency. The story would withstand any checks Gates could initiate. A perverse irony somewhere there, Braden had refelected, in using one espionage organization as a cover for one even more clandestine.

"I imagine there's some ill-will on the part of many of your colleagues at the direction some of my activities are taking," Gates ventured.

"I suppose so, sir," Braden tried to keep his voice noncommittal. He did not understand the purpose behind this interview and was impatient for it to be over with. He did not want to like this man he had been ordered to kill. But, despite himself, he felt drawn to Gates' obvious sincerity and integrity.

"No hard feelings on your part, I trust, though?" Gates' grin was open and engaging.

"No, sir."

Gates chuckled. "That's good. I've reached the point where I wonder if you fellows are for me or against me. I almost expect a CIA hit squad to target me any day now."

Braden felt himself tense ever so lightly. Did the man know? He met the guileless gaze openly and in it was only humor. He looked away without answering.

Gates' expression became serious as he studied Braden then. "What do you think about God, Eric?" he asked after a moment.

Braden stared at him blankly, nonplused. "He and I don't have much to do with one another, I guess," he said finally.

"I think you're wrong, Eric, if you could only see that." There was a fervor in Gates' voice that had not been there even during his speeches condemning the American intelligence structure.

The man was a fanatic, Braden thought. But everything about Gates, from his intelligence and charm to his obvious dedication, belied that idea.

He gazed at Braden with disarming intensity. "Do you ever go to church, Eric?"

"No, sir." Braden had recovered enough to answer woodenly.

"Do you own a Bible?"

Braden thought of his modest library in his house. There was a Bible there with the other literature. "Yes."

"Good," Gates said with satisfaction. "Do you ever read it much?"

"No, sir." How long was this absurd interrogation to last? Braden wondered.

Gates' expression had turned thoughtful. "You know, you might try reading it. Take it with you when we go to London." His penetrating gaze seemed to discern Braden's derisive thoughts. "And if you should happen to forget it, there'll be a Gideon's Bible in your hotel room. Begin in the New Testament; read one chapter a day and pray that God will reveal himself to you through His Word."

The man's intensity was disconcerting. Braden wanted to draw back, to break a strange spell which seemed to have ensnared him, but he felt himself caught, held immobile.

"Let me give you a few verses to start with," Gates went on. "Think about what they mean to you personally. Romans 3:23 tells us that '...all have sinned and come short of the glory of God.' "

Braden felt the words go into him like a knife. He fought to keep his face straight as Gates continued implacably.

"And over in John 14:6 Jesus said, 'I am the way, the truth, and the life; no man cometh unto the Father but by me.' And finally, Romans 10:9 lays it out plainly, 'If thou shalt confess with thy mouth the Lord Jesus, and shalt believe in thine heart that God hath raised Him from the dead, thou shalt be saved.' Remember those verses, Eric. They may be the most important thing you ever hear. And start reading the New Testament tonight, like I suggested, then maybe we can talk a little bit more about it later." Gates drew back slightly. "I like to have these little talks with the people who work for me. I think it helps things."

"Yes, sir."

Braden made it a point not to read his Bible that night. Nor did he bother to check his hotel room for a Bible in the few spare moments he had once they reached London. He found himself working hard to avoid direct contact with Gates whenever possible. In truth, it was not difficult, since the Senator's schedule was a busy one, and most of Braden's time was occupied with the myriad details of planning and putting into place a comprehensive security system, because the security precautions had to be authentic; to do less than a professional job would only arouse suspicion when the system failed at a single crucial point.

Andruss, as usual, had been correct in his evaluation, Braden discovered as he immersed himself in studying options and strategies. Piccadilly Circus was like the hub of a giant wheel with a number of converging streets as its spokes. The motorcade bearing Gates, his wife, and two young daughters, as well as the Crown Prince and his glamorous wife, would emerge from one street, pass diagonally across the hub, and exit opposite its point of entry. A dozen cars would be involved and the Circus itself would doubtless boast an admiring crowd held at bay by bobbies and barricades. The other streets would be blocked by police cars or U.S. military vehicles. A good enough setup and fairly standard procedure in the terrorist-conscious London of these days. But like any system, it could be circumvented by duplicity from within.

A car laden with explosives, coming fast down one of the converging streets at a strategic time, would have a clear shot at the motorcade and the limousine bearing Preston Gates and his family, provided, that is, that there were no roadblocks to prevent access to the Circus itself, and provided the driver was willing to risk almost certain self-destruction in the ensuing explosion.

The driver was. Braden made contact with the Palestinians in a seamy backwater district of London late the first night in that city. There were five of them, housed in a rat-infested tenement that looked like a relic of the Blitz. The building stank of fear and dissolution and despair. There were no other occupants, the terrorist leader, Ahmed, told Braden with a scabrous grin. He and his men had seen to it. Braden did not ask for details, and Ahmed did not volunteer them.

Ahmed was a short, wiry man with a grin that split his sparse beard and hinted at the twisted decadence of the man's mind. He was the only one of the terrorists Braden considered a pro. The other four were scum, degenerates and perverts who made even Braden's flesh crawl.

Ahmed had been trained in violence, perhaps in Cuba or Libya, and although belief in the Palestinian cause might partially motivate him, he almost certainly was receiving high wages from some source for his mercenary skills.

The others, Braden realized, were psychos, nutcases to whom the cause or whatever payment they received were only excuses, licenses to engage in the senseless violence and mayhem they craved. More than once in his career Braden had come up against such men in the dark secret war in which they were all combatants. Now, he thought with a cold sickness, they were his allies. What had happened to the idealism that had prompted him to become a United States secret agent? To the earnest desire to change the world for the better?

"Your plan is excellent," Ahmed said in his sibilant, accented English after hearing Braden's explanation and studying an annotated map of that part of the city. "You think like one of us, Braden. You should join our ranks." He grinned his decadent grin across the dilapidated table at which they sat.

I already have, Braden thought, and felt the nausea heave up within him. "I'll pass," he said aloud. "Will you have any problem acquiring a vehicle or explosives?"

Ahmed's smirk told him how stupid the question had been.

"What about a driver?" he forced himself to continue.

"We have a brother in Allah who has been waiting for such an opportunity." Ahmed's inflection gave just the slightest touch of scorn to the religious reference. He raised his voice. "Syed."

The man — almost a boy, actually — who entered the room was taller than Ahmed and handsome, with smooth, dark skin and curly, black hair. He wore cheap casual clothes, as did Ahmed, and had an Israeli-made Uzi submachine gun slung over his shoulder with studied casualness. Apparently the Palestinians' anti-Jewish beliefs did not extend to any prohibition against using their weapons.

Although the single naked light bulb hanging from the ceiling cast only poor illumination, Syed halted just inside the room, blinking. Braden stared at his eyes and saw the dilated pupils. When Syed finally came forward, his movements were jerky, frenetic. A hophead, Braden thought, looking for the ultimate high. The dilated eyes had a wildness to them that was unnerving. So might have been the gazes of the Japanese Kamikaze pilots or the thugee fanatics of old India in whom self-preservation had been relegated to a minor priority.

Syed halted at the table. He did not seem to look directly at either of the men seated there. "We have a target for you, Syed," Ahmed said, almost as if he were speaking to a child. "You will drive the vehicle that will destroy an enemy of Allah. Are you prepared for this honor?"

"I will destroy the infidel dogs!" Syed cried unexpectedly. His trembling became even more pronounced.

Braden glanced sharply at Ahmed. "I wouldn't trust him on a bicycle, much less behind the wheel of a car," he said coldly.

"He will be ready to do the job when the time comes," Ahmed assured him.

Braden looked back at Syed, and those wild eyes met his. He had to resist the sudden almost overwhelming compulsion to draw his .38 and shoot this rabid animal of an Arab where he stood. Syed, plainly addicted to drugs, and clearly insane, was one of the most dangerous individuals he had ever met, Braden realized. He did not take his eyes off the man, for the sudden conviction grew in him that should he do so, Syed would unlimber the Uzi and turn it on him, or else lunge for his throat with throttling hands and rending teeth.

"Syed! Leave us!" Ahmed's voice cracked like a whip.

For a moment Syed stood frozen, even his tremors disappearing. Braden tensed. And then the young Arab turned his head, spat onto the filthy floor, then wheeled and left the room. Braden kept his eyes on him until he had disappeared. He looked back at Ahmed. "One of your holy warriors?" he asked drily.

Ahmed would not be provoked. "Syed does not like Americans," he apologized. "As a professional, you understand. Regrettably it is sometimes necessary to work with amateurs, even unstable ones."

One pro to another. Braden felt his gorge rise. Something about Ahmed made him think suddenly of Andruss. He stood abruptly. "Make your plans," he said coldly. "But keep your mad dog on a leash until then. I'll be in touch." He turned and walked out, neither knowing nor caring if Ahmed replied.

Back in the hotel room, Braden angrily poured himself a drink. Straight Scotch. Normally he did not drink on assignment, but this was not a normal assignment. Not normal at all.

As he lifted the glass to his mouth, he saw that his hand was trembling, shaking like that of Syed, the psychotic young Arab. He set the drink down hard, untouched.

There were no answers to be found in the bottle. Even between assignments, he reflected, it was becoming harder and harder to find refuge in sleep, even with the tranquilization of alcohol. The faces of people, some dead, some living, but all, he thought, victims of his actions in one way or another, came out of the darkness to haunt his dreams. Would the faces of Preston Gates' daughters hover over him in his anguished nightmares a few nights hence?

No answers in the bottle, he thought. So where were the answers? With Preston Gates' God? He found his eyes drawn to the lamp table. Impulsively he crossed to it and yanked the drawer open. There was the Bible, just as Gates had predicted. He picked it up. And what else had Gates said? Read the New Testament? He snorted at the thought. The outdated scribblings of fanatics. Better the bottle than the empty platitudes they could offer. He slammed the Bible down on the table.

But even with the bottle, he got little sleep before the day of the motorcade. Gates' crowded schedule and the open, unaffected style of the man had made him a high security risk and kept Braden busy in his capacity as advisor and coordinator.

On one of the occasions when he had spoken personally to Gates, the Senator had commented on his haggard looks and advised him to get some rest. Braden wished he could comply with the suggestion.

Piccadilly Circus, with its bewildering display of advertisements, billboards, and buildings, was bemusing even in the daylight. At night, Braden knew, the display of blinking, flashing lights was dazzling.

Now, however, the crowds here held at bay by uniformed bobbies and wooden barriers. They lined the circumference of the Circus, pressing forward eagerly to gain choice spots from which to view the dashing American Senator and the darlings of the royal family.

Braden had been careful to see to it that the crowds did not block the mouths of the converging streets. No one — not the bobbies nor the American military personnel involved —had questioned his orders. It was almost too easy, he reflected bitterly.

He glanced at his watch as he stood near one of the barriers adjacent to the street he and Ahmed had decided on. He had met only once more with the Palestinian leader, refusing a further meeting on the excuse of the increased security risks their meetings produced. If Ahmed had detected his growing revulsion, he had not mentioned it.

Syed had not been visibly present at the meeting, for which Braden had been thankful. The face of the psychopathic young Arab had come to haunt him even during his waking hours. He scanned the crowd now, half expecting to see the man's handsome wild-eyed face glaring insanely at him.

But of course Syed would not be in sight. He would, Braden knew, already be behind the wheel of his deadly vehicle not far distant, perhaps even now negotiating the narrow streets to reach his destination. Braden looked again at his watch. He had not really seen it the first time he looked. Five minutes. By that time the motorcade should have entered the Circus and Gates' car would be almost in line with the chosen street, passing broadside to it.

He looked back over his shoulder at the heavy U.S.

military armored car parked blocking the access road. James Fletcher was behind the wheel of the vehicle, a young freckle-faced private whom Braden had chosen to be his unwitting accomplice in murder.

In a few minutes, when the motorcade entered the Circus, Braden would use his walkie-talkie to order Fletcher to move the armored car to a different location. A tragic miscalculation, he would later say, that had resulted in a means of access being opened to the fanatical Palestinian car bomber who would barrel down the unblocked street and crash his vehicle into Gates' limousine.

A minute had passed. There, he could see the first car in the motorcade making its entrance into the Circus. A restless stirring passed over the crowd. Gates and his family were in the third car. Would his daughters feel anything when the explosives-laden vehicle careered into theirs?

The second car was now visible. Braden looked at his watch. He recalled with startling clarity the moment earlier in the morning when Gates, busy in his preparations, had caught his eye. "Sorry we haven't had a chance to have another talk," he said to Braden. "But if you get a chance, try reading the Bible like I mentioned. We can visit about it later if you'd like."

Braden had turned wordlessly away. Now he could see Gates' car clearly. Little American flags flew from the hood. Syed would be approaching. Braden fought the impulse to turn and look down the street behind him.

What do you think about God, Eric?

Braden lifted the walkie-talkie and thumbed the transmit button. "Private Fletcher?" he said into the voice grid.

"Yes, sir?"

"Report to me immediately. On foot."

A moment's pause. "Yes, sir." Fletcher was a good soldier.

The motorcade was well into the Circus now. The crowd noises had increased. Braden watched the cars crawl forward.

16

He could see Gates' classically handsome profile. The Senator waved at the crowd and smiled broadly.

"Private Fletcher reporting, sir," said the voice at his elbow.

Braden turned slowly and looked back down the street past the armored car. Even as he looked, a nondescript panel truck burst into sight from a side street, making the screeching turn on two wheels. It fishtailed wildly, straightened out and bore down on the armored car with a roar of supercharged acceleration that was audible to Braden even above the tumult of the crowd.

"Down!" Braden shouted and hit Fletcher at the knees with a body block, taking him down, sprawling atop him, hearing his startled cry of protest, aware of his thrashing muscular body. Braden covered his head. The metallic crash of impact was an infinitesimal prelude to the explosion.

The heat and wind of the blast tore at Braden, its sound smashed at his ears. He had time for the fleeting thought that he had been right. Syed had been just crazy enough to smash his explosives-laden van full into the armored vehicle blocking his path.

Braden made it to his feet and helped a dazed Fletcher up beside him. The force of the blast had been largely blocked and absorbed by the sturdy armored car, he realized.

He and Fletcher had been nearest to the explosion. There did not appear to be any casualties among the crowd.

Thank God, Braden thought fervently, and even standing in the midst of the pandemonium which was rapidly beginning to sweep the Circus, the significance of that thought struck him rigid.

Later he would recall only vaguely the remainder of that day's events. Although the investigation would undoubtedly continue for some time, it seemed unlikely that the initial conclusion would be refuted. A psychotic terrorist, thwarted from reaching his target by the elaborate security provisions, had, in a fit of suicidal rage, driven to his own destruction.

Braden's coincidental order to Fletcher had saved the young soldier from becoming yet another U.S. military casualty of a terrorist attack. There were no fatalities, only minor injuries.

Braden's ears were still ringing slightly in the hotel room that night. He had received congratulations from Gates himself on the thoroughness of his security arrangements and the successful prevention of a terrorist attack.

But he had cut his own throat in thwarting the attempt, Braden thought. Andruss would never accept whatever story he offered to explain his failure. And, at best, his actions had only been a stopgap maneuver. Andruss would only send him or someone like him out to try again.

Braden sat and stared at the bottle and dreaded the future he could foresee in it. When the dreams got too bad, when the bottle no longer offered its treacherous solace, would he, one day, simply react too slowly to an assassin's bullet, deliberately leave himself open to the thrust of a killing knife rather than face another day in the lonely desolation of his life? Why even wait if that was the case?

He dropped his eyes to the floor. *What do you think about God, Eric?* the question asked itself in his mind. He buried his face in his hands. God, he begged silently, show me where you are. Show me how to find you.

After a time he lifted his head. Through the bottle, distorted by the amber glass, he saw the Bible lying on the lamp table where he had left it. What was it Gates had said? he wondered numbly. What were the verses he had quoted? "For all have sinned and come short... I am the way, the truth and the life... That if thou shalt confess with thy mouth the Lord Jesus and shalt believe in thine heart..."

Slowly, awkwardly, Braden reached for the Bible.

1

Andruss held the letter for a long time, his lean, austere features quite expressionless, the paper motionless in the thin fingers of his hand. At last he laid the paper back on the empty expanse of his polished desk and looked up. As ever, his dark eyes betrayed nothing. "I don't believe I quite understand."

"It should be plain enough. I'm quitting. That's my letter of resignation." In his own ears Braden's voice sounded as emotionless as that of Andruss himself.

The older man did not respond immediately. He looked back down at the letter as if to reread it, but Braden knew that in that first glance the full contents of the instrument had been absorbed as completely as data keyed into a computer terminal by an expert. He watched as Andruss' long fingers, like enormous hairless spiders, shifted the paper, precisely centering it on the desk—no pens, no papers, no blotter, not even a phone, just the single sheet of paper constrained by those arachnoid fingers.

Was there ever anything on that desk? Eric Braden wondered. Did Andruss conceal whatever he was working on whenever he summoned one of his agents into his presence? Or did he simply sit behind that cleared desk, his enigmatic mind functioning on some plane of its own, engaged in the delicate machinations that all too often sent men like Braden out into the merciless kill zone of the midnight world in which they lived and loved, fought and died?

He wanted to shift his weight, but to do so would only be to alert Andruss to the tension coiling within him that made him exert a conscious effort not to grit his teeth or let his hands clench into fists.

There was no place to sit, indeed, no other furniture at all in the sterile office — only the metallic desk with Andruss looming behind it, grim, and dark, and foreboding. Andruss could dominate most meetings of which he was a part by the sheer raw force of his character.

Braden felt the impact of that charged vitality now as Andruss directed his gaze up at him. "You realize, of course, that this is against Operational Policy."

Not a question, and Braden did not respond because there was no question but that he was beyond the nebulous restrictive boundaries of the enigma called Operational Policy. He did not know of anyone who had ever resigned from the Operation. He also knew that he had to do it.

"If you no longer desire and are no longer capable of field work, you will be retired from it and assigned an administrative position." Andruss might have been and probably was quoting from some obscure manual. "Certainly you are qualified."

"I'm not talking about retiring from field work," Braden said slowly. "I'm resigning, quitting, leaving your employ."

Andruss seemed not to hear him. "You have been one of our top agents for over twelve years now. The Operation recruited you following your tour in Viet Nam with the Special Forces, as I recall. Your survival index and field apti-tude have remained consistently high. You have been a major asset to the Operation, one that will be difficult to replace. Further, our policy just does not permit an agent to resign. I think you should reconsider this move very carefully."

"I don't give— I don't care about your policy," Braden snapped. "I don't need to reconsider. I've made up my mind.

What might have been distaste flicked across those harsh features. Andruss made some indetectable adjustment to the position of the letter on his desk, then regarded Braden coldly. "I suppose there really is no avoiding the underlying cause of all this — your religious experience." He said the last two words as if shaping them actually hurt his mouth.

Braden felt himself slipping, felt his iron control weakening. "It wasn't a 'religious experience.' I was born again, saved. There's a difference."

Andruss' gesture was a study in contempt. "Semantics, Braden. Word games. That is really beneath you, you know."

"No games. I've been reborn." In his own ears Braden's words sounded trite, pedantic, a meaningless litany recited by rote. "I've committed my life to Christ—"

The look of scornful pity in Andruss' eyes cut him off cold, and the feeling of hopelessness seemed to overwhelm him. Why was it so hard, he wondered despairingly, to speak of the one thing that had so recently become centermost in his life, so difficult to tell others of the miraculous changes within his very soul? He could expound at length on methods of toppling a Communist-backed dictator, speak with authority on ways to kill a man with a single blow, but when it came to this subject the words escaped him, left him all but stammering in his inability to communicate what he knew and felt. Was it like this for every new Christian? Or had his background, the unsavory life of deceit and violence he had led, made him irretrievably different?

"Let us be objective." Andruss had apparently decided to ignore his feeble efforts at witnessing. "The life of an agent is one of the most stressful that could be imagined. The tensions, the pressures, can be extremely dangerous and can produce varied results depending on the individual. You have lived with these pressures for twelve years now and have shown little or no discernible effects until recently. Obviously," Andruss paused and his dark eyes seemed to penetrate into Braden's skull, "the stress caught up with you. You are suffering from some kind of mental or nervous backlash from the years of tension you have undergone. It is understandable — and there are solutions other than resigning. Let me set up an appointment with one of our Reappraisal Teams—"

"No." Braden took cold pleasure in cutting him off for a change. "I don't need any of your trained psychotic head shrinkers probing my ego." He felt stronger, more in control of himself and the situation now that the discussion had shifted directly from the topic of his conversion.

Andruss obviously picked up on the change. He exhaled, apparently realizing that he had lost a point, if not several. "I wish you would reconsider, Braden. It will be a blow to the Operation to lose you." Staring at him, Braden felt a chill. It was Andruss' first sign at acquiescence, yet strangely Braden was only aware of a vague unease, a sense of something, somewhere, out of joint.

Andruss looked back down at the letter and pretended to read it again, although his eyes did not shuttle back and forth as they should have. A wariness stole over Braden. He felt the sense of control over this meeting slipping once more subtly away from him.

"I will make the necessary arrangements." Andruss returned his gaze to him and Braden again felt himself probed, analyzed, and somehow violated. "Some paperwork is required and certain parties must be notified." Andruss fell silent.

"Thank you," Braden heard himself say distantly. He waited a moment longer, but Andruss had looked away from him and did not seem disposed to carry the conversation further. "I'll check back with you tomorrow." Andruss ignored him. Somehow, in the very act of Andruss' capitulation, the man had gained the upper hand.

Braden was at the door when Andruss spoke again. "Until we have this finalized, I would appreciate it if you would remain silent within this organization concerning this matter. I would not like for your actions to set a precedent.

"And one other thing, Braden..."

Andruss' pause was long enough that Braden felt constrained to turn back toward him. "Yes?"

"What will you do? Where will you go once you have your freedom? Do you really believe that you can function in the civilian world after this long?"

Where would he go? Braden's mind repeated the question. Andruss was not raising a new objection, but it was easily his most telling, and, like a master strategist, he had waited until the very last moment of the confrontation to strike with it.

"There really is no place else for you, Braden." Andruss' voice had softened. "You have no home but the Operation. Surely you realize that."

And the man was right, Braden reflected. What else was there for him but the jeopardous half-life of an agent? What else had his training, his experience, prepared him for? He would be an alien in the civilian world where his skills at survival — so essential to him as an agent — would be worthless or perhaps, even worse, a liability.

"The Lord provides," he said, but could not have told from where the words came or why they seemed to instill in him such a sense of peace.

Andruss' mouth tightened almost imperceptibly. "Very well," he said coldly. "I can see there is no dissuading you."

For a second time Braden had been dismissed. This time he made it out of the office and strode down the short, sterile corridor which connected Andruss' office with the rest of the labyrinthine headquarters of the Operation. The sterility was deceptive. The corridor, he knew, was infested with observation mechanisms and defensive devices to prevent unwanted visitors from reaching this innermost sanctum of the Operation's chief.

He exited the corridor into the reception area, unable even then to shake the feeling of unseen eyes watching him, of a dissolute voyeurism that was somehow contagious, afflicting him with its foulness. How had he lived and thrived in this environment for twelve years?

Resolutely he forced his mind into a neutral mode, submerging the emotions which welled within him and which would be all too apparent to the trained eyes of those he passed, should he allow them to show on his face.

He made his way toward the central elevators serving the building. From the outside it was a nondescript four-story brownstone, but inside it contained a bewildering maze of corridors, offices, and subterranean levels. The ground floor was occupied by a number of legitimate businesses, with the upper floors ostensibly providing additional office space. The entire facade was a complex exercise in deception, in delusion and bureaucratic sleight-of-hand that had effectively concealed the Operation's existence from even the liberal press, which, in intelligence circles, was as great a threat as any hostile foreign power.

Braden was eager to be out of the building, his mind insisting on replaying in fragmented slices his conversation with Andruss. The elevator doors opened as he approached it, and the man in the cell-like cubicle grinned.

"Yo, Eric," he said.

Braden's preoccupation slid reluctantly away. "Hello, Robert." He stepped quickly between the elevator doors as they began to close. Of all people he might have met just now, he reflected sourly, surely Robert Chandler was the least desirable. Even when Chandler had been the top student in the Self-Defense and Survival courses taught by Braden over four years ago, the man's perception had been uncanny, particularly for a novice.

"You going out?" Chandler's grin was still in place.

Braden felt a chill touch him. Did Chandler know of his resignation?

He met the guileless gaze of Chandler's eyes, then saw Chandler's hand hovering over the buttons and realized that he was being asked what floor he wanted, if he was going to the ground floor to leave the building. The relief actually made his knees weaken.

"You all right?" Chandler's grin never altered, but he had caught Braden's reaction just the same.

"Fine." Braden made his voice brusque. "Ground floor."

"I was just heading down to the target range," Chandler said as they descended. "You have time to join me? See if you've still got it?"

Something nipped at Braden's mind, then scurried away into the darkness of his subconscious. Again he met Chandler's gaze and remembered the younger man as his student, in a sense his protege. Chandler had changed little in appearance in the years since he had been recruited out of Harvard law school. He had gone on to demonstrate a surprising flair for the covert activities of the Operation, a flair he had nurtured with merciless dedication.

He was tall, well-built, with dark curly hair and handsome features marred by eyes that were too small, too close-set, and, to a trained observer like Braden, too dangerous, too prone to light up with fiery satisfaction at a karate blow delivered with expert precision, at the blast of an incendiary bomb, or at the staccato roar of an automatic weapon.

Those eyes had never changed, Braden thought, except to grow a little harder, a little more dangerous over the years of Chandler's active status as a field agent. And the years had been busy ones for Chandler. Braden had seen him occasionally after the younger man had passed the training courses, had even worked with him briefly on an abortive military affair in Central America. But he had heard of the daring exploits, the cool, hard precision of the man under fire—physical or mental—which had raised him through the ranks in a remarkably short time. In the secret wars they both fought, Robert Chandler had become something of a legend, an expert at violence, deceit, and manipulation.

Was he somehow practicing such deceit now, manipulating him in some covert fashion? Braden found himself wondering with a stab of disquiet. But there was no way the other could know of his conversation with Andruss, and to refuse his invitation might only lead to suspicion he could ill afford. He remembered Andruss' request not to leak the details of his resignation to any other member of the Operation. So, all right, he thought. One last time by the rules.

"Sure," he said aloud to Chandler. "You're on."

2

Braden hefted the Smith and Wesson .38 Military and Police Revolver with the four-inch barrel. It felt heavy, somehow awkward in his hand. Which was absurd since it was his own gun, one used in several assignments and innumerable practice sessions until he had often thought of it as a part of himself—a lethal extension of his own character.

"Still using that toy?" Chandler's grin was mocking, as if, perhaps, he had detected Braden's unease. He drew his own weapon smoothly from its shoulder rig, a Metalife Custom L-frame .357. "Like it?" Chandler prodded. "This baby is something special."

Braden lifted his .38, arm extended, gun hand cupped in the palm of his other hand. He took a preliminary sight on the chest of the frontal human silhouette at the far end of the range. It had not been that long since he had practiced here, but somehow it seemed as though an age had passed. They were in the target range in one of the underground levels of the Operation's headquarters.

"Sloppy, Eric, sloppy," Chandler chided. "You look all tense. Loosen up."

He was right, as he had so often been right when he had finished head of the class in the courses Braden, as a senior field operative, had taught in the interims between assignments. Already proficient in karate and guns as hobbies,

Chandler had adapted to the strenuous training regimen with an almost appalling ease. He had easily outclassed the other students and had kept Braden constantly on his toes to keep from slipping up and being outclassed himself.

Now he felt Chandler's eyes on him as he donned a set of ear protectors. "Go ahead," the younger man's voice came to him muffled.

There were combat tactics—standing with your back to the target and spinning to fire—and fast-draw techniques, but Braden didn't feel up to such maneuvers. He wanted this idiotic competition over and done with. But he couldn't afford to make himself look too bad.

In one smooth motion then he swept the gun up into firing position, triggering it rapid-fire as fast as he could pull the trigger, feeling it kick like a live thing in his hands, hearing the blasts even through the mufflers as a single sustained roar.

His arms felt suddenly weak and he lowered the .38.

He was aware of Chandler's gaze on him, but did not meet it. Still he thought he sensed a wraith of surprise, as if Chandler had noticed that slight awkwardness which had plagued him.

Chandler did not speak. He hit the button that carried the target forward for examination. Braden fumbled a little as he used a speedloader to replace the spent shells. He watched wordlessly as Chandler spread one big hand across the chest of the target figure. It just covered the six holes there. Chandler glanced at him without expression.

Braden replaced the .38 in the shoulder rig, shifting the straps slightly to make it ride more comfortably. He watched as Chandler stepped over to position himself in line with the next target, the younger man standing loose and relaxed. Braden kept his own features expressionless.

Then Chandler's hand darted beneath his sport coat, and he was spinning, the big L-frame .357 coming out, level and firing even as he completed his turn. There was no discernible separation in the blasts and they seemed to pound in Braden's skull even after Chandler straightened and lowered the .357, still staring at the target as if it might fire back.

Then Chandler glanced over at him, and in those narrow eyes Braden caught a flash of that wild exultation he knew of old. Chandler grinned like a skull, and Braden had no doubt that the other's performance had been detectably faster than his own.

To escape that grin he turned and pressed the recall button.

Chandler had gone for the head—a more difficult target than the torso—and when he lifted his hand, his palm alone covered the single gaping hole the six bullets had left in the silhouetted head.

He turned back to Braden and dawning surprise mingled with the savage glee in his eyes. "I beat you," he said tightly. "The grouping's closer and I'll bet my life I damn well shaded you on speed. You're getting old, Eric."

"So are we all." Chandler's exuberance, his excitement over the senseless competition, made Braden feel old. "You want something to drink?" he asked and turned abruptly away before Chandler could challenge him to another round.

The canteen was located on another sublevel of the basement. It was almost deserted and Chandler's gaze was intense as he studied Braden across the beer he had ordered. Braden sipped at his Coke.

Chandler shook his head. "A Coke, by God. You've changed, Eric. There's all kinds of rumors about you now, you know that? Some kind of religious experience or something?" His inflection turned it into a question.

Here was another opportunity, Braden thought. He could tell Chandler what had happened to him, explain it to him so he would understand. He remembered Andruss, the mocking scorn which had met his feeble efforts to witness. "Maybe I am just getting old," he said tonelessly.

"No, there's more to it than that." Chandler's inflection

was thoughtful. "It's funny. You seem softer somehow, not as hard, like you've lost the edge. But at the same time you seem—I don't know—stronger, maybe."

Braden sipped his Coke wordlessly, keeping his face impassive. He watched Chandler as the younger man took a long pull at his beer then set it down. His nostrils flared and his eyes seemed suddenly on fire. Braden felt his own body go tense.

"Have you ever thought about it, Eric? Ever wondered what would happen if we went up against each other? How it would turn out?"

"Then I'd have to take you down," Braden said flatly.

Chandler let out a short, harsh bark of laughter and some of the wildness that had been in his eyes was in the sound. "That's more like it. There's the old Eric Braden. Never give in. Training, discipline and guts will see you through. You remember preaching that to us novices, Eric? We ate it up."

Yes, Braden thought, I suppose I did preach to them, but in the end none of those things had been enough. They never had been. He had fooled himself for years—fooled how many agents?—with that same doctrine in training, sending them out to survive or die armed only with a humanistic gospel of self-reliance that, he recognized now, was ultimately more deadly than all the automatic weapons, all the knives, all the varied instruments of death and destruction on the planet. Deadly not in a physical sense, although that, assuredly, was part of it, but in a spiritual sense as well.

"I think I could take you, Eric," Chandler's voice was a feral whisper. "Maybe I couldn't back in training, but that was a long time ago, and I've been around since then. You saw me on the range. I'm better than you now. Admit it."

"I'm not a target on a firing range," Braden said softly. "I shoot back."

Chandler's grin was cold. "Maybe I'll get a chance to see someday."

"Pray that you don't," Braden said.

He stood up and the old insticts were there moving his body sidewise so that he did not turn his back on Chandler as he left the canteen. It seemed he could still feel Chandler's eyes like icy daggers embedded in his spine as he headed for the elevators.

A wariness was in him. What had Chandler been after? Why the taunting, the brazen challenge? What had motivated Chandler? Some long-nurtured jealousy concealed beneath his casual, daredevil air? And if so, what had summoned it forth now of all times? Did Chandler know he was leaving the Operation? Had he acted thus because he knew he would soon lose whatever chance he had to settle his obsessive desire to outdo his teacher?

How could he have found out? Only Andruss had known and he, Braden, had met Chandler immediately upon leaving Andruss' office. So what was going on? Had Chandler simply gone over the edge, goaded into madness by the hairtrigger life of a field agent?

He had left the building now, and the smog and the heat seemed to smother him like the decaying embrace of a clam-my shroud. He had parked some distance from the head-quarters — standard operating procedure to make spotting a tail easier.

He was sweating, and the bulk of the .38, once almost a part of him, was now an uncomfortable burden beneath his coat. A narrow alley cut between a brownstone and a warehouse, offering a short-cut to his car, and he strode down it, staying near one wall by ingrained habit. Recalling Chandler's mirthless grin, the unholy fervor in those smallish eyes, a chill touched Braden there in the heat.

A subliminal portion of his brain registered the sound of a car motor starting on the street behind him. It grew louder, and another higher level of his mind assessed it as it crescendoed to a roar.

Reflexes were moving him even as the sound of the

motor mingled with the clanging, scraping sound that grated at his nerves. The car had swung into the alley behind him. A massive grill, like the snarling grin of some great demonic skull, bore down on him as he flung a single glance back over his shoulder. One side of the bumper was just grazing the warehouse wall, maintaining a screaming contact with it so there could be no chance of his flattening himself against the wall to escape. He would be ground into the wall, borne down to be smashed into lifelessness beneath those churning wheels.

There was no place to run; the car would be upon him within a second. The alley's width was only some six feet greater than the car, and its onrushing bulk seemed to fill it from wall to wall. Braden saw the sparks flaring from the contact of the bumper against the wall.

His hand was in his coat, closing on the familiar butt of the .38 even as he hurled himself sidewise, taking the impact of his shoulder and rolling, his impetus carrying him in front of and clear of the car as he came up onto his feet, his back against the far wall. The .38 was out, his arms swinging up into the firing position, feet swiveling into the stance, and there was no hesitation, no awkwardness now because this wasn't the firing range, this was the real thing, and hesitation spelled death.

The barrel of the .38 came into alignment with the face of the driver of the car in the instant before it swept past, and in that infinitesimal clocktick of time Braden shifted his arm so that, as the .38 roared, the windshield to the side of that recognized face exploded.

The car rushed past him now — a dark, late-model Continental — and he shifted his aim again and pumped a bullet into each of the driver's-side tires as they went past him, the double roar of the .38 merging with the thunder of the engine.

Then it was past him and he swiveled to keep it in his sights as it traveled on down the alley another fifty feet, the punctured tires disintegrating on the spinning rims. Then the passenger-side wheels ran up on a loading ramp jutting from the warehouse wall, lifting the car up on its rims for a long teetering moment as its momentum carried it on down the alley like a vehicle in a stunt show. Finally it toppled over onto its side and tilted the rest of the way over with a grinding crash. Upside down, on its flattened roof, it skidded a few yards further and came to rest.

The sudden silence was almost a physical shock. Braden's ears rang shrilly from the blasts of the .38.

He glanced up and down the alley. No one else was in sight. The whole affair had lasted only seconds, though his adrenalized reactions and perceptions had made it seem much longer. He still probably had a few moments before anyone responded to the sound of the crash and the shots, assuming they had been heard at all.

He moved swiftly forward, .38 still at the ready. There was no sign of life in the car as he approached. He was not particularly worried about an explosion. It was only on television that cars exploded like giant firecrackers at the slightest of impacts. Not that this had been a slight impact by any stretch of the imagination.

Not slight at all, he thought ruefully as he eased himself cautiously down into a flattened sprinter's crouch to peer into the overturned vehicle. And certainly more than sufficient to end the life of the driver whom he had spared in that fleeting instant as he lined up his first shots.

He could not, in that brief glance, ascertain the exact cause of death. But there was no doubt that the mangled body was without life.

Nor, he thought grimly, as he came smoothly erect, was there any doubt that his flash of recognition of the driver had been correct. He knew the man who had just tried to kill him.

Braden holstered the .38 and strode quickly from the alley.

3

The two men in the sterile office looked up as Braden entered, and he saw the shocked looks on their faces and cold disbelief in their eyes.

"Excuse the interruption, gentlemen," he said with an icy grin. "I didn't wait to be announced. I figured as a senior field agent I had pretty much carte blanche around here." As he spoke he stepped to one side of the door so that his back would not be to it.

He was watching them closely, not sure just what to expect. Andruss sat motionless behind his barren desk, fingers frozen on its surface. Chandler stood beside him, just now straightening, his attitude that of a man surprised in the middle of a conversation by the subject of that conversation. Neither man spoke, but after an instant Andruss' eyes flicked downward ever so slightly.

"Don't try it," Braden said. "Keep your hands in sight, push yourself back away from the desk. No hidden buttons, no silent alarms." Andruss complied, rolling his swivel chair back from his desk slightly. His eyes regarded Braden coldly, and now a new element was added to that harsh intensity — a dark and brooding malignancy.

"If you're wondering how I made it in here past all your little booby traps in the corridor, just remember that I know this place as well as you do, maybe better."

When neither man responded, Braden kept talking. "But you're really surprised to see me here at all, because you never expected me to come back. You must know by now that your little try at me didn't work and that your would-be assassin is dead. It was a clumsy try—amateurish really. I'm surprised at you. A hit-and-run in an alley."

Some of the rage he felt had slipped into Braden's voice now. "Yes, I saw the driver and I recognized him, and I had time to kill him, but I didn't—one of the side-effects of my new religion—mercy. That's something you wouldn't understand. I could have killed him, and I didn't, but he died in the wreck anyway."

Braden paused and drew a harsh breath. The other two men continued to watch him silently and he went on, "I would have thought you could have done better, but then you were working on short notice, weren't you? You set me up right here in your office. You must have suspected the reason I made an appointment to see you—there have been enough rumors flying around, I'm sure. So you arranged to have Chandler here ready to delay me long enough to give you time to alert Sanger to get ready for me. You must have signaled Chandler somehow while I was still here. He met me at the elevator and I should have caught on then that something was wrong, because he said he was heading down to the firing range, yet he was riding up in an elevator to the top floor."

Another pause. Still no response. "He was on his way to meet me, but I didn't realize it. But then why should I suspect that my senior officer and a fellow agent were planning to kill me? Of course you did tell me that my resignation was against Operational Policy. So just what is the policy? Kill off any agent foolish enough to try to resign?"

Even knowing what the answer to that question had to be, Braden felt a kind of numbing shock at the bland affirmation he could read on Andruss' face.

"Such a severe remedy is rarely warranted," Andruss

said as if explaining a fine point of corporate policy. "Generally a burned-out or disillusioned agent is willing to accept a desk job and eventually a pensioned retirement in a sanctioned rest home. You can see our side of it, Braden." One pallid finger tapped the air in soft emphasis. "You are too experienced in the field not to realize the potential danger if we were to allow Operational employees to resign at will. The possibility of leaks, inadvertant or deliberate, would be far too great to permit."

"So you kill them off. Neat. Saves a lot on pension payments."

Andruss sighed. "Termination is always our last resort, Braden, I can assure you. It was not easy for me to issue the order on you. I did try to dissuade you, you know."

"Only to give your hit-man time to get his ambush set," Braden said savagely.

"You got lucky, Eric," Chandler spoke for the first time. His grin was as insolent as ever. "That won't happen next time. I tried to warn you. Nobody leaves the Operation and lives. Nobody. Not even you."

Braden looked at the younger man for a long, gauging moment. "Of course," Braden said then. "You're not only in on it, you're the chief executioner. That's how you came up through the ranks so fast, by doing Andruss' dirty little missions for him, killing your own fellow agents."

Chandler's mocking smile was a chilling confirmation.

"Chandler has proven himself well-suited to such tasks," Andruss added. "He has the skills, the training—much of which you gave him—and, more important, the proper attitude for such work.

"Not many agents do, I've found. Certainly you never had quite the characteristics I look for in what I call my personnel terminators."

Braden stared at them and the lurking horror, hovering on the fringes of his mind, crept loathsomely in to possess his soul, leaving him transfixed, mute.

"You were a fool to come back, Eric," Chandler said.

"Maybe," Braden's voice was hollow. "But I had to know for sure."

"Why, you ought to be proud of me, Eric. After all, you trained me, and it takes a good agent to be sent out after other agents."

"It takes an amoral, cold-blooded pagan," Braden said flatly.

He saw the surprising spark of anger flare in Chandler's eyes, saw his hand start to move. Then Braden's own hand blurred and he had the .38 out and leveled before Chandler's hand had even disappeared under his coat.

Shock replaced the anger in Chandler's eyes, and Braden felt his mouth pull into a mirthless grin. The old habits, the old reflexes, stirred in him, and his finger tightened on the trigger. He could kill them both now, should kill them, surely. They would make relentless, deadly opponents, and by their own admission were determined to see him dead. To let them live now, when he had them under his gun, would be madness, the play of an amateur. For if the tables were reversed now, he knew, Chandler would not hesitate.

Slowly then his finger relaxed its pressure. No. Chandler would not hesitate, but he, Braden, had already hesitated. If his new-found faith meant anything, then there had to be a difference between these men and himself—a difference not only inside himself, but one that could be, had to be, outwardly visible in his actions.

"Listen to me," he said hoarsely. "I'm no danger to you. I won't publish my memoirs; I won't cause any leaks, inadvertant or otherwise. I'm not some unreliable rookie. I know how to keep my mouth shut, how to maintain a low profile. I've done it for twelve years now."

"I'm sorry, but it's not an acceptable risk," Andruss said.

"What about this?" Braden gestured with the .38. "Is it an acceptable risk?"

"You won't use that unless we force you." Andruss'

voice was mild. "And neither of us intends to do that just now."

Chandler had been right, Braden thought. It had been a mistake to come back here, a fool's play. He took a step back toward the door.

"I'll come after you, Eric," Chandler's eyes held that wild gleam that had illumined them earlier. "You can't run fast enough to get away. You can't find a hole deep enough to hide from me. I'll be behind you no matter where you go. You remember that."

"I'll remember it. You remember this: Don't come after me. Leave me alone. I'm no threat to the Operation. You wondered if you could take me, Chandler, what would happen if we had it out. Well, you had your chance just now and you didn't even come close. No games, no target practice. Just plain and simple—you come after me and I'll take you out."

"Better do it now, Eric. Next time I won't give you the chance."

"You didn't give me this one. Both of you, remember what I said." He kept them under the barrel of the .38 until he was out of the office.

He left the building without incident; they would not make a play for him there where he was almost as much in home territory as they were. Besides, he thought ruefully, it wouldn't do anything for Operational morale to have a veteran agent gunned down in headquarters, no matter what explanation they concocted.

Outside he caught a cab, giving the driver a direction at random. He had not returned to his apartment following the failed assassination attempt. Nor could he do so now. All his old haunts had to be considered off-limits. To all intents and purposes he was a fugitive now, and he knew better than to underestimate the opposition.

Andruss would have his house and all his hangouts, few though they were, covered within the hour. Agents could be assigned to be on the lookout for him even now without knowing the reason for the order. The entire city had become a trap for him.

But it was a trap which speed alone would not get him out of. Cunning would be required as well.

He had gone by his bank and withdrawn all his deposits in cash after the attempt on his life. He had even cashed in the certificates of deposit, taking the penalty, acting on the honed reflexes of a trained agent, guessing, even before he returned to confront Andruss, what the score was and taking initial precautions to cover himself.

Several miles from Operation headquarters, in a mixed residential and commercial section, he paid off the cab and walked. No one followed him. He entered a chain fast-food outlet and ordered a soft drink, taking it to one of the back booths. He stayed there two hours, losing himself in the plastic anonymity of the convenience restaurant as evening slowly descended and the headlights of the rush-hour traffic began to reflect harshly off the large, tinted window.

The Operation was limited in manpower, but it was thorough. All means of public transportation would eventually be covered and any traces he left would be picked up. He considered stealing a car, but that would only make a mockery of the new faith and lofty ideals he had espoused so ardently not long ago in Andruss' office.

When he finally left the fast-food restaurant he found a nearby thrift shop and purchased old jeans, a jacket, a shirt, and a tote bag. He used the bathroom of a service station to change, putting his sport coat, slacks, and dress shirt in the tote bag. The .38 in its shoulder rig he donned under the jacket.

He caught a city bus, sitting near the back as it lumbered along the night streets. He changed buses once, then alighted near the junction of two major highways at the city's edge. He had to walk a quarter of a mile along the side of the westbound highway until he reached his destination.

The giant neon sign read "Truckers Village." He went past the behemoth shapes of the semi's in the gravel lot and entered the restaurant. He found a seat in another corner booth, this one smelling of sweat, cigarette smoke, and beer. The bleached-blonde waitress took his order for a cheeseburger and soft drink and left him studying his fellow diners.

The truckers were a mixed lot, from middle-aged veterans to long-haired rednecks who told their crude jokes too loudly and laughed too long when they were finished. After a few glances in Braden's direction, they ignored him. He was not too much different in appearance than one of their ilk. The waitress brought him a greasy burger and tepid soft drink. He ate and drank mechanically, then settled back against the cracked plastic of the booth and continued to watch the truckers.

It was almost an hour before he made his choice — a young man with short hair and shifty eyes beneath a billed cap with a truck logo on it. An independent, Braden had surmised from his conversation with two others. He owned his own rig (the payments were too high) and was not bound by the myriad regulations and red tape which smothered those drivers who worked for the big companies. And he was planning on driving through the night to get back to a live-in girlfriend.

When he left the cafe and headed back out toward the saurian bulk of his old Peterbilt, Braden paid his bill and followed. The trucker's name was Max, and for a hundred dollars cash he was willing, without too many questions, to have a stranger ride shotgun with him as he headed west.

Braden settled back as Max jockeyed the eighteen-wheeler out onto the highway and worked it up through the gears. Once he was in the left lane and had the speedometer needle hovering near seventy, he glanced over at Braden.

"You on the run?" he asked without too much interest.

Braden studied the receding glow of the city lights in the side mirror. "After a fashion," he said.

Max grunted. "Yeah, I know what you mean. Time to move on, right?"

Braden didn't answer, and after a moment Max shrugged and turned back to his driving. Yes, it was time for him to move on, Braden thought. Time to run, far and fast, until he ran out of places to run or until somebody caught up with him. A fragment of a Bible verse touched his mind: "The Son of Man hath not where to lay his head."

4

"Obviously you will have the full resources of the Operation at your disposal," Andruss said. "It does appear that Eric made it clear of the metroplex area despite our best efforts. The man is very good at this, an old hand. You would do well to remember that."

"I'll remember it," Robert Chandler said grimly. His legs were becoming tired from standing, even in his customary relaxed posture, before the older man's desk.

Despite the informality his unique status with Andruss conveyed upon him, he would never have done what he would have liked and hitched his hip onto the edge of Andruss' barren desk. He did not think the Operation's head had ever kept him in a briefing session quite this long. He hid his growing impatience and studied Andruss surreptitiously.

"The harm Eric Braden could do to us is incalculable," Andruss continued. It was a theme upon which he had been dwelling for some time. "We simply cannot run the risk of him undergoing some kind of divine compulsion to reveal all he knows to the press or to some government figure such as Senator Gates. The ramifications of his disappearance are unthinkable."

Andruss was standing, which was unusual, and the two days which had passed since the failed attempt on Braden's life had plainly taken their toll on him. Braden's desertion had hit him hard. Chandler could not remember ever having seen his superior quite so agitated, although, admittedly, what passed for agitation in Andruss would only have been remarked as a slight case of nerves in any other man.

"I'll find him," Chandler asserted aloud and felt the grim eagerness well up within him. "He won't get away again."

Andruss' incisive eyes seemed to probe into him with physical impact, and it took a distinct effort not to flinch.

Braden's unexpected actions had had their effect on him, too, Chandler had to admit. He recalled Braden's awkwardness on the target range, contrasted with the heart-numbing speed with which he had reacted when Chandler had tried to get the drop on him. It still left him a little awed to think about it. He had been confident of his ability to beat Braden, particularly after his religious experience. Indeed it had been the rumors of whatever change had taken place in Braden that had aroused in Chandler the old competitive drive, quiescent since his days of training as a student of Braden. This desire to top the master had driven him to excel under the man's tutelage in a futile effort to prove himself superior.

The drive had reawakened now, leaner, harsher, no longer geared to meaningless classroom rivalry, but metamorphosized into a gnawing passion to confront Braden on the only field of competition which, in the end, had any real significance: life or death, killed or be killed, one-on-one, with survival the prize.

The old Romans had had it right, he thought, with their gladiatorial games. When else was a man more alive than when he faced death at the hands of one who was his peer? So must the ancient gladiators have felt as they confronted their opponents on the bloody sand.

Belatedly he realized Andruss had fallen silent, was staring at him intensely. He realized that he must have allowed his emotions to become visible on his face, in his eyes. And he also realized, as Andruss slowly seated himself, that the man approved of what he saw there.

"I really believe you will take him, Robert," Andruss said softly.

"I'll take him," Chandler heard himself affirm.

But he remembered again Braden's appalling speed, the sensation of staring at Braden's gun leveled at him and knowing he had been beaten. But he had been overconfident, he knew, not anticipating the Braden of old to materialize so unexpectedly in the stranger his old mentor had become. He would not be so overconfident again.

And he had allowed Braden's taunt to anger him. What had Braden called him? A pagan? Someone without religion. Why should that have sparked the sudden rage within him? He dismissed the thought as irrelevant. He would not let rage or any other emotion get in his way again. Going up against Braden, he could not afford to.

"I should, of course, have anticipated an occurrence like this following that wretched affair in London involving Senator Gates." Andruss seemed to be speaking almost as much to himself as to Chandler. "I always suspected something was wrong with Eric's explanation that the private inadvertently disobeyed his orders to move the armored car. And Eric was never the same after that incident. We are fortunate that the remaining members of the terrorist cell were all slain when the police traced the bomber to their headquarters. Otherwise, they might have linked the Operation to that assasination attempt."

He looked up suddenly at Chandler. "You will need to dispose of this matter with Eric as soon as possible, in any event, since I will want you to go to Central America when Gates visits there and handle that incident. If I cannot send you, it will be necessary to dispatch Hansen and a team to take care of Gates. That would be an unfortunate development for a number of reasons, not the least of which is the fact that it would require a greater number of our personnel."

"I'll find him," Chandler repeated. "I know how he thinks; I can anticipate his moves."

"Don't be too sure of that," Andruss stated warily. "His motives have changed, I believe."

"His motivation is survival now," Chandler said, brushing the objection aside.

But a small voice in the back of his mind whispered that he himself had noted the change in Braden. "Look," he went on quickly. "I've studied our files on him. I don't have to chase him down. I can intercept him." He continued to speak, outlining what he had gleaned from the Operation files on Braden. Their detail and extent had surprised even him, but they had provided the information he needed, and he recounted his plan to Andruss.

As he spoke, the conviction grew in him that what he was telling Andruss was nothing new to the older man. Clearly Andruss had already perused the files and come to certain decisions and conclusions himself.

Chandler fell silent when he finished, and Andruss regarded him for a long moment. "Excellent, Robert," he said at last. "Your plans are not too dissimilar from what I would propose. But when you find Eric" —his voice hardened—" do not hesitate, do not give him even so much as a chance to speak to you. Whatever the circumstances, dispose of him immediately and have done with it. Do you understand?"

It was a peculiar order and Chandler had time to wonder what had prompted it. "Yes, sir." he answered.

Andruss' gaze seemed to weigh and evaluate him on some obscure set of scales. "Very well, Robert. Keep me advised."

Gratefully Chandler left his office. His mind insisted on replaying the details of the plan he had devised. The files which had given him the information he had used had been so extensive as to leave him with the belief that there was little about Braden that he did not know.

Not for the first time since viewing the files, he reflected that the presence of such a comprehensive background on Braden could only mean that there was a similarly comprehensive file on him as well. It was not a pleasant thought.

There were certain parts of his life, certain personal habits and idiosyncracies, he liked to think were private even from the Operation. He doubted now that such was the case.

Anger stirred in him. It was Braden's fault that he had learned these unpleasant facts about the Operation. He felt a rekindled surge of eagerness to have it out with Braden, to go up against him, one on one. He remembered the session of target practice with Braden on that last day. He had beaten Braden then, beaten him clearly and decisively. Even Braden himself had all but admitted it.

He would beat him again when the opportunity came. Only this time it would be for real.

His plan for catching up with Braden allowed Chandler time for a final session of target practice. This time he bypassed the target range itself and headed for the small room which housed the computerized simulator. The idea of shooting at a cardboard target had little appeal for him. He wanted at least the illusion of having a target that could shoot back.

Would Braden shoot back when they confronted each other? he asked himself. The veteran agent had spared both himself and Andruss when he had gotten the drop on them in Andruss' office. He did not think the Braden of old would have been so merciful. But Braden had changed. His religious experience had worked subtle and as yet undefined changes in him.

What would drive a man like Braden — a hardened professional whom he had tried for years to emulate—to give up on his career and risk his life trying to break away from the espionage business?

Andruss attributed it to stress, to nerves, the accumulation of years spent living on the edge of survival, finally manifested in a nervous collapse expressed as some kind of spiritual awakening.

That conclusion boded ill for his own future, Chandler mused. Was this what lay in store for him in another five or ten years down the line? Perhaps it would be possible to talk to Braden before he killed him, Andruss' explicit orders not withstanding. Before he killed the man, he needed to understand what peculiar motivations had driven him to turn rogue.

He shrugged off his preoccupation as he reached the small room with its battery of terminals and keyboards. He was glad one of the technicians was there. He did not like to program the simulator himself. It took away the vital element of the unexpected from the automated training exercise.

The technician, Dickson, nodded at him. "Hi, Mr. Chandler."

Dickson, Chandler noticed, would not meet his gaze. Few of the other operatives would these days. He wondered idly what they could read in his eyes. He had also become "Mr. Chandler" to many of them lately. He was not sure he liked it.

"Set it up," he ordered as he replaced the .357 with a replica, identical in size and weight, which fired an infrared beam instead of bullets. A toy, and not as satisfying as the real thing, but necessary for use in the simulator.

"What difficulty factor?" Dickson asked.

"Four," Chandler said flatly. The highest.

"Yes, sir." Dickson began to work the keys on his terminal.

Chandler hesitated a moment. "What's the record score?" he asked.

Dickson glanced up. "Ninety-five percent accuracy, sir."

Chandler felt his lips tighten. Someone had beaten him in the weeks since his last visit. "Who set it?" he asked, already knowing with grim foresight what the answer would be.

"Eric Braden, sir."

Chandler turned sharply away. "Level four," he repeated and went through the doorway into the simulator cell.

The computers had already projected the three-dimensional image of the survival environment onto the four walls so that it was as if he stepped through the doorway directly into a desolate street in some benighted section of a big-city slum. Empty windows of deserted tenements gaped blankly down at him. The stripped body of a car rested on blocks. Bottles and trash littered the street. There were flaws, of course. By studying the images closely it was possible to detect their unreality, realize that the scene was nothing more than a sophisticated video projection. But still the sensation of reality was strong.

Chandler advanced a few steps toward the center of the room, shrugging his shoulders to loosen his sport coat. No two sequences were the same, or at least he had not encountered exactly the same scenario twice. He guessed that the potential sequences programmed into the computers were virtually limitless.

He turned slowly, allowing himself to become absorbed in the scene, to accept it as reality. Behind him where the door had been, the street stretched several blocks. In the distance he could see a busier avenue, where vehicles flashed past. Overhead was a leaden sky. He wondered if this was a reproduction of an actual scene in some nameless city. It did not matter; for him, now, it was reality.

A flicker of movement to his left, and he was spinning in a crouch, hand taking the .357 replica from his shoulder holster as he turned. Framed in a doorway, a long-haired street gang member leveled a sawed-off shotgun at him. As the .357 came into line, Chandler fired. The weapon made a kind of whining bark of sound and the gang member fell backwards into the doorway and disappeared.

Chandler swung around fast, eyes scanning doors and windows for a possible follow-up. Nothing. It was impossible to anticipate the computer. He could only react.

He holstered the gun. Another opponent, this one in an upper-story window with an automatic weapon. Again he scored, then pivoted fast and nailed a terrorist before the latter could throw his grenade. Again he waited, alert, ready. A minute passed. Another. The attack when it came was on three fronts. He went flat, firing as he did so, rolled, fired again, reversed directions, and came up on one knee to catch the last ambusher with a snap shot.

Moving, reacting, on a kind of adrenalin high now, he could feel the precision of his moves, the accuracy of his aim. As the next armed figure appeared it seemed to him to have Eric Braden's face. He gunned it down before it could move.

He turned and held his shot just in time to avoid hitting a child who had come from behind the stripped car. There were other innocent bystanders, appearing unexpectedly sometimes in conjunction with the hostile images which lurked in windows, emerged from alleys, descended on a fire escape.

When the street scene finally wavered, then vanished, leaving only the opaque walls, Chandler blinked in surprise, and whirled reflexively, seeking other enemies. There was nothing. The training session was completed. He had, he realized, become so caught up in the illusion that he had forgotten that it did not represent reality. But he had survived; he could feel it without even looking at his score.

He was grinning as he emerged from the room, and Dickson, the technician, flinched away from that grin.

"Well?" Chandler demanded. "What's my score?"

Dickson's fingers moved over the keyboard. He looked up after a moment. "Ninety-seven, sir," he said. "You beat him."

Damn right, Chandler thought. Now for the real thing.

5

Coming in on I-40 from the west, you could watch the modest collection of skyscrapers that composed downtown Oklahoma City materialize out of the shimmering heat waves. Some years before, an urban renewal project had claimed most of the older buildings, Braden recalled.

They had been replaced with a haphazard and ill-advised assemblage of gleaming towers and giant rectangular blocks stood on end, among which the few remaining throwbacks to traditional urban architecture stood out in awkward contrast.

Viewing the skyline from the window of the eighteen-wheeler in which he was a passenger, Braden tried to assess it as a stalking ground. It was a scenario in which the role he could conceivably play might be either that of hunter or hunted.

The highway, elevated for several miles along this stretch, swept past the outskirts of the downtown area, separating it, like some unacknowledged but impassable barrier, from the rugged industrial area of giant mills and factories to the south.

Beneath the city a complex system of air-conditioned pedestrian tunnels, miles in length, linked most of the major downtown buildings and formed a shopping concourse lined intermittently with small restaurants and businesses.

Not far off the highway, at the southwest corner of the urban area, were the green berms and the giant gleaming cylindrical greenhouse tube of the exotic Myriad Gardens, a park-like project only now in the final stages of development.

Braden watched the panoramic view slip past the grimy window of the tractor-trailer rig. He had reached his destination, he thought, but the knowledge brought little relief from the tension which seemed to coil now constantly in his nerves and sinews.

His eyes were gritty from lack of sleep or sleep snatched in shabby, oppressive surroundings. His skin felt oily, his hair lank and tangled from dried sweat. An annoying ache had, over the past couple of hundred miles, gradually made itself felt in his spine. The almost nonexistent suspension system of the old Mack rig in which he rode was the punishing cause. The days of hitchhiking and hiring rides with disreputable truckers had taken their toll on him, mentally and physically.

Still, he reflected, he was glad to be here at last, although he made no effort to have the burly taciturn driver of his current transportation halt the rig to let him out. His route to reach this "little big city" in the Southwest had been too circuitous, involving an elaborate and monotonous criss-crossing of this part of the country as the passenger of various truckers, for him to make a direct approach to his target at this late stage of the game.

Not that he thought his route had been traced by any of the covert observers which he had no doubt were attempting to pick up his trail across the country, and, he suspected, throughout the world. The surveillance network, like a massive encompassing web which Andruss and Chandler could command, was mercilessly effective. Braden knew. He had utilized it all too often himself in tracking human prey.

But that same familiarity had also given him confidence that his own unlikely method of travel, and the further ploys of overshooting and backtracking to his goal, had enabled him to elude the net. Still, he would not relax his vigilance.

Interstate Highway 40, running east and west, intersected with north-south I-35 just east of the downtown area. Two of the nation's major traffic arteries met in a bewildering maze of ramps and cutoffs, with traffic slowed to a crawl by seemingly perpetual road construction on one lane or another. Similar construction, Braden recalled, had been going on when he had last passed this way some years before.

The trucker's route took him north on I-35, skirting the sprawling northward expanse of Oklahoma City. At a truck stop where they had lunch, Braden paid off his erstwhile chauffeur and bid him farewell, eliciting a noncommital grunt of acknowledgement. He left the fellow fingering the bills and hungrily eyeing one of the overage prostitutes who obviously frequented the truckstop.

Braden's head ached. He felt exhausted, soiled mentally and physically. He had been acting almost on reflex, relying on the ingrained training and experience he had received over the desolate years in the field to keep him moving ever toward his goal, but in such a way as to baffle and evade any pursuit or observation.

That training and experience had served him well, he believed, but his seeming success engendered no resultant feelings of satisfaction or accomplishment. Something in that lack disturbed him deeply, added an extra level of depth to the numbing exhaustion already weighing him down. But the reason for his unease, for his emptiness of spirit, eluded him in the shadowed areas of his mind, and he could only scowl impotently at the harsh flickering flare of sunlight reflecting off the passenger cars and pickups blasting past him on the highway.

He walked, not trying to hitch a ride, but heading methodically more deeply into the city through the maze of industrial parks and undeveloped patches of woodland which served as illegal dumps for the encroaching industries.

Eventually a bus took him to the downtown section. He tried to relax in the cracked plastic seat of the poorly ventilated vehicle, studying his fellow passengers. Not many at this time of day—a couple of mid-management sorts, one of them female; a heavyset black woman; a brace of urban teens; and three part-time work-away-from-home housewives. No alarms sounded in his mind, no warning bells rang. His fellow passengers were as innocuous as they appeared.

He had seen no real sign of pursuit or observation since beginning his flight. He had not even felt that tingling awareness which he had learned to trust in warning him of impending danger. Had his moves been that good? he wondered. Had he really succeeded in eluding the hounds which Andruss would have wasted no time in putting on his trail?

And if so, why this nagging discouragement that appeared to have taken root in his soul?

He caught himself frowning at a massive, steepled church crowded in among lesser office buildings, and felt a quick automatic stab of self-disgust.

But he was too tired to analyze it. He left the bus behind him and negotiated the sidewalks toward the imposing modern facade of the Sheraton Century Center Hotel. He had spent enough time on the run in the blue-collar stratum of society, he had decided. Time for a change in tactics and environments.

There were few pedestrians. In this heat, most of the business populace would keep to the subterranean tunnels and elevated crosswalks which connected most of the major buildings.

He was not followed.

If the exclusive hotel frowned on a rather shabby registrant without luggage, nothing to that effect was said when he paid for the night in cash. Oklahoma, nucleus of the Oil Boom, had more than its share of wealthy eccentrics.

In his room, Braden luxuriated in a long shower, and then shaved off his several day's accumulation of whiskers. Growing a beard might conceal his facial features, but it would not conceal them from a trained observer, and would actually make him stand out in a crowd, pulp fiction concept of disguise notwithstanding.

Clad in slacks and sport coat redeemed from the tote bag he had purchased after leaving Andruss' office that last time, he spent a time in the cool, indirectly lighted confines of the elegant restaurant and club located off the plush lobby of the Sheraton. There were few customers, and he saw no one and nothing to disturb him.

Clean now, refreshed, some of his exhaustion having slipped away with the layers of grime, he relaxed in the cool, affluent surroundings. With his goal apparently almost within his grasp, he knew he should feel something—relief, pride in his professional expertise, even satisfaction.

Why then this numbing, desolate depression, this emptiness of the soul which he had thought himself rid of with his break from the Operation?

He heard one of the businessmen in the club curse, and felt like using the words himself. He recalled the reflexive frown he had cast at the church he had passed on the bus, and a sense of betrayal crept over him.

Was this all his new life offered him? Hiding and running, even the sense of commitment and satisfaction brought by his confrontation with Andruss and Chandler long since dissipated?

"The Lord provides." He remembered his defiant words to Andruss. Well then, where were those much-vaunted provisions that the television evangelists spoke of?

He had given up everything he had, he thought bitterly. Yet not even the wary, self-reliant solitude he had known in the field as an agent could approach the empty, lonely desolation he felt now.

Prayer was beyond him, and, besides, he found himself doubting that any plea he uttered would even be heard, much less answered. But that portion of his mind geared to survival over the years still functioned, warning him that to persist in this malignant brooding was only to court self-destruction, whether by his own hand or that of another.

He paid for the soft drink he had consumed and left the hotel, the harsh afternoon heat bludgeoning him across the eyes as he emerged. He could have stayed inside and managed to reach his destination through the tunnel and walkway system of the concourse, he guessed, but he welcomed the casual brutality of the heat as a physical assault he could cope with, and, in coping, try to disregard the mental and spiritual assault he seemed to be undergoing.

He took a moment to get his bearings.

In its time, before being outdone by the shiny new buildings, the tower of the First Interstate Bank of Oklahoma had been the tallest building in the city. An old-style skyscraper, a long-time city landmark, it had escaped the urban renewal mania, and now stood as an anachronism among its more progressive brethren. Now even its status as a landmark had been all but destroyed by the encroachment of the taller buildings which, when viewed at certain angles, obliterated it from the skyline. Braden found himself feeling a curious affinity for the old structure as he headed toward it.

The tower and the lesser buildings of only slightly later vintage which were connected with it formed a complex that occupied most of a city block.

The bank itself was the successor to the failed First National Bank of Oklahoma City, which had been owned for generations by one of the state's wealthiest families, and had long been a bastion of Oklahoma banking. Ultimately, however, even it had not escaped the purge of Oklahoma banks which the failure of Penn Square Bank and the collapse of the Oklahoma energy and agriculture industries had heralded. The out-of-state holding company of First Interstate had acquired the failed bank's assets, less the bad loans kept by the FDIC, and now stood as the strongest bank in the state.

Braden had followed the fortunes of the bank with a subjective interest, motivated by the account he maintained there under an assumed name. Over the years, in his assignments, opportunities had come to him, opportunities to claim substantial amounts of cash from extralegal sources.

A successful operation against a dope ring in Turkey, whose activities had indirectly threatened America's national security, had given him access to some of the liquid profits of the ring, concealed in accounts in various American banks. He had never reported it but had instead engineered a transfer to a personal account of his own he had established.

He had not robbed anyone, he had rationalized at the time. The money had constituted ill-gotten gains, and he had had as much right to it as anyone. There had been no repercussions from the Operation, and he had kept the funds invested at high rates.

Similar opportunities had presented themselves on other occasions, and he had taken advantage of them, creating what he had thought of as his retirement fund, maintaining it in the Oklahoma bank—a spy's IRA.

Such practices, he knew, were not uncommon among veteran intelligence operatives. A shift in government policy, a realignment of political forces, a new man in the Oval Office, and any of a myriad of other conceivable scenarios could easily result in an agent, even an entire intelligence organization, falling from grace, condemning its employees to bureaucratic limbo, stripping them of pension and retirement rights, leaving them with no recourse, hamstrung by the clandestine nature of their employment.

Braden had seen it happen more than once to fellow inhabitants of the underworld of intelligence and security. He would not, he had vowed, allow it to happen to himself.

So he had created his retirement fund, adding to it over the years, careful never to reveal its existence to anyone. He was confident that he had evaded even the stringent security measures placed on him as an agent of the top-secret Operation, and had succeeded in his goal of having a windfall waiting for him should his career fall prey to the constantly shifting and treacherous political undercurrents.

And now he had a use for it, although not, he reflected, such a use as he might ever have imagined. The contents of the account and the accumulated interest it had earned would serve to take him to virtually any country he chose and establish him there, if not in luxury, then at least in comfortable security.

He had even paid taxes on the income, using an elaborate fictitious identity. His planning, his execution, had all been flawless. The Operation, he was sure, had no knowledge of his nest egg's existence.

The lobby of First Interstate was an imposing cavernous space with enormous pillars supporting the ceiling two stories above, and genuine marble adorning the walls. Braden took a moment to scan its occupants, then secured a withdrawal slip from the customer service desk and took his place in line at one of the teller's windows. He felt naked, exposed in the vast room.

The attractive young female teller accepted the withdrawal slip with a smile, then blinked as she read the amount.

"In cash?"

"Yes, please."

Her composure restored, she ran her fingers over her keyboard, then gazed at the screen hidden from Braden's view. Her smooth forehead furrowed in a frown.

"I'm sorry," she said, giving him a puzzled look. "We're showing a zero balance in that account. There's nothing in it."

Braden stared at her dumbly, understanding the words, but rejecting them. He opened his mouth to protest.

"I think your account's been closed, buddy," the softly mocking voice said at his elbow.

A chill gripped Braden's heart. He turned and found himself staring into the narrow eyes and handsome face of Bob Chandler.

6

"You didn't really think the Operation wasn't aware of your little windfall account, did you? Andruss has had it monitored for years. The assets, by the way, have gone into the Operation's coffer. They'll be put to good use. Why it might even be financing my trip here and my hotel bill while I've been waiting for you," Chandler taunted.

Braden could only stare into those mocking eyes and feel the cavernous lobby closing in upon him with claustrophobic pressure.

The teller, with one last puzzled frown, had addressed herself to the next customer as Braden stepped mechanically away from her window to confront Chandler.

"Not a bad try, actually." The younger man's voice was soft, sibilant. "But you need to watch that FDIC insurance limit, especially what with all the bank failures in this state. You can't be too careful, you know."

Chandler was attired in a tailored sport coat over a knit shirt with coordinated designer jeans above rubber-soled shoes. He was poised and confident, but his stance, the placement of his feet, the slight angling of his limbs, betrayed an electric current of awareness charging through his body. He was primed like a cocked and loaded pistol on a hair trigger, Braden thought, but he made no move to go for the big .357 that was undoubtedly concealed beneath the tailored jacket.

Chandler hadn't killed him, hadn't even tried to. And Chandler was enough of a pro, Braden knew, to have shot him down even there in the lobby in front of witnesses and most likely have succeeded in evading whatever pursuit materialized.

That was what Chandler should have done. That was what Braden had trained him to do, or better yet, to have concealed his presence and stalked his prey until an opportune moment presented itself for a quick, anonymous hit.

But Chandler had done neither. Instead, he had chosen to reveal himself, to actually approach Braden and taunt him with his own utter failure to elude the grasp of the Operation, and it was this fact which shifted Braden's mind back into gear.

He had been outwitted and outmaneuvered, played for a fool, but he was still alive, and now was not the time to dwell on his defeat. Rather it was time, with every sense alert, to confront this man who had vowed and been ordered to kill him.

"You wondering why you're still breathing, buddy?" Chandler cocked his handsome head slightly, using it to indicate the spacious lobby. "Too open in here, too many witnesses. We'll just step outside. There's a nice quiet alley I've already picked out. No witnesses that way."

The mocking eyes appraised Braden, gauging him like a fencer testing his opponent by the touch of his blade.

Braden could feel the vibrant current in the man. Chandler was waiting for him to make some move against him, to give him the excuse, the opportunity, to actually try to take him out.

"How about a drink?" Braden asked casually. "For old time's sake."

He was watching those slanted eyes, and he saw the surprise leap there. Whatever Chandler had expected from him, it had not been this. But he recovered quickly and an untamed wariness replaced the bafflement in his eyes.

"Sure, buddy," he said then. "I'll even buy, seeing as how you're short on cash." He laughed, the sound a little too loud, a little too harsh.

The Whitehall Club, where they headed, was a posh restaurant and club occupying the top two floors of the Bank of Oklahoma Building some two blocks south of the First Interstate Tower. They walked beside one another, neither of them willing to have the other behind him. Braden wondered if the few pedestrians they passed could sense the tension coiling between them.

"You staying at the Sheraton?" Braden worked to make his voice as offhand as possible. He had taken a little of the initiative away from Chandler by his casual acceptance of disaster and defeat. Those ingrained reflexes of survival had carried him through. He could not afford to lose any of the ground thus gained. He felt Chandler's sidewise glance.

"No, the Skirvin," Chandler named the classic old downtown hotel. He was puzzled, Braden knew, but he was playing along.

"You been in town long?"

"A couple of days." This time Chandler's look was direct, flicking quickly away, however. He seemed about to say more, but fell silent.

Games, Braden thought. Superficial sparring that only mirrored the true life-and-death conflict lurking between them. His mind, like a runaway train, kept trying to jump the tracks, to derail into a wasteland of fear and desperation. He forced it back on track. But he had let the conversation lapse for too long.

"Andruss has known about your little account all along," the bravado was back in Chandler's voice. He was recovering from Braden's oblique offensive. "He even knew where the cash to fund it came from. You can't keep secrets from the Operation. You ought to know that."

"And it's something you ought to remember." Braden said calmly.

Chandler laughed that harsh laugh in reply. "Me? I don't have any secrets. An open book, that's me." They passed the elaborate metallic sculpture that stood outside the bank, water flowing constantly through its shallow tilting troughs into the blue pool at its base, and they crossed the lobby of the bank. Not as large as that of the First, nor as elaborate, it was designed on more modern lines. It didn't appeal to Braden.

They stood in front of the elevators and Chandler showed his teeth in a smile that had nothing of warmth to it, as if he was enjoying the charade. Just two businessmen on their way to dinner. Braden realized that whatever brief advantage he had gained had somehow slipped away. If anything, they were now on even terms.

Why was he even doing this? Braden found himself wondering. Why hadn't he simply fled when Chandler had first accosted him in the bank. He knew with a sickening despair, that, unless he killed Chandler, he would have to evade him. Chandler might be willing to play games for some unfathomable reason of his own, but, of a certainty, he would not willingly let Braden escape him again.

In the club, seated at a small, round table sheathed in marble next to the floor-to-ceiling windows with their panoramic view of the city, Braden ordered a soft drink while Chandler, with a sneer, ordered Scotch.

Oklahoma City spread out below them. The growth to the north had spawned modern office towers, silhouetted at random intervals against the late afternoon sky. In a few more years Oklahoma City might have a whole new skyline. Would he be around to see it? he wondered.

"I told you I'd catch up with you, Eric. I told you that you couldn't escape." Chandler was almost gleeful in his gloating.

Maybe that was all Chandler wanted — to gloat. He certainly had reason enough. "Andruss would be proud of you," Braden admitted. "How many of our associates have you killed, anyway? I never trained you to betray your own people." Chandler just grinned that mirthless grin.

"Does it matter? Besides, I'm not betraying anyone. I just follow orders."

"There's a good defense for you," Braden said drily. Faintly he heard the chime of an elevator outside the club arriving at this, the top floor of the building. He still was not too sure of his own motives in promoting this meeting, unless it was simply to postpone the inevitable showdown.

"Defenses are for weaklings. I don't need one. I'm good at what I do. I enjoy it. That ought to be enough for anyone. It was always enough for you."

Braden shook his head. "Don't put me down on your level," his voice was hard. "I never enjoyed the killing. I did it when it was necessary; I trained others to do it, but I never enjoyed it."

Chandler stared at him hard, as if trying to peer into his soul. At last he leaned back slightly in his chair, toying with his drink, although his eyes and body remained alert.

"You know, I still can't figure you out, Eric. You don't act crazy, even now, but you really have flipped out. There's no way Andruss can risk you running around loose thinking you're Billy Graham, or something. Who knows when you might have some divine revelation that tells you to spill your guts to the *Washington Post* or some such liberal piece of trash? You'd tear the Operation apart."

There could be worse things, Braden thought, but he didn't speak the words aloud, because suddenly he knew the reasons for being here in this place and perhaps they were not his own motivations after all.

"Look," he began, but then stopped because he had no words for what he was trying to say. But he had to try. "Something happened to me. I've been on your side of the fence, been there a lot longer than you have. You think you're good, a real pro, but I've been all the way around that same block and back again. You remember that when you try to sit in judgement of me."

Braden heard the passion in his own voice as if that of a

stranger, and Chandler had recoiled slightly from it. The words were there now, whether his own or from some other source was no longer important. "But something happened to me, like I said. You can call it a religious experience, call it being saved—there are all kinds of buzz-words. I don't know about all that; I'm still new to all this. But I knew there was a change in me. It changed my perspective somehow, made me see things differently, plainer, made me realize that there's more to life than serving the Operation as a hired gun. There are higher things, more significant priorities..."

"Like Jesus Christ?" Chandler cut him off with savage scorn. "Like God?"

"Christ Himself had an answer for that," Braden shot back. "It's what he said to Pilate, 'Thou sayest it'." From somewhere in his superficial Bible studies, he had plucked the words, surprising even himself.

Chandler's slashing gesture of disgust might almost have been a blow directed at unseen enemies.

"Look," Braden tried again, "don't you think I know how I must look to you? I've seen things like this happen to people. I've always thought they were crazy. Maybe, deep down, I envied them a little bit, even while I thought they had lost their minds. They always seemed so certain, so confident they had found an answer to some vital question I never even knew existed.

"Well, I understand now. And they were right, those people I thought had lost their minds. They did have the answer. And now I have it too. Not all the answers, but the only one that really matters."

"Christ, Eric! You sound like some damned fanatic!"

"That's one thing I'm not and never will be."

Chandler stared. "A fanatic?"

"No, damned. Can you say the same thing?"

The younger man's face twisted into a mask that was no longer handsome at all. In that instant, Braden realized that there would be no further reasoning with him at this point in time. He had given it his best shot and succeeded in provoking only a murderous rage that flared dangerously in Chandler's eyes. He was beyond listening now, beyond anything save the savage fury surging in him. The games were all over now.

Dimly Braden heard the chime of the elevator, and in that same moment he saw Chandler's hand start its grab for the big .357 and he knew that the man planned to kill him here and now. He gripped the edge of the heavy table and upended it, coming up onto his feet as he did so, ramming the edge of the table hard into Chandler's body.

Chandler went over backwards, chair and all, his drink flying, his gun undrawn. Braden's own hand started its reflexive stab for the butt of the .38. He could take Chandler out, end the game now and for real.

But his hand never completed the movement and instead he turned and raced for the doorway, hearing the startled protesting shout of the bartender, dreading the blasting sound of the .357, remembering Chandler's bewildering speed that day in the firing range.

But he made it out through the doorway, down the brief corridor to the elevator foyer. One of them was there, as the chimes had told him, its doors just beginning to slip automatically shut. He plunged between them, rebounding off the opposite wall of the empty cubicle. For a moment the doors hesitated, the electronic eye activated by his hurtling body. Then they continued to close.

Braden stabbed a finger at the lowest button and felt the conveyance begin its descent. He did not know how close behind him Chandler was. He had not seen another elevator waiting, which meant the younger man would have to take the stairs down the full sixteen floors. But Chandler was in shape. Even starting late, he could give the elevator a run for its money.

Braden stabbed helplessly, impotently at the button again. He had hit the button for the basement level which opened, as he recalled, into the labyrinth of corridors of the underground concourse. In its maze, he thought, lay his best prospect of escape.

Would Chandler anticipate him? Would he descend nonstop to the concourse, or would he take the time to stop first and check the lobby on the ground floor? Or would he guess that Braden had gotten off on one of the intervening floors and waste further time checking that alternative?

Braden couldn't count on it. He had to assume the worst.

Thankfully the elevator did not make any intermittent halts in its descent. Braden drew the .38, holding it down alongside his leg so it would not be immediately obvious to any innocent bystanders waiting when the lift stopped.

Twice now he had passed up opportunities to kill Chandler. Did that make them even, or was he one up on Chandler? Idiotic thoughts. Whatever emotions had motivated Chandler to postpone a showdown were long since gone, submerged in the flood of kill lust he had seen in those small eyes. Chandler would give him no more breaks, and Braden tightened his grip on the butt of the .38. He himself might not have the option of hesitating again.

7

A shot rang out behind him, its blast merging with the ugly metallic shriek as the bullet ricocheted from one of the parked cars in the underground garage. Braden veered automatically to evade the second shot, but he didn't slow, racing for the double glass doors which opened into the concourse on the other side of the garage.

The lowermost elevator foyer had disgorged him into the garage. He had seen no one; Chandler had not beeen waiting in ambush. He had replaced the .38 in its shoulder rig.

He did not draw it now. Chandler must have been close behind the elevator. Nor had he been fooled by any of Braden's options. *He knows how I think,* Braden's mind gasped. *I trained him that way.*

He reached the glass doors and flung them open, lunging through them and the next set. The underground corridor, its walls painted in various neutral pastels, angled off in front of him and to his right, blocking his view. It ran straight to his left. He went that way, running hard.

The upper half of the wall on his left was a window looking out into the parking garage. He would be in plain sight to Chandler on the other side of it, and as he realized this, he flung himself forward and down into a shoulder roll, even as another shot shattered the glass above him, showering him with fragments as he rolled up onto his feet and pelted on.

Chandler wasn't the only one who could anticipate his opponent's moves.

He dodged through a dogleg in the corridor and out of the makeshift shooting gallery into a more populated stretch of the concourse. Although pausing to shoot would have slowed Chandler slightly, but he would not be far behind.

Braden slowed his frantic pace, aware he was drawing stares. There was more traffic here. It was late afternoon and the office people were in motion, departing their jobs.

Braden was breathing hard, although his actual exertions had not been great. Adrenalin pumped through his system, opposing the effort he made to slow his breathing, to calm his nerves. After three misses, Chandler would have to cool the gunplay, particularly with this much pedestrian traffic. But Braden harbored no illusions that his stalker would give up.

He moved at a swift walk, only a little faster than some of the people, shifting adroitly to sidestep and bypass them. He noticed a small video camera mounted near the ceiling and recalled that the halls of the concourse were monitored by security guards from a central communications center—another element to contend with.

Marginally, it played to his advantage. Chandler would not want to allow himself to be video taped gunning down his prey, although Braden himself could ill afford to be detained for questions by curious police. He hoped that the transmitted images of two men, moving rather more quickly than usual in the crowd, one in the wake of the other, would not alert the guards to the life-and-death stalk going on right in front of them.

He glanced back once just before negotiating another dogleg through a set of glass doors. He had a brief glimpse of his pursuer some twenty yards back.

Chandler's face was set, implacable. There was no sign of his gun, but he moved with one hand hovering near his lapel. Braden felt a chill that touched the marrow of his bones.

He had come to a kind of crossroads with a number of

corridors disgorging into a central area between the entrances into small shops, and the glass front of some kind of banking or finance facility. One of the overhead video cameras seemed to stare straight at him. There was map of the whole concourse system in a glass display case, names of businesses with accompanying arrows attached to the wall. He had time to look at neither.

He forced himself to move, to choose a corridor almost at random. He looked back again as a turn in the hallway hid him from sight of the intersection. Chandler had not yet appeared. Perhaps for the moment he had eluded him.

He passed a single glass door with the obscure name of a club stenciled on it and gloom behind it. On impulse he entered, finding himself in a long narrow cocktail lounge, poorly lit to conceal its sleazy character, and occupied by various business types having a first or last drink before heading home for the day.

He found a booth in the far corner and occupied it, ordering a nonalcoholic fruit drink from the overly made-up waitress clad in a too-tight leotard getup. Perhaps Chandler would find him here, but at least this vantage point would allow him to see him first. He could not stay here long, but for the moment it provided a refuge, a breathing place.

He sipped the drink — a mixture of some lemon-lime carbonated beverage and orange juice that seemed to pull at the insides of his mouth.

He didn't know how familiar Chandler was with the layout of the concourse. If he had, indeed, had a few days to wait, almost certainly he would have used the time to familiarize himself with the stalking ground.

Braden's own knowledge was faded by the years that had passed since he had last been here. Outdated too. They almost certainly would have added new extensions, new branches. The place had been a confusing maze to begin with. He might be better off leaving it, taking his chances outside.

It would be easy to underestimate his opponent, just as he had done up until now. All his planning, his elaborate tactics, the long hours on the road to reach here, had been futile, useless. He had played right into Chandler's hand. Andruss, like some evil, omnipotent chess master, had moved a knight to take a pawn.

But the pawn had once been a knight himself.

He finished the drink and ordered another, but did not touch it. The club was almost empty now, and he guessed the concourse, as well, would be mostly cleared of people. He wondered how late the guards maintained their automatic surveillance.

He had spent enough time here. He paid for his drinks, then slipped back out into the hallway. Nothing happened. No one shot at him. The hallway was empty.

He headed back to the intersection and into another corridor, passing few people, glancing back frequently as he went. His hand ached to grip the butt of the .38, but he did not draw it.

He did not need to return to his hotel room. He had left nothing there worth the risk of having Chandler anticipate his return and be waiting there in ambush.

He needed to get out of the downtown area, to keep moving. And, he decided, he wanted to stay in the tunnel system as long as possible. At least down here he had a better chance of seeing whatever came at him.

He paused briefly to study a display map of the tunnels, but could glean little from it. He found a corridor which he thought corresponded to one on the map and headed down it. Soon, he imagined, they would be closing the tunnels for the evening. He moved more quickly, trying to stay on the course he had selected, although in this subterranean urban maze, it was easy to become disoriented. He passed the glass fronts of closed shops and once took a wrong turn that brought him to a dead-end area of little sidewalk-type cafes, now eerily empty.

The pastel carpeting muffled sound, but at times he stopped to listen and heard nothing untoward. He had not passed anyone else for several minutes, and he began to picture himself as a rat turned loose in the same maze as a hungry ferret. Quickly he banished the image.

He reached a portion of hallway where tile replaced the carpeting. Pausing, he slipped off his shoes. Someone, something, was nearby. He could sense it. Somehow Chandler was on to him, had picked up his trail, perhaps hearing him pass by some side corridor. The hallway curved gradually so that he could see only a short distance behind him.

He went ahead, moving silently in sock feet. When he was well out of sight of the beginning of the tiled floor, he paused to listen. At first he heard nothing. Then, even above the pounding of blood in his ears, he caught a brief squeak, as of rubber against tile.

Braden smiled coldly. Chandler was back there close behind him, but he had made a mistake. He had not removed his shoes before stepping off the carpet, relying on his rubber soles to allow him to move in silence.

Not good enough, Braden thought, and the .38 came into his hand in a smooth, natural movement. Time to show Chandler what it felt like to be the hunted, to remind him that just because he stalked a Christian didn't mean that the Christian was either helpless or a pacifist.

There were no cameras here to record him. He positioned himself against the far wall, shoes tucked in his belt, arms extended in a shooter's stance, and waited motionlessly. There was a chance, a bare chance, that whoever was back there behind him was an innocent bystander, but deep down in his gut he knew better.

The fluorescent lights cast poor shadows. He saw a flicker of movement and had an impression — no more — of an approaching figure, hugging the inside wall, moving in a cautious feline crouch. It was enough. No innocent pedestrian would have reason to move in such a fashion.

Braden fired three times, pulling the trigger as fast as he could, sending the bullets back down the curving hallway to ricochet off the outside wall opposite the oncoming figure. The echoes slammed back and forth down the corridor.

He took two swift steps across the width of the corridor, respositioning himself to avoid any return fire. The figure was gone. The follower had never fully appeared, and Braden had not gotten a good look at him. He did not need it. He slipped the .38 back into its holster, snatched his shoes from their awkward place in his belt and, turning, ran hard down the corridor in the direction he had been going.

Chandler would be a bit more cautious about following him now, he thought with grim pleasure. He had not aimed to kill, or even to wound, but the warning would be plain.

The shots might or might not be investigated. He reminded himself that if he stayed too long in the concourse it could well become a trap.

At a branching of the corridor he paused long enough to replace the spent shells in the .38 and to slip his tieless shoes back on his feet.

The safest time to emerge from the tunnels would be after dark, but that was still some time off. He needed a place of refuge until then, and Chandler, even slowed by the warning shots, would not be far behind him.

He did not think the map he had briefly viewed had included this area where he now found himself. Surely this was a new addition to the tunnel system, perhaps attaching it to the giant display greenhouse in the nearby Myriad Gardens.

He moved quickly into one of the branches. The tilework here looked newer than in the other choice. He had gone some hundred feet before he came to a sawhorse barrier with a sign denying access to the public. Beyond was unfinished concrete floor disappearing into darkness.

Braden slowed his pace, but kept going. He had a small penlight on his keychain, but was reluctant to use it. A gleam of light would show up for a long way to someone coming up behind him. He guessed there was a temporary lighting system of some sort for the area, probably extinguished when the construction crew called it a day. If he searched, he might be able to locate the breaker, but he doubted that he had time. Besides, the darkness would delay Chandler even further.

The corridor ran straight now, and after a time he was forced to use the little key light intermittently. He passed tools and supplies, and once what he thought was a rat skittered away in the darkness.

Overhead the acoustic ceiling panels ended abruptly, although the metal framework intended to eventually hold them continued on ahead into the gloom. Braden halted, considering.

There were no sounds in the darkness. He used the penlight again to inspect the framework overhead. There was some two feet of space between the wide strips of the grid and the true ceiling above. What was above that ceiling? Sunlight? A busy street? The basement of an office building? Freedom and safety?

He dismissed his musings and clicked off the light. Crouching, he sprang upward, his hands closing on the metal gridwork. He pulled himself up, and like some great ungainly spider worked his way in over the acoustic ceiling panels already in place, careful to keep his weight distributed on the metal and not let it rest on the fagile panels.

Teeth gritted with effort, he made his way further back, then managed through a series of contortions to turn himself about so that he had a view past the end of the ceiling tiles into the darkness of the hallway below.

The continuing strain on his muscles was becoming a burden. He shifted himself about until he found a position of relative comfort with chest, belly, and shins resting on intersections of the wide metal strips. He was glad they were wide enough and sturdy enough to support his weight.

It was hot, and he tasted dust when he breathed. He

forced himself into an neutral mode, concentrating on remaining motionless, on disregarding the pain in his bones and joints and muscles. After a time he entered almost a trance-like state, although his senses remained alert.

There was no way Chandler could detect his presence. If he came along the corridor, he might guess, but short of the impractical method of firing at random up through the ceiling, there was no way he could come after Braden without first exposing himself.

Clinging there in the stifling darkness, Braden waited.

8

His watch measured it only in hours, but he was certain an eternity had passed. An eternity of dust, and sweat, and subtle isometric exercises to keep his circulation going.

It would be dark outside now, he knew. No one had come this way; he was certain that in that stygian silence he would have heard even Chandler had he passed in the corridor below.

Cautiously he began to ease himself forward, grimacing in pain, but careful to maintain silence. When he dropped to the rough concrete floor, he had the .38 in hand, swiveling in a crouch, almost expecting the roaring flame of Chandler's .357 to stab at him out of the gloom.

Only darkness, and the sound of his heartbeat.

He moved swiftly to the wall and flattened himself against it, pausing to orient himself. He had no idea where his nemesis was, but he thought he knew in what direction the unfinished tunnel was headed. He used the key light once, then catfooted on into the darkness, gun held at the ready.

He came to a set of heavy metal doors, locked with a chain and padlock. He stood and listened for a long time, but could detect no betraying noise beyond the doors. At last he extracted a pocket knife which, along with a conventional blade, had several other more esoteric extensions. Working by feel, he selected one and inserted it into the heavy padlock.

When the padlock clicked open, he paused again before returning the lockpick to his pocket. He eased the chain loose without clatter, palmed the .38, and pushed down on the door handle. A dim crack of light showed around the edges of the door, seeming intolerably bright to him after his hours in darkness.

He waited, then eased the door open just far enough for him to slip through, finding himself in a foyer area with nonfunctioning escaltors leading up to twin glass doors. A single light bulb provided illumination in the foyer.

He ascended in a crouch, going almost flat on the last few motionless steel steps to peer through the glass. For a moment he could not discern the identity of the various shapes, and then he realized he was peering into the Botanical Tube, the giant cylindrical greenhouse in the Myriad Gardens. His guess about the tunnel's destination had been correct.

It was like peering into a jungle. Numerous species of tropical verdure had been planted in garden-like plots at irregularly staggered levels. Palm trees loomed tall in ghostly silhouette above various forms of lush foliage. Just inside the doors a pathway took a wandering route among the displays.

Moisture had condensed on the inside of the doors, making observation difficult, but he still stayed prone for long moments. He saw nothing to alarm him. There could be another door, or doors, at the far end almost two hundred feet away, which, presumably, opened to the outside world, and there lay his escape route.

He used the lockpick again, feeling the warmth of the glass beneath his fingers. He had time to recall before the lock clicked open that the original designers of the greenhouse had completely overlooked the fact that the temperatures inside an enormous glass tube in the summer in Oklahoma would reach levels that were far above anything that could be endured for any length of time.

This had caused abandonment of the project for over a year. Work on the elaborate landscaping of the Myriad

Gardens around the Tube had ceased and the grounds had become shabby and overgrown while the necessary redesigning was plotted and further modifying construction completed. The exhibit was still not ready to open as a tourist attraction.

He opened the door just wide enough to allow him entrance, and stepped into a wall of humid heated air redolent with the scents of dozens of tropical plants. He crouched low and stepped to one side, off the path into the yielding soil of one of the exhibits, to avoid being silhouetted against the doors.

As he moved, an explosion stabbed a roaring flame at him from one of the elevated areas about half way down the structure.

The bullet punched a hole in the glass beside his head. If he had not been moving as he entered, it would have caught him dead center. Even as the glass was still falling, he flung himself, diving sidewise, triggering one wild snap shot in the direction of the muzzle flash. He landed in soft soil and rolled over and over through the tangling growth, feeling leaves and branches slap at his face, pluck at his clothing.

Then there was nothing beneath him and he fell some two feet to a lower display, coming up onto his knees behind the barrier made by the higher exhibit's retaining wall.

He peered into the gloom of the vast artificial forest. Chandler had been waiting for him! The man had known, guessed—how didn't matter—where he would emerge from the tunnels and simply waited in ambush. He could see no sign of him, nor hear any sound. Chandler would have shifted positions following his botched shot. He could be moving even now, or waiting in concealment for Braden to expose himself again. The fact that there had been no further shots signified that he had lost track of Braden in the darkness.

The only illumination in their shadowy stalking ground came from the lights of nearby buildings and street lamps, shining dimly through the thick glass. Headlights from passing cars on the highway flickered faintly in eerie reflection.

Braden lowered himself into a prone position and began to work his way back from the retaining wall. He could not return to the tunnels, and Chandler, knowing this, would be alert for him to try for the far doors to the outside. But time would be working against Chandler, perhaps forcing him to carry the attack to Braden rather than simply waiting in ambush. A gun battle in the greenhouse could not be expected to go unnoticed for long.

Braden snaked his way from one exhibit to the next, moving silently so that not as much as a leaf was disturbed by his passing. He had learned how to move in brush in the jungles of Indo-China. Moving undetected through this landscaped artificial forest was child's play by comparison.

There was no sign of Chandler. Most likely, Braden decided, the other man was staying put, waiting in a position which gave him clear coverage of the exit, gambling that the single shot had attracted attention from outside.

He had worked his way some two-thirds of the way to the exit when he paused next to a small, nonfunctioning waterfall to take stock. There were, he saw now, two sets of doors at the end of the structure, almost beside one another. Obviously, once the greenhouse was open to the public, one set would serve as an entrance and the other as an exit. Chandler would have entered through one set and most likely would have left both sets unlocked so as not to block his escape route.

Braden scanned the dimly seen exhibits on the other side of the tube. Chandler was over there, waiting and watching. When Braden tried for the doors Chandler would have an open field of fire.

Braden's mind meshed, calculating odds, probabilities, evaluating Chandler and Chandler's knowledge of him. The younger man would expect his mentor to follow the precepts he had taught, which meant that Chandler would be waiting for him to work his way under cover as near to the doors as possible before making a try for them.

So all right. Where was Chandler? Where would he position himself to permit the best coverage of both sets of doors without exposing himself unnecessarily? Braden's eyes scanned the far side of the tube, not seeking details now, but assessing terrain, lines of fire, available cover. If he were in Chandler's place, setting up this ambush, where would he himself be now?

There. Amidst a clump of smallish trees bordered by heavy ground cover in an exhibit set almost directly opposite his own position part way up the inner curve of the tube. If he was Chandler that was where he would be, ready to fire the instant a figure materialized next to the doors.

Braden removed the cartridge case from the single shot he had fired in the tube and replaced it. He had two speedloaders on him, but he had already partly depleted one when he had reloaded back in the concourse. He eased out of the now ragged sports coat and spent a fruitless moment straining his eyes to detect some hint of Chandler's presence. Nothing, but he was certain Chandler was there. He had to be there.

Put your money on it then, Braden thought, and began a stealthy descent from the exhibits where he himself was concealed.

He crouched behind some exotic shrub next to the pathway. The humid air seemed to enfold him, stifling his breath, condensing on his flesh to mingle with the sweat already soaking his body and clothing. If he had guessed wrong, he would most likely be dead within the next couple of seconds. And there was a good chance of that anyway.

He came out of cover sprinting, firing across his body as he ran, pumping shells up at those odd trees and their surrounding ground cover, laying down a cover fire as he pelted for the doors.

On the fourth step, he let go of the coat in his left hand, flinging it billowing behind him as a distraction. He thought he heard a return shot, mingled with the drum roll of his own

.38, might have felt the wind as a bullet whipped by him, but in the headlong frenzy of his rush, he could not be sure.

Then the hammer fell on an empty chamber as the doors seemed to charge toward him. They opened outward, he saw, and he put his shoulder down, praying in that last instant before impact that they were actually unlocked.

He hit with jarring impact, felt the door swing open as glass beside his head shattered in concert with an echoing blast from behind him. He dived forward, across the foyer, his outstretched hands, one of them still gripping the .38, shoving hard against the outermost door. It too gave and he tumbled out into the relatively cool air of the Oklahoma night, coming smoothly up onto his feet.

He ducked low and darted around the front of the greenhouse, almost flinging himself down the concrete steps he encountered there. Below him was a small kind of amphitheatre extending into the huge fish pond which nestled in the center of the hill-like berms of the Myriad Gardens.

Halfway down the steps, he slapped a hand onto the round metal bannister and transformed his momentum into a vault, landing with flexed knees that thrust him once more into a run.

The enormous tubular greenhouse actually bridged the pond, and he ran under its shadowy bulk, using the last speedloader as he did, staying on the sidewalk which encircled the pond. For a moment the absurd structure's entire weight seemed to hang suspended over him. Then he was out from under it, turning to leap and claw his way up the steep grassy side of one of the berms.

He found purchase with both feet and paused. Blind flight might take him only back into the sights of Chandler's .357. He was half clinging to the thick grass which covered the berm, his feet resting in a shallow indentation. The curving mass of the greenhouse loomed hugely above him. Chandler had disappeared.

On the far side of the Botanical Tube, the fish pond and

its surrounding berms extended probably fifty yards or so. The sidewalk completely encircled the irregularly shaped pond. Flights of steps ascended the surrounding berms at intervals and spiderweb-like bridges spanned the air above the water.

Tall poles with floodlights provided harsh illumination to some areas of the park, leaving others in dark shadow. The lights were reflected unsteadily from the surface of the water.

Braden recalled that the pond was supposedly connected by a subterranean channel with a nearby river which provided a ready supply of murky water. It was stocked with ornamental giant goldfish. In the past, the park had served as a haven for winos and transients who sought relief from the elements at the base of its sheltering berms. The pond had proven a hazard to some of these addicted part-time residents, and the bodies of more than one such unfortunate had been fished from the depths of the pond.

If he wasn't careful, it would be his own body being fished from there, Braden thought grimly. He strained his senses in the warm night breeze. He could see the lighted spire of the Interstate Tower and the luminescent cubes and blocks surrounding it like gawdy undesirable suitors.

Chandler might be catfooting along the sidewalk in his wake. Or, conceivably, he might have circled around the front of the greenhouse to haunt the heights of the berms above Braden's head. Braden tilted his head, but saw no ominous shape silhouetted against the skyline.

In the distance he heard a siren.

He froze, knowing that Chandler, wherever he was, had also gone rigid at the sound. Their running duel, he was certain, had at last attracted the attention of the police.

Would Chandler cut and run? Braden asked himself. Or would the younger man's obsession with this hunt drive him to make a last try for his target? Slowly Braden began to work his way up the berm. The single siren had become two, then three, and they were undeniably converging on the park.

Braden drew a deep breath and hauled himself up the last few feet, squirming over the crest of the artificial hill so he would not be skylighted. Lying there prone in the grass, he saw a figure some fifty feet away sprint into the brightly lit deserted boulevard. Before he was halfway across, a police car skidded around the corner, its siren screaming, its revolving light casting wildly shifting patterns. As it straightened out, a spot light from it nailed Chandler as if he were on stage. A mate to the first patrol car slewed around the other corner. Chandler seemed to hesitate, then he came to a halt and lifted both hands above his head. Every line of his body radiated disgust at this turn of events.

Braden slipped back over the crest of the berm and began to make his way rapidly toward the nearer, east end of the park. Now was the time for him to move, while Chandler and the police were occupied with one another. Chandler would eventually be able to pull strings to get released, but in the meantime, he would be detained, with no way of keeping tabs on Braden.

Further, Andruss would be displeased upon learning of the episode. Operation agents active within the country were not supposed to attract the attention of local law-enforcement authorities.

Braden slipped away from the park without incident, although other police cars were gathering as he left the area. Downtown Oklahoma City was mostly deserted at night, and he stayed to the shadows as he circled several blocks back to the west.

As the urban renewal projects had expanded the downtown section, the small area of skid row bars and porno shops had retreated westward. Braden crossed into these sleazy environs and, in his battered attire, merged with the populace of winos and addicts, prostitutes and hard-eyed men who watched the police lights around the Gardens with vested concern. They glanced nervously at Braden, then pretended not to see him.

In a filthy restroom in a grubby bar, Braden peered into a cracked mirror wedged between coin-operated condom dispensers and did what little he could do to repair his appearance. It wasn't much, but at least when he walked into the nearby bus station, he was the object of only a few disinterested stares.

The first available bus out of town left in a half hour, and he was on it, not interested so much in its ultimate destination as in seeing the night skyline of Oklahoma City disappear behind him.

There were few passengers, and those desired company no more than Braden did. He had stuffed the flexible straps and holster of the shoulder rig into a pocket. The .38 he had stuck in his belt where it rode uncomfortably beneath his shirt tail. Surreptitiously now, he shifted it to a more satisfactory position and settled back in his seat.

His eyelids were heavy, and as he was lulled into a doze by the motion of the bus, he realized that, throughout the long game of cat and mouse with Chandler, he had never once come intentionally close or even seriously considered killing the younger man. His every move had been directed toward the goal of escape. He had never slipped into an offensive mode, and that was contrary to every fragment of training he had ever received or delivered himself: kill or be killed.

Without even being aware of it, he had violated that most basic of tenets, had shown mercy when he could have killed. The Eric Braden who had trained Chandler, who had thrived in the ruthless, darkside world of counterespionage, would never have spared an enemy who was trying in turn to kill him.

But then, didn't the Scriptures say something about every man being a new creation in Christ?

He was smiling slightly when he finally sank into sleep.

9

"We can hold you as long as we like, one way or another, you realize that don't you? If nothing else we'll go ahead and press charges under John Doe and worry about identifying you later. Under the circumstances, there's no way you'll get bail."

Listening to Detective Sergeant Fredrick Lossman speak to him, watching the detective's puffy face, Chandler decided that the man meant what he said. He was suddenly glad that he was not a common criminal facing Lossman on his own. Even with the as-yet-unfelt power of the Operation looming near, dealing with Lossman was not a pleasant experience. He regarded the Oklahoma City detective and grinned wordlessly.

Lossman reddened. "All right, go ahead and play it cute, hotshot. We'll see how long you keep on grinning."

In truth, Chandler did not feel at all like grinning. The interrogation room was small enough to be claustrophobic, and the stale air only added to the effect. He had spent most of the last five hours in the room, following the degrading process of being booked. He had adopted a role of passive resistance by simply refusing to cooperate. He was playing a waiting game, and he thought that Lossman had guessed as much and was not pleased by it.

He had utilized his one phone call to dial the emergency number reserved only for situations such as this. He had given a cryptic report to the sexless impersonal voice which had answered, and then settled back to endure the interrogation and wait.

And the waiting was growing irksome. He had now gone over twenty-four hours without sleep. He was tired and dirty and his nerves had been stretched to their limit by the long hunt in the tunnels and its humiliating aftermath.

He knew that by now—midafternoon — Andruss would have word of his predicament and would be working behind the scenes, pulling obscure strings to secure his release. He knew Andruss would not be happy with his performance and wondered perversely if his superior was deliberately delaying his release as a subtle form of chastisement for his failure to take Braden out when he'd had the opportunity.

It was just another score to be tallied against Braden's name, he decided bitterly. To have been so close to his quarry, to have actually had him in his sights, only to lose him, was infuriating. And he *had* blown it, he admitted ruefully. Not only in disobeying Andruss' orders to shoot Braden down instantly, on first contact, but in letting his anger spur him into reacting impulsively and acting hastily without sufficient planning.

Once again Braden had succeeded in angering him with his talk of God and damnation. But he did not think Braden had planned it that way. The veteran agent had appeared sincere in his efforts to explain what had happened to him. Chandler's anger had seemed to spark of its own volition. He was not a man given to introspection, but recalling that conversation now, he again felt that murderous rage rise up in him. Let Braden have his psychotic religious experience. He would not allow him to escape the next time they faced one another. And there would be a next time, he vowed silently.

"Calm down, boy," Lossman's gruff voice intruded on his thoughts.

The policeman's features had lost a little of their earlier cool and he realized that he had again let his emotions become apparent to another. He was getting bad about that.

He remembered Dickson, the computer technician, back at Operation headquarters and his ability to read his expressions. It could easily be a fatal mistake for an agent to allow his emotions to be so readily discerned. He tried another grin on Lossman but knew he did not quite pull it off.

The detective studied him shrewdly. "You know, if you'd unbend a little bit and give us some help, we might be able to pick up whoever it was you were playing high noon with. It can't be too much fun for you sittin' here knowin' he's out running around scot-free."

Chandler silently damned the man's perception and was surprised to realize that he was actually considering the offer. The need to bring Braden down, by whatever means, was a consuming drive within him.

Again he refused to respond. There was no percentage in bandying words with this hick cop. And in his present mood, he was smart enough to know he just might let something slip if he allowed this cunning detective to goad him into conversation.

Lossman shrugged with elaborate casualness. "Makes no difference to me, but you must really have a mad on for that guy, whoever he is. You all played gun tag all over the concourse and the Gardens. It's a wonder nobody was killed."

An interruption. A young detective stuck his head in the door and spoke to Lossman, who gave Chandler one last glare and then followed the messenger out. Chandler sat and waited. Maybe this was Andruss taking action at last. He had been denied access to an attorney, he mused. That might be a violation of his rights, but he was not sure. He had stopped keeping track of the court decisions. His victims had no rights except what he gave them, so the law was irrelevant to his actions and those of the Operation anyway. Unless, as in this particular instance, it could provide a loophole through which to wriggle out of a ticklish situation.

It was some time before Lossman returned, and when he did his face told the story. He stood looming over Chandler where the latter was seated in a hard-backed chair and glowered down at him. "I don't know how you did it, hotshot, but you're out. Somebody big is pulling strings for you somewhere. Times are bad when punks like you have connections."

Chandler stood up so abruptly it made Lossman step back to avoid him. "That's right, I've got connections," he said easily. "You remember that. Because if you don't, and you try something stupid, like putting a tail on me, I'll have your job and you'll be off this police force so fast there'll be a vacuum. You got that?"

Lossman's face had gone red again. "You get out of town, boy," he gritted, "or we'll be seein' each other again, connections or no connections!"

Chandler brushed past him and went out the door. Processing his release took almost an hour, and he did not see Lossman again. Outside of the old building housing the Police Headquarters on the outskirts of the downtown area, he paused a moment, savoring his freedom.

His clothes were a mess and he knew he looked little better than any of the transients frequenting the city. He would need to report in to Andruss soon, and he was not looking forward to the experience. But there were a few preliminary steps he could take now, he reflected grimly, even though they had lost their best lead on Eric Braden.

The Operation's knowledge of Braden's secret account had been the best bet at intercepting him. That chance was gone. It would be a chase from here on, with himself as the tracker. And he may as well start now trying to pick up the trail.

He knew where the sleazy bars and the porn shops and the flophouse hotels were clustered, ironically, not far from the police station. Even though it was mid-afternoon, the first bar he entered boasted several dubious customers. Chandler took note of two burly hired-muscle types at a corner table.

They stared at him with flat, empty eyes as he entered. He did not like having them behind him as he approached the bar.

The bartender was middle-aged with oily hair combed straight back from a hollow-eyed face. Chandler appraised him covertly as he ordered a drink. The whiskey was cheap and harsh. He drank it and had to resist the urge to buy another. He had found himself more prone to drink lately and knew he needed to watch himself. He had seen more than one agent lose his life, directly or indirectly, to alcohol or other chemical addictives.

He caught the bartender's attention with a move of his head. He placed a bill on the bar, holding it there under his hand so that only the denomination was visible to the bartender's avaricious eyes. Those eyes finally came up to his face.

"Yeah?" the bartender's voice was rasping.

"A passport," Chandler said sotto voce. "I need a passport."

The hungry eyes flicked down to the bill, then away. "Try the Immigration Office." The bartender started to turn away.

"Hey." Chandler's voice was still low. "This isn't open to negotiation. The price doesn't go up."

"Get lost," the barkeep grunted.

Casually Chandler flicked his glass off the bar so that it shattered on the floor. The bartender turned back sharply to-ward him. "The thing is," Chandler explained reasonably, "I offered to pay you in the first place. Now it starts to cost you."

The man's head turned ever so slightly toward the back of the room and behind him Chandler heard the scrape of a chair being pushed back. He took two fast steps along the bar to carry him clear of the bartender and turned, coming lightly up on his toes. The two thugs had gotten to their feet and started around the table toward him.

Chandler grinned, and now he didn't care if his emotions

showed. "Come on," he said with genuine pleasure.

For a moment the two men stared at him. Then one of them cut his eyes toward the other who shook his head a slight negative. Wordlessly they turned toward the door. Behind him Chandler heard the barkeep curse. He moved so that he could keep an eye on the man.

"Now," he said, turning back to the bar when the two thugs were gone. "Let's start over. I need a passport; a good one that can pass Customs with no problem."

In the end the barkeep could only give him a name of someone who might know someone who could help him. It was a start, and he had not expected much more at this stage.

If Braden opted to leave the country, which seemed likely, he would need a clean passport. And in Oklahoma, a crossroads for international drug traffic, a forged passport should not be particularly hard to come by.

Chandler knew he could follow up on it later, and there were other options to pursue, but for now, he decided, it was time for a shower and a change of clothes back at his hotel.

As he headed in that direction, something caught his eye. The martial arts school occupied an older brick building and displayed signs boasting that its curriculum included karate, tae kwon do, kung fu, and some other art Chandler had never heard of. It did not look particularly reputable which, he supposed, was only to be expected of an establishment located in this part of town.

He hesitated. The frustration and tension coiling in him demanded a release. He found himself hoping, as he crossed the street, that there would be a class in session, so that he could have a live opponent.

There wasn't; the training room of the dojo was deserted. He found the rugged caucasian owner in his seedy office clad in a soiled karate gi complete with black belt, his feet up on his desk as he studied a magazine probably featured in one of the nearby porn shops.

For a nonrefundable deposit of ten dollars, the owner

had no objection to allowing a fellow student of the martial arts to work out in the dojo. Chandler paid without complaint, but mentally condemned the man as a mercenary. Most dojos offered used of their facilities to visiting students or masters free of charge.

He found a stale-smelling gi in a shabby changing room and donned it with distaste. He knotted a white novice belt around his waist in the traditional gesture of humility for a visiting master.

Formally, he bowed onto the training floor. There was a heavy punching bag suspended by a chain from the ceiling, and he addressed himself to it without warmup, disdaining the elaborate exercise sequences, or katas. He wanted the feel of impact with a target, even an inanimate one.

He punched the bag—a dazzling series of alternating left and right straightarm blows—then pivoted into a reverse roundhouse kick, the heel of his naked foot denting the heavy canvas of the bag at head level, setting it swinging on its chain. He dropped back into a riding-horse stance, snapping out a backfist blow that thudded hard against the bag on its rebound.

Sweat began to flow from him as he worked, alternating sequences and styles, kicking techniques and hand strikes. And, as in the simulator room back at Operation headquarters, he could feet the rightness of his moves, sense the flawless precision that powered each blow, each kick, sent home to the heavy bag.

He had been a black belt at karate before ever joining the Operation. The martial arts and hand-to-hand instuctors there had refined his early style which he now recognized as amateurish. Then had come Braden, older than some of the instructors, perhaps not as flawless in his katas, but when it came to full contact competition, when there were no holds barred, able to beat them all.

Braden had honed Chandler's skill to an even finer edge until Chandler had been a match even for him. And in the ensuing years, in the crucible of the life-and-death world of counterespionage, Chandler's abilities had been forged to an even greater temper. He could take Braden now; he could feel it. Armed or unarmed, it would make no difference when they met again.

Indeed, Chandler found himself hoping that their final encounter would be hand-to-hand. The satisfaction of beating Braden like that, on his own terms, would be even greater. But he would not give Braden that option by choice. To do so would be to make a fool's move in a professional's game.

He kicked the bag again, lashing out sidewise with his foot, and again, the movements so fast even his own eye could not follow them. The bag rocked and swayed. If it had been a man—if it had been Braden, he thought with gleeful savagery—he would be dead.

Dimly he became aware of another presence. The burly owner of the dojo had entered the training room and was watching his performance silently, arms folded across his broad chest. Chandler had not seen him enter, and a part of his mind was displeased with this lapse. His concentration on his vendetta — what better word? — was making him careless. But such concentration on his mission and target was vital, he knew, if he was to succeed.

One last spinning kick, and he straightened, breathing faster, but not really hard. He felt strong and light on his feet.

The exercise had purged his system of the accumulated stress and frustration. He smiled insolently now at the karate instructor.

"A white belt," the man snorted. "Who're you trying to kid?"

Chandler gestured toward the center of the room where a sparring ring had been laid out in black tape. "How about it?" he challenged. "You game? A little free-style?"

For a moment longer the instructor regarded him. "Not a chance," he grunted at last. "Not even on a dare."

Chandler grinned and went back to the bag.

10

The town of Cromwell was located on an obscure two-lane blacktop road off I-40 somewhere east of Oklahoma City. There were a couple of churches, a few houses, and a kind of combination convenience and general store which displayed horse halters and sweet feed for livestock adjacent to groceries and soft drinks.

There were no motels, but there was an elderly black woman who would rent a small shack to a stranger, although her conversation frequently turned to the fact that she possessed a shotgun, apparently permanently loaded with heavy lead slugs, which she kept near the door to her sagging frame house.

Braden had ended up there some twenty-four hours after his flight from Oklahoma City, following a switch in buses and a good hike from the highway to the town. He had reoutfitted himself with shells for his .38, a cheap suitcase, and several changes of casual clothes from a larger town, with an Indian name, which boasted a Walmart discount store. He was careful with his purchases; he had counted on having access to the account in Oklahoma City, and consequently, had not been as prudent with his spending as he might have been. He was nowhere near broke yet, but he knew the funds he had would most likely have to last him for some time.

He had also taken the opportunity to purchase a Bible. It had come as something of a shock to him to realize that he did not have a Bible among his possessions. In his flight from Operation headquarters, he had neglected to take the one at his apartment. It and the apartment were forever out of his reach now, he reflected grimly.

Buying a new one had made him feel good, but, lying in the cot in the rundown shack and trying to read the tome in the light of a single naked bulb, he found little solace in the heavy prose and antiquated poetry of the King James translation.

His effort to escape the Operation had been a comedy of errors and miscalculations so far. Somewhere in the Scriptures, he knew, the Lord promised protection and guidance to His children, but such verses as contained those promises escaped his untutored efforts at Bible study.

Braden had committed himself to the Lord, given up everything to follow Him, as Jesus had requested of the rich young man. In return he had been hounded and almost killed, betrayed by a comrade who now sought him with all the skills of a trained assassin. Perhaps the Lord had delivered him from that deadly game of stalk and kill, or perhaps he had escaped Chandler thanks to his own skills and experience. He hadn't felt the Lord's protective presence when the shells from Chandler's .357 had been whistling past his head.

His one source of funds was irretrievably beyond his reach, and Andruss, with seeming omnipotence, had proven himself capable of anticipating his every move. Such divine blessings and guidance as he had received thus far had been scarce indeed, he thought bitterly.

With a snarl of mingled disgust and impotence, Braden laid the Bible aside. He rose and pushed open the screen door and emerged into the sultry night air. He could see the lights of other houses, and heard what had to be an ancient pickup go by out on the road. He hoped Mrs. Jacobs, his landlady, didn't see him, decide that he was aprowl with less than good intentions, and seek to resolve his doubts once and for all with her shotgun.

He circled wide out toward the road. A group of local teenagers, exercising their rights of freedom and rites of puberty on Saturday night, had gathered at the store down the road. The sounds of their voices and the occasional revving of a souped-up engine seemed remote.

Across the road he could see the dark shape of the small stone church. The cross atop its steeple was starkly silhouetted against a rising half moon. The sign out front gave the name of the pastor and the times of the services. He had looked at it earlier.

He knew he should go there in the morning, but he found himself devising reasons to avoid it. How would the local congregation react to a stranger in their midst? Isolated, used to privacy, they would probably resent his presence. His previous sorties to church had been to large denominational gatherings where he could lose himself in the crowd.

Here he would be open, exposed, the object of intense and critical scrutiny. For a man on the run, it was suicidally foolish to subject himself to such exposure.

And how was he supposed to act among them? What did one do or say to other Christians? He knew how to set a charge of plastique so as to demolish the building, but as to how to enter it as a worshiper, he had no real idea.

He slept fitfully on the hard cot, dreading the morning, equally angry at himself and at a God who put His followers in such absurd dilemmas. Dawn found him almost eager for the morning services if for no other reason than to have the ordeal over and done with.

He dressed in slacks and an oxford shirt, deliberately forcing himself to wait until his watch showed a scant minute before the designated hour of ten a.m. to leave the shack and stride quickly across the road before he could lose his nerve.

The sound of a hymn reached him as he approached, and even before he could make out the words, the sound of the voices raised in praise touched some chord deep within him. It was with a kind of eagerness that he opened the door at last and entered.

The sanctuary was not large, and the congregation fit it comfortably. Braden took a seat in a back pew. Surprisingly, few of the people seemed to take notice of him. An elderly man across the aisle — obviously a farmer who had come to town with his wife to church — smiled at him with a simplicity of greeting that left him feeling awkwardly inadequate. He managed a nod and a feeble grin in return.

There were more hymns, a prayer, and an offering to which he contributed a small bill. A pretty teen-age girl, accompanied by the pianist, sang a solo with more heart than skill. She was obviously nervous at performing, and Braden found himself admiring her courage.

The pastor was a heavyset man with a ruddy face that nevertheless radiated a kind of warmth that Braden found immediately appealing for some reason he could not define. His name, Braden had seen on the sign, was David Carrol. As he took the pulpit the congregation grew silent.

"We have a guest with us today, and I'm sure you've all been looking forward to hearing him. We all know him in a sense—our church helps support his work down in Mexico. I've had the pleasure of knowing him personally for years, and he has been a blessing to my life. Those others of you who know him, I think, will share my sentiments."

A few people in the congregation said, "Amen," and Braden blinked.

"I could keep on talking," the pastor continued, "but you get to hear me every week, so I'll turn it over to our guest and brother in Christ, Howard Dennison."

The man who ascended to the pulpit was gray-haired, well into middle-age, but he was tall and rugged with a craggy face that bespoke a life not unfamiliar with harder times. Curious, Braden examined the bulletin he had picked up when he entered. He scanned the brief paragraph he found there. Howard Dennison was an American missionary in the remote Mexican village of Puerto Madero. He ran his own mission there, ministering to the local inhabitants, relying in large part on financial support from stateside churches such as this one.

Braden found himself listening with interest as Dennison spoke.

"Some of you know my story." His voice was deep. "My background isn't something I'm proud of, and, yet, in a sense, I am proud of it, because it bears witness to what the Lord can do with even the lowest of sinners if they will only commit themselves to him."

"Amen," the old farmer across the aisle from Braden said with feeling.

Dennison's appearance didn't lie. He had known hard times. As a teenager, he recounted, he had been active in the street gangs of Chicago, graduating finally to armed robbery. He told of a life marked by drugs and alcohol where violence and degradation were the touchstones of success.

Convicted for his crimes, he had done time in the brutal maximum-security prisons of the fifties, surviving there by strength and nerve, and eventually becoming a kind of warlord among the convicts.

"Then one day I met a man," Dennison said. "He was a pastor of a little mission in the roughest part of Chicago, and he would come once a week to the prison and preach and witness to anyone who would listen. There weren't many, but he always came back. For some reason, maybe because I was a leader, he always wanted to visit with me alone."

Dennison paused for effect and with a rueful grin continued, "The warden would let him have his way, so every week whether I wanted to be there or not—and believe me, brothers and sisters, I never wanted to be there—I would find myself having to either listen to this man or ignore him, and it got harder and harder to ignore him.

"He said something to me once, something that stuck in

my mind. He told me that even when I got out of prison, I didn't have any chance or hope of finding any satisfaction in life. You see, he knew I had no intention of ever going straight, that I would be back in business as an armed robber or even worse as soon as I hit the street. He told me I could never be happy because I had a contract with death—what he called a covenant with death."

Braden felt a cold chill, like the very touch of the Grim Reaper, work its way up his spine.

Dennison resumed his story. "Up until that time I had thought of the Bible as an antiquated, outdated history book with no possible relevance to my life. But that preacher insisted that the Scripture was given for our instruction—to teach us object lessons and show us how to live our lives today."

"He began to tell me about a period in Bible times when Judah was menaced by the overpowering might of the Empire of Assyria during the latter half of the eighth century B.C. Ahaz, the King of Judah, rather than looking to God for protection, had sought the good graces of the Assyrian monster waiting to consume his kingdom. It was during this time of idolatry and sorcerous practices that the prophet Isaiah came striding onto the scene with a warning of what was to come.

" 'And your covenant with death shall be disannulled, and your agreement with hell shall not stand; when the overflowing scourge shall pass through, then ye shall be trodden down by it,' so warned the prophet Isaiah in the eighteenth verse of the twenty-eighth chapter of that book."

An ominous tone had entered Dennison's voice. "Isaiah knew; he had been told by God: Only darkest doom and blackest destruction awaited those who made covenants with Assyria, who made covenants with death. The Lord God, he told them, would obliterate those covenants, would void them utterly, and the people who took part in them would be naked before His wrath!"

The words slipped away from Braden, left him locked in a coldness like that of the grave. A covenant with death, he thought. Wasn't that, in truth what he had had in all those years with the Operation? What better words to describe the unholy commitment he had made of his life to the cause of killing and destruction?

But in his submission to Christ, he had rejected that covenant and lifestyle, turned from it. Or had he?

When he had fled the Operation, seeking to transform his newfound faith from words into action, he had, he realized now, not rejected his former life at all. Rather, he had sought out the material gains that life had given him in order to finance his new life. He had been unwilling to break his "covenant with death," unwilling to give up the material things it had given him. He had not truly trusted in the Lord. He had trusted instead in but another face of death. He had accepted the Lord's gift of salvation, but had refused to allow the Lord to provide for him in this life.

And, in clinging to his past life, he had only succeeded in walking blindly into the trap that had been set for him.

Dennison was still speaking, and the words slowly began to make themselves heard in Braden's ears. "I left prison; I served my time and was finally released. And I went out of there with every intention of going back to the life I had led before, of reconfirming my covenant with death. But it seemed like I had hardly hit the streets when I saw this little shabby mission, and I realized that it was the one that the pastor had told me about in prison.

"Something drew me to that mission. At the time I convinced myself that I wanted to go there and gloat, to fling that man's words back in his face and show him how much time he had wasted on me. But, I'm here to tell you today, his effort had not been wasted."

So that was why his attempted flight had been so disastrous, Braden thought. Because he had relied on himself. And, of course, the flip-side of it all was that if he truly wanted to be free of the entangling coils of the Operation, he would have to rely on God to grant him that freedom through whatever means He desired to use.

He sat there in dawning realization, barely listening as the missionary continued with the story of his salvation in the little Chicago mission, and his subsequent descision to start a mission of his own.

"I had been down in Mexico when I was younger," Dennison said. "I had business that I don't like to talk about even now that took me down there. But I had liked the country and the people, and when the Lord told me that that was where He wanted me, I didn't argue."

Dennison's ministry had suffered from the beginning. "I was an ex-con. No denomination was going to sponsor me as a missionary. But the Lord called me, and I answered in faith, because I knew that in His infinite resources He would provide whatever I needed. I began to travel in the Southwest, calling on churches like this one, telling them my story, asking for their help, and a few of them responded.

With his sparse financial backing and a strong faith in his calling, Dennison had headed south. Across the border, he had encountered more obstacles, until in Chiapas, the southernmost state in Mexico, he had found himself in the fishing village of Puerto Madero.

There had been a hunger there, and the simple townspeople had not been hostile to a lone gringo who came among them with a message of salvation.

Braden recalled his feelings of bitterness—had it only been the night before? Small wonder that he had felt the pangs of betrayal and desertion. But it had been he who had betrayed and deserted God, not the other way around.

He had to rely on God. Only then could he hope to escape the global clutches of the Operation. His Lord would provide, he had told Andruss and Chandler. Okay, Lord, he thought. Acid test. Show me where I am to go, what I am to do. I won't argue now.

"I've been in that village now for twenty years," Dennison's voice penetrated Braden's reverie. "But the work is not done; it is far from done. So I've come back to this church, to the other churches which support me, to ask for help. Not for financial help this time—though that is always needed—but for volunteer help. People who are willing and able to go back down to Puerto Madero with me, to pay their own way, to devote a week, or a month, or six months, or even their lives to doing the Lord's work in a foreign land.

"Are there those among you like that, who will take up your crosses? I think there are, and when I begin to pray in a moment, I want you to pray too. And if the Lord tells you to respond, listen to Him. Don't let it be your own decision; let it be His. But if that is His will for your life, then when I begin to pray, I want you to get up and come forward, to make that commitment. I'll be waiting for you. Let us pray."

Dennison bowed his head and began to speak, but Braden never heard the words. Somehow he found himself on his feet and moving down the aisle to where the misssionary waited.

11

"Who are you?" Howard Dennison asked from where he sat behind the pastor's desk in the latter's cluttered office at the back of the church. "Oh, I know you said your name is John McAllister, but you aren't a member here. Brother Carroll doesn't know you. He said he's never even seen you before this morning. So who are you?"

There was no hostility in the questions, Braden thought, but there was the strength of a man who had seen the world from two polarized extremes of perspective and had not let his faith in one of those perspectives blind him to the reality of the other. Howard Dennison was not a man who would be easily fooled.

"I'm a man who needs a second chance," Braden said. "A man who has had his own covenant with death."

He had, on impulse, given the fictitious name when asked. The appearance of his name on any passport or visa list would draw the hounds down on him. The lie had been necessary.

There had been no other volunteers to Dennison's plea, and, following the close of the service, the two of them had retired to the pastor's office where Dennison sat now and studied him with dark, probing eyes. Braden met the man's gaze cleanly.

Up close, the lines of Dennison's tanned face spoke even more eloquently of the rigors of his life. He was powerfully built and appeared to be in good shape. It was a safe bet that in his younger days he had not been a man to mess around with. He probably still wasn't.

"If you died right now," Dennison spoke deliberately, "do you know that you'd go to heaven?"

"Yes," Braden said flatly.

"How do you know? What are you depending on to get you in?" Probing, diagnostic questions—sharp and fast. Not a man to mess around with indeed, Braden thought.

Braden didn't falter. "I know I'm going to heaven because God told me so when I accepted Christ as my Savior. He put the knowledge into my heart. But I guess I can't quote you the right verses that back up what I say."

Dennison seemed to muse for a moment. Apparently Braden had passed whatever obscure test the man had subjected him to, because after an interval he asked, "Ever been to Mexico?"

"Yes."

Again that hard, appraising stare, and Braden braced himself to be asked what kind of business had taken him there. But Dennison came in from another tack. "Ever do any mission work?"

"No. Is that a prerequisite?"

"Not really." Dennison almost smiled. "The Lord knows it wasn't in my case. I might ask you how long you've been a Christian, but I don't know if that has any real relevance either when you come right down to it. I will ask you this: why do you want to come?"

There was a limit, Braden reflected, as to how far he could push this man with evasive answers, and the truth of it was he did not want to push him at all. Only a fool would deliberately antagonize a potential benefactor. But Dennison would be a fool to accept him if he knew the whole truth. "When I sat down in there," Braden replied, "I had no idea you existed. And even when you spoke I didn't know you were going to ask for volunteers. But I felt like what you said was meant for my ears alone, and when you did call for volunteers I found myself walking down the aisle."

Braden paused, fumbling for words. "I guess what I'm trying to say is that it wasn't my decision; I had my mind made up for me."

Dennison might not have heard him for all the expression that showed on his rugged features. "Can you pay your own way?"

There was a kind of rhythm to the questions: spiritual concerns alternated with practical matters, as if Dennison hoped to throw him off stride in one realm or the other.

"Yeah, I can pay."

"Where do you live?" Apparently spiritual affairs had been abandoned for the moment.

Braden's head throbbed. He didn't want this man as an enemy, but he didn't know if he could avoid incurring the other's enmity. He felt a sudden stab of misgiving at whatever impulse had goaded him into responding to the missionary's plea. Had he really been following the will of God?

"I guess you could say I have no permanent address at the moment." His answer sounded lame even in his own ears.

Dennison frowned, but it might have been only a deliberate ploy to increase the pressure. "What are you doing in Cromwell?"

Braden shrugged, liking this less and less. "Just passing through."

Dennison echoed the words. "A little off the beaten path aren't you?"

Braden had no answer. He was defeated and he knew it. And he hadn't even wanted this to be a conflict. He could only shrug in reply.

Dennison sat regarding him until he appeared to realize he was not going to get any more of an answer. Abruptly then he came to his feet, swinging away from the desk to stand gazing out of the window.

Braden stared at his broad back for a long moment. It

was hard for him to get up from the chair where he sat, but he did so anyway and turned toward the door. He felt tired and scared and lonely.

"One thing," Dennison's voice stopped him at the door. He turned back and found the older man facing him across the desk. "I have to ask you," he said. "Are you wanted by the law?"

"Not like you mean," Braden answered after a moment.

"You don't make it easy on a man, do you?"

"The Bible says somewhere that you will find trouble in the world."

Now Dennison did grin slightly. Some of the tension went out of his big body. "That it does. So how long would you be willing to stay down in Mexico?"

"Say six months."

Dennison's eyebrows lifted. Wordlessly he turned once more to the window, and this time Braden waited. At last the big shoulders lifted as the man drew a deep breath. When he swung back around, he shook his head. "This is crazy. No missionary in his right mind would take you on as an associate. Your answers are evasive, though I don't think you want them to be. You're no stranger to violence. I can tell that by the way you move, by something that's in your eyes, or maybe something that isn't there. You're running from something or someone, but not from what we conventionally call 'the law.' And I want to believe you even while you're dancing around the truth—skillful dancing, I'll admit, but dancing nevertheless...."

Braden didn't respond. He only waited.

Finally Dennison continued. "But I have a good feeling about you, and I'm hoping it was sent by the Lord and isn't the result of my selfish desire for someone to help lighten the workload."

Braden's spirits lifted hopefully. Could this discourse possibly be headed where he hoped it was?

"I think you are being as sincere and truthful as you

believe it is possible to be under the circumstances. You're wrong, but we won't go into that right now. God knows I needed a second chance at one point, and I guess that's why I'm going to take a chance and give you one. I'll leave it to Him to deal with you if I'm wrong about you. Welcome aboard, John."

He came around the desk then, extending one calloused hand. Braden gripped it hard and swallowed. "I go by Eric," he said.

Dennison, it turned out, had another church in eastern Oklahoma he was scheduled to visit on Wednesday night before returning to Mexico. He would handle the necessary details, and Braden arranged to meet him at the airport with a passport and cash for traveling.

The passport presented a problem. Braden had three in his possession, taken from his house in his preparations for flight. But none of them were in the name of John McAllister. Further, he knew the passports had been produced by the Operation and Andruss would be aware of one of them being used within twenty-four hours of that use.

It was possible, Braden knew, to get into Mexico on considerably less than a passport, but not for a prolonged stay. And, should he need to leave that country for another it would be a wise precaution to have a passport that could pass official scrutiny.

He rented an ancient Ford from his landlady. She insisted on referring to the transaction as a simple loan of the vehicle, but made a point of informing him that his deposit was nonrefundable. He clattered out of Cromwell on Monday afternoon.

The stretch of north-west Tenth Street in Oklahoma City had not changed much. If anything, it had only slid to lower levels of decadence. A mixed residential and commercial area, it had gradually been taken over by small businesses consisting predominantly of rough bars, sleazy porno theatres, and tawdry sex shops.

He parked the old Ford in the gravel lot of a cinderblock bar surmounted with the cartoon-like image of a scantily clad girl which would light up and probably blink on and off after dark. In the hard sunlight it looked grotesque.

The inside of the bar was dim, with cheap neon advertisements for various brands of beer, and a pool table, currently being put to use by two drugstore cowboys. A few other patrons occupied tables or booths.

Braden found a table near a wall where he could watch the door. The waitress, wearing a dirty costume that showed cleavage and stubbled legs, caught his gaze with a look that was lewd rather than suggestive. He ignored it and ordered a soft drink. She glared, then slunk away.

The barkeep was young, emaciated. Braden guessed that if he cared to look closely enough he would find needle tracks on the thin arms. He studied the man briefly, then turned his attention to the other patrons. There was no one here to interest him. He left the soft drink in the slightly greasy glass untouched.

After that all of the bars seemed the same — different versions of Southwest barroom decor peopled by losers and grafters and hustlers of both sexes. His eyes began to burn from stale cigarette smoke which rubbed his throat raw. He avoided the porn shops and theatres. The clientele and employees of those sinks of iniquity were too engrossed in their own sordid brands of decadence to be able to give him the information he sought.

In the fifth bar, he sat and watched the bartender for longer than in any of the previous places. The man was in early middle-age with rawboned heavy shoulders and an incongruous beer gut beneath a stained T-shirt. His flat rectangular face carried a stamp of cynical experience. He seemed to run a kind of unofficial answering service, picking up the phone with an almost contemptuous sweep of one big hand, usually on the first ring and rarely letting it interfere with whatever else he happened to be doing. He would listen, speak a few terse sentences, and then terminate the conversation abruptly.

A couple of times disreputable sorts sauntered in, glanced furtively about, then exchanged brief whispered conversations with the laconic bartender before departing. In both instances, something — money or some other form of consideration — exchanged hands, with the bartender as recipient.

He had found his man, Braden decided. He left his table and approached the bar, careful to leave the edge of the ten dollar bill in his fist showing as he rested it on the formica counter.

"What'll it be?"

"Sid Tabor," Braden said, sotto voce.

For a moment the man's eyes appraised him, then dropped briefly to his fist and the bill it contained. "He know you?"

"I did business with him a few years back. But he doesn't need to know I'm coming."

The bartender's statement as to his concern over whether or not Tabor knew anything at all was obscene.

"Keep it that way," Braden said. He moved the bill slightly.

The bartender gave an address, and, at Braden's slightly raised eyebrows, gave terse directions to it.

"Thanks." Braden left the bill on the bar. One big hand consumed it.

He waited until he was at the door to look back. The bartender had turned toward the battered phone and was reaching for it. Braden moved fast and the man gasped as Braden's hand clamped on his wrist, halting his fingers inches from the phone. He started to jerk his big body around and then his eyes met Braden's

"You better be calling your mother, pal," Braden said low and hard. "Because if anyone, including Tabor, is expecting me at that address, you better hope they kill me, because if they don't, I'll be back to see you. Understand?"

Something in Braden's eyes had made the man go pale. His own eyes darted frantically. He managed a weak nod.

Braden smiled once without mirth. He went sidewise out of the bar so that the barkeep would not be out of his sight. The few other patrons, he saw, were pretending that the whole brief affair had never happened.

He found the frame house in the nearby low-rent neighborhood without trouble and parked the Ford two houses down from it. For a few minutes he sat there, surveying the surroundings. He saw nothing to alarm him.

He did not know who the barkeep/information broker had been planning on calling. Maybe Tabor, maybe some completely unrelated party. Or, just possibly, Bob Chandler.

With no leads, the Operation agent would be waiting for the sophisticated resources of the Operation's intelligence machine to provide him with one. In the meantime, he would have put out word among locals like the bartender of his desire to find someone answering Braden's description. It didn't matter. Braden had seen the look in the man's eyes, smelled his fear. He did not think the bartender would be contacting Chandler or anyone else to inform them of his whereabouts.

When Braden had set up his supposedly secret retirement account, he had utilized the dubious skills of Sid Tabor in establishing his false identity. A forger and sometime computer thief, Tabor was a small, bespectacled man whose decided lack of enthusiasm upon finding Braden at his door made the latter even more certain that Chandler had put out feelers for him.

A hundred dollars persuaded Tabor to allow Braden the use of his lab and scrivener's tools for the necessary period. Braden could have, he was certain, persuaded the little man to do the work himself, but he did not want the forger aware of the details of what he did and able to pass those details on to an interested ear.

When he headed back to Cromwell, leaving a richer but considerably unnerved Tabor behind him, he was the possessor of a purportedly year-old passport in the name of John McAllister.

12

"We're going to extend the invitation a little longer." Howard Dennison projected his voice so that it carried clearly throughout the small church sanctuary with its one hundred or so occupants. "Because I feel that the Lord is asking someone to respond, is urging you to take the first step, to commit yourself to the mission field in some manner. It's not important whether or not He wants you to accompany me. That might be it, I don't know. Or it could be giving yourself over to full-time mission work. That is between you and God. But I urge you to make that decision whatever it is—for your own peace, your own spiritual growth. I know there are unanswered questions. But the Lord will supply the answers if you will let Him. Don't turn Him down now that He is asking."

Dennison paused long enough to draw a breath, to gauge the effect of his words on the crowd. "The organist is going to play one more stanza," he continued then. "And if no one comes, you will have closed the invitation."

The organist, a middle-aged choir member, took her cue and began to play softly. Dennison resisted the urge to keep talking. The congregation was growing restless; he had kept the invitation open for a long period with no results, and it was already past the time when most of the crowd would have anticipated being out of church. They were all probably dedicated Christians—otherwise they would not have been here in this growing urban church on a Wednesday night. Even so, some of them were becoming impatient at the length of time he had held them.

But his own conviction of a need in the congregation had been undeniable. He had not made it up. He would not stoop to manufacturing an excuse to prolong the invitation as some pastors and evangelists did. No, he had felt the presence of the Lord even as he spoke of his mission work. He had sensed that there were those in the congregation who were wrestling with a decision regarding the mission field, exactly as he himself had wrestled those long years before. He empathized with that struggle, but he had done all he could to provide a chance to resolve it. If the person or persons being called by God chose to disregard the Lord's will in their lives, then the resultant consequences would be of their own choosing.

The church was on the outskirts of Tulsa, the state's second-largest city, and catered to a brotherhood of mostly younger professional types who had realized that they could not allow their careers to be the highest priority in their lives. It satisfied Dennison to know that there still were young, dedicated Christian couples even in the complex, mercenary, commercial world of modern business. But the satisfaction was offset by the frustration flexing itself within him now.

The frustration had begun to grow when he left Cromwell with only one volunteer of dubious reputation to accompany him back to Mexico. It had burgeoned as he delivered his message this evening and sensed the refusal to respond on the part of at least one member of the congregation. Obviously, to some the dedication only extended so far, he thought bitterly.

The man who called himself John McAllister — obviously not his real name — had at least responded out of what appeared to be a genuine conviction. He had not denied the call to step out in faith and go to the mission field. But Dennison also sensed that the man had had few other options open to him; there had been a sense of hunted desperation all too familiar from the old days before his own conversion.

Perhaps if this John McAllister had a nice cushy condo to go home to, and a high salary awaiting him in some professional position, like these people did, he would not have been so eager to accept Dennison's offer.

And just what sort of volunteer had the Lord sent him? he wondered now. His initial excitement over a recruit—which were few and far between the past years—had faded in the cold light of practical reality. What did he really know about this man he was going to inflict on his congregation? Almost nothing, of course. Only that he could handle an interrogation like an old hand, was plainly no stranger to violence, and seemed to possess the furtive air of a hunted quarry. All of which could just as easily have described himself when he had taken his first faltering steps in following God's will for his life.

But his uneasiness could not be so summarily dismissed. Was it safe to take this man back to the mission he shepherded? What of Cristina, his assistant? Did McAllister, or whatever his name was, offer any potential threat to her or the children? He didn't know, couldn't know. And it was becoming awfully hard to trust in the Lord on this one.

His old friend David Carroll, pastor of the church in Cromwell, had been able to offer little reassurance when questioned. "I don't know who he is, Howard," David had admitted. "Never had him in the congregation before, either. I had heard there was a stranger rooming in old Mrs. Jacob's shack, but I'd never visited with him. I planned to go over and talk to him Sunday afternoon. It surprised the life out of me when he showed up in church."

"What do you make of him?" Dennison had urged. The two men had been in Carroll's office Monday morning discussing the stranger's commitment to Dennison's need.

Carroll shrugged uncomfortably. "Hard to say. On general principles I wouldn't trust him; he's got someone or something he's running from, and you've only his word it's not the law.

"I know, I know..." he held up both hands to forestall Dennison's interruption. "I said that was on general principles. Since talking to him and praying about it, I'm prone to think he means what he says. He seems dedicated and sincere. But it's really anybody's guess as to how stable he is. I just don't know what to tell you except to pray about it. I'll be doing a lot of that too."

Good advice, Dennison admitted now, but advice he had done far too little in the way of following. He had, instead, gone to McAllister's landlady, Mrs. Jacobs, a sometime churchgoer, to get her impressions of her tenant.

"He be a good man." She nodded at the accuracy of her own evaluation. "He jus' not know it yet. But you give him time; he work out."

Great, I got the town psychiatrist, Dennison thought sourly. Aloud he asked, "Has he given you any trouble since he's been here?"

"Him? Shoot, no!" Mrs. Jacob declared firmly. "He not that kind. I done told ya. Wouldn't let nobody stay here noways unless I trusted 'em. But don't worry, pastor. Ain't nobody goin' to give me no trouble as long as I got ol' Henryetta here loaded for bear." She patted her ever-present shotgun with fond confidence and cackled gleefully.

McAllister was lucky he had survived to make his commitment to mission service, Dennison reflected drily. He thanked his hostess, invited her to church and took his leave.

Her evaluation of her tenant had been much more favorable than either his or Carroll's. Did she see more in this McAllister than either of them did? Or was her evaluation no more than the workings of a near-senile mind?

And an even better question: if he himself had so many doubts about his new recruit, why in the world had he consented to letting him go back to Mexico with him? Even if he was trustworthy—and that had not yet been established in spite of Mrs. Jacob's endorsements—McAllister was obviously a new Christian and almost certainly had a lot of growing to do before he could be of much help to the Lord or Dennison, or to anyone else for that matter.

Perhaps, he concluded, it would be better all the way around if McAllister just did not show up at the airport tomorrow. He would be going back alone then, all his prayers and hopes for a worthy volunteer notwithstanding. But he was used to it after this long. And certainly there did not seem to be any members of this congregation willing to take him up on his offer.

The organist had almost completed the final stanza of the invitational hymn, Dennison realized, coming out of his reverie. And, rather than thanking God for having given him a volunteer, he had used the occasion to put together a nicely packaged argument as to why it would be a mistake to have anything at all to do with McAllister.

Shame stirred in him, shame at his lack of faith in the Lord's choice, shame at his own temerity in presuming to second-guess God's will. In the few moments that remained before the invitation was over, he bowed his head. Lord, he prayed, I don't understand your choice, but then that really isn't necessary. Grant me the proper attitude to accept your will in this matter, knowing you can use all things to further your ends. And use me as a witness in this man's life, so that through our working together in your name we may both be drawn closer to you.

The pastor dismissed the congregation and Dennison watched them leave. He felt better for having committed the problem to God, but the stubborn doubts as to the value of his new volunteer on the mission field still gnawed at the back of his mind.

He heard his name and looked up from his preoccupation, realizing that the pastor was speaking to a couple who had lingered following the close of the service. As he noticed them, the pastor motioned for him to join them.

He pushed his own worries to the back of his mind and went over. The couple were both in their early thirties, he handsome, she attractive, both dressed in expensive, no doubt stylish, clothes. They looked at him a little nervously, he thought, as he approached.

"Brother Dennison, these are the Maxwells, Alex and his wife Sandra. Alex is a deacon, and Sandra teaches Sunday school for the grade school girls."

Dennison acknowledged the introductions, shaking Alex's proffered hand. Sandra, too, extended her hand in a businesslike fashion, surprising him a little bit, and he shook it too.

"They wanted to visit with you some," the pastor went on unnecessarily. He made a casual withdrawal, leaving Dennison alone with the pair.

Sandra seemed about to speak, then abruptly stopped and glanced quickly at her husband. Alex avoided her glance, as well as that of Dennison, and shifted his feet uncomfortably. Dennison had the sudden impression that neither one of them was used to feeling awkward or having trouble finding the right words in any social setting.

"Let's sit down over here." He ushered them toward the front row of pews. They went gratefully. If nothing else, a pastor learned quickly how to cope with awkward situations, Dennison had time to reflect.

By the time they were seated, Alex had plainly decided on a forthright approach to the problem. "Brother Dennison, we wanted to talk to you some about what you said about the, um, mission field..." He let it trail off helplessly, his directness dissolving almost immediately.

Sandra stepped in to fill the void. "We've been thinking a lot about mission work," she said earnestly. "We feel like maybe we're supposed to be doing something more than what we are. When you were talking tonight—what you said in the invitation—it was like maybe you were talking to us. But..." Now it was her turn to break off self-consciously.

"It's not as if we aren't active here in church," Alex chimed in. "You heard the pastor; I'm a deacon and Sandra teaches Sunday school We go out on the visitation programs when we get home from work early enough—"

"That's really kind of the problem," Sandra took her turn again. "Alex is an attorney and is in line for a partnership at his firm. And I'm a CPA and just started work at a big accounting firm. So I can't really take any time off just now, and neither can Alex because of the promotion and all."

"It's not as if we aren't interested in mission work," Alex had come in on cue. "It's just right now, our careers won't let us do anything about it. You understand...?" He seemed to have second thoughts about that question and went hurriedly on before Dennison could reply. "But we've given it some thought, and we've made some plans. In a few years — we can't be certain just when because it depends on so many things — but in a few years when we get our careers a little more stabilized, we're going to take some time off and do some volunteer mission work." He nodded in firm confirmation of their nebulous decision.

Careers permitting, of course, Dennison added silently.

"It's just not possible for us to do that right now," Sandra added her support. "But in a few years it will be different."

It wouldn't be different, Dennison thought. Their lives would become centered more and more around their professions, excluding, at last, even their church activities. Their drive for affluence and success would become the central theme of their lives, claiming more and more from them, including, possibly, their marriage itself. Christians, children of God, their lives would most likely be wasted, spent on an unending and ultimately meaningless quest, all due to their commitment to make their own decisions, their refusal to acknowledge God's calling and will for their lives.

"That's what we wanted to talk to you about," Sandra was continuing in the same earnest tone. "To explain how things are."

"We've always supported your mission," Alex's voice had acquired an undertone of defensiveness now. "Ever since we've joined the church. We've sent money each year."

Dennison murmured amenities. They weren't going to listen to him anyway; they had already made up their minds. And if they had listened to his sermon they had already heard what they needed to do. These few extra minutes after church to patronize the visiting missionary were no more than a salve for their consciences. Dennison felt a deep and abiding sadness for them.

Yet he had to try, even if their ears were already closed to his words. "The prophet Ezekiel told the Israelites that they were all, each one of them, responsible as an individual for the choices each of them made. They couldn't blame their forefathers or anything else. It all came back to each individual making a choice and, ultimately, having to accept the consequences."

They were staring at him blankly. This was plainly not the kind of answer they had wanted or expected or even understood. But it was all he could offer. Everything else had been said, and they had chosen not to hear it.

He watched them leave. Sandra gave him one last puzzled glance. Alex did not look back. Were they the type of volunteer workers he had been looking for? he asked himself. Successful, able to manipulate prosperity and people with equal ease?

Instead, the Lord had given him only a man who needed a second chance.

He found himself comparing their shallow dedication with its worldly trappings, to the simple strength and untutored desire to serve that he had sensed in the man who called himself John McAllister. Alex and Sandra had chosen to serve their careers. McAllister had chosen to serve the Lord.

Dennison remembered his silent heartfelt plea made only moments before. The Lord, he thought gratefully, answered some prayers sooner than others.

13

"I wondered if you would show up," Dennison said once they had settled into their seats on the plane. He chuckled. "To be honest, I almost hoped you wouldn't."

"I almost didn't," Braden confessed.

Dennison raised an inquisitive eyebrow. "Second thoughts?"

"More like third or fourth." Dennison's receptive expression made Braden go on, though he was suddenly sorry that he had spoken up at all. "Dennison, I mean, Pastor...What do I call you, anyway?"

"Howard's fine."

"I told you back in Cromwell that I'd never done any mission work. That was an understatement. I just have the vaguest idea of what a mission even does. I can work with my hands. I'm good at athletics. Other than those things, I don't know that I have much to offer."

Dennison's grin was engaging. "If you really were led by the Lord to come forward last Sunday, then He'll see to it that you pick up all you need along the way, whether it's from me or from someone else. And, rest assured, whatever talents you have, we'll find a good use for them."

Mayhem and death are my best talents, Pastor, Braden thought disspiritedly. Care to put them to use? Got any athe-ists you need terminated? A rival church you need blown up?

"Look what He's done with me." Dennison might have read his thoughts. "I was as useless a human being as you can imagine. Don't sell yourself or your Savior short."

The words could have been almost trite, but they gave Braden a curious feeling of comfort and reassurance.

Puerto Madero, Dennison told him, was located on an infamous beach noted locally for treacherous undertows and unpredictable riptides. "It wasn't always like that," Dennison's voice went reflective. "When I first saw it, it wasn't much more than a sleepy little fishing village out in the boondocks not too far from the Guatemalan border. They had a nice beach too, and gradually built up a localized tourist trade—a kind of low-key resort for Mexican citizens who didn't care or couldn't afford to go mingle with the gringo tourists in Acapulco and Cancun. The population swelled for a few years there, and the town prospered—a few of the locals still fished, but most of them, including a whole new influx of outsiders, lived off the tourist trade in one way or another."

"So what happened?"

Dennison's grin was rueful. "The Mexican government, seeing this thriving little resort, decided that it was the perfect spot for a naval base—God knows why—and I'm not being profane."

Braden had to smile. He found himself liking this man, enjoying his company. It had been a long time since he had had any kind of relationship that might even remotely qualify as friendship. Unless you counted Chandler. And Chandler was trying to kill him. "The navy ran the tourists off?" he prompted.

"Not directly, and not intentionally. But they built their base. They brought in their excavating equipment and dug a channel from the beach back to where they built the actual facilities. Only trouble was, when they opened this manmade channel, it created a whole network of riptides and undertows that hadn't existed before. A couple of tourists were drowned before anyone realized what was happening."

Braden smiled. So government bungling wasn't peculiar to the United States.

"After that, understandably, the tourist trade declined. And to top it off, a hurricane hit shortly afterward and took out a good portion of the beachfront real estate, including a bridge across the bay and the nicest of the hotels." Dennison shook his head. "The tourists left, but the support population they had attracted didn't. We've got somewhere around ten thousand people jammed into an area a mile long by about a half-mile wide. With the economy in the shape it is, they don't have anyplace else to go now. And, of course, the naval base is still there, but it's done little to alter the financial climate of the general populace."

"Governmental bureaucracy at its best," Braden responded. Something in his caustic tone caused Dennison to glance at him sharply. He had to watch it, he warned himself. Faced with Dennison's easygoing geniality, it would be all too easy to let slip more that he could afford to.

Seen from the air, Mexico City, still not recovered from the devastating earthquake which had leveled a good portion of it, looked much like Braden imagined London after the Blitz must have appeared. Always a dirty, grim, gray city capped by a layer of alien atmospheric smog and soot, to which had been added dust from the quake, the city was even more unappealing now. Braden was glad their stay there was short and that they were able to make their connecting flight on Aero Mexico to Tapachula in Chiapas.

Even Dennison seemed subdued by the air of shell-shocked desperation that seemed to pervade the populace in the airport. "We got off lightly in Puerto Madero, thank God," he confided. "Some heavy waves, not much else, although we felt it. I spent a good two weeks here in the capital helping with the rescue and cleanup efforts. It was grim."

By reflex, Braden found himself examining the faces of the other passengers on the Aero Mexico flight as he and

Dennison were seated. He thought he had made a clean escape this time. Even if Chandler learned of his visit to Tabor, all that would tell him was that Braden was now in possession of a new passport of which the Operation had no record. And that bit of information was virtually useless, since Chandler would have no guarantee that, even possessing such a passport, he would use it to leave the country.

His .38 he had disassembled, distributing the pieces throughout his luggage. Other than his foray into Oklahoma City, he had done little except stay close to his temporary lodgings in Cromwell, half expecting Chandler to appear at his door momentarily.

But there had been no alarms, and now, having found an unexpected comfort and pleasure in Dennison's company, he began to hope that he could relax.

"How big is your mission?" he asked once they were airborne. The question sounded inane even to him. How did one ask questions about a mission?

Dennison seemed to sense his discomfort. "Not large really, although we've had several former members, who came to know Christ through our mission, go on to start their own churches, a couple in Puerto Madero, the rest in other outlying villages."

Braden nodded helplessly. He made a very poor Peter or Paul.

"When those members of my mission went out and formed their own churches, it was a real blessing to me, because that's how it's supposed to work. I can't reach everyone in southern Mexico; logistics prevent it, not to mention that some Mexicans won't give the time of day to an American, much less listen to him present the Gospel. But they might listen to their own countrymen with the same message. That's how it works with a mission, how it's supposed to work with any group of believers; each individual takes the message to those that he comes into contact with. Some of those accept the message and continue to spread it, like ripples in a pond." Dennison's face had lit up with a kind of inner glow as he spoke. His voice had grown imperceptibly louder. Braden felt strengthened by the man's enthusiasm—no—his spirit.

"Christians in the United States have access to resources no other group of believers in the world can match. That's why it's so important that we use these resources to reach other parts of the world."

Here was a concept of foreign intervention new to him, Braden thought. His own missions (what a perversion of the word!) into other countries had generally been for the purpose of intervention, but intervention based on mayhem and coercion, subversion and terror. Granted, some undercover intervention was necessary in a world where other nations were increasingly hostile, in methods both covert and overt, to the interests of the United States. But the necessity of it did not justify the murder of a loyal operative who wanted only to retire.

"You do everything yourself?" he asked, still unable to quite envision the situation into which he had so blindly committed himself.

"No. I couldn't. I've got an assistant, Cristina Rodriguez, a widow. She might surprise you. She takes care of abandoned or unwanted children and serves as my right arm. She's running things while I'm gone, in fact. And some of the church members help out when the need arises. By the way, I've never asked you, but do you speak any Spanish?"

"Si. Yo Hablo espanol," Braden answered, slipping fluently into the tongue. And six other languages, besides, he thought, compliments of the organization that's now trying to kill me.

"Good! We really will put you to use." Dennison cocked his head. "You must have spent quite a bit of time down here to become that fluent."

"I just have a knack for picking up languages," Braden said, deflecting the probe, if probe it was.

They landed at the city of Tapachula and left the plane by old-style portable steps rolled out to it. A gaggle of people were behind the low metal railing waiting for the disembarking passengers. Dennison cast a grin over his shoulder at Braden. "There's Cristina."

Braden couldn't tell who he meant, but as they reached the gate a tall, young woman with long, black hair and a full, statuesque figure met Dennison with a quick hug.

The missionary disentangled himself. "Cristina Rodriguez, let me introduce our newest lay missionary, John McAllister. He goes by Eric, however."

"Oh, good! I've been praying you'd find someone. You're an answer to prayer, Mr. McAllister." Her smile flashed dazzling white against her dark complexion and she extended a firm hand to shake his.

Up close, he could tell she was probably in her thirties. Her dark eyes were vibrant and alive with the kind of strength and warmth he was beginning to associate with Dennison. "That's a new experience for me," he heard himself say, "and please, call me Eric."

"A new experience? You mean mission work?"

"No, being an answer to prayer."

Again that infectious smile. "Well, you better get used to it here, Eric."

They left the airport in an old four-wheel-drive International Scout with Cristina competently at the wheel. She was not at all what he had pictured when Dennison had mentioned a widowed assistant, Braden mused, glancing at her from where he sat in the back seat. Was there more to their relationship than what there appeared to be on the surface? he caught himself questioning silently, and then wondered why he cared.

They headed south on a two-lane blacktop road across flattish semi-arid terrain that bore a surprising resemblance to south-central Oklahoma. Cristina kept up a running commentary on the state of affairs at the mission. Luis and Ramon had both settled down (two of her juvenile male charges, Braden guessed), and Rosa had finally had her baby— a boy — whereupon Pablo, the proud father, had promptly gone on a celebratory binge that ended with him in jail in Tapachula with a half dozen stitches in his scalp. Dennison groaned.

Rosa, Cristina explained to Braden, was a faithful church member who had come to know the Lord at the mission. Her husband, a part-time fisherman, however, was something of a reprobate and the constant despair of his spouse.

Her English was almost without accent, and Braden guessed that she had been schooled or at least spent a lot of time north of the border.

Oh, but she had forgotten the really good news. Old Senor Cantavas had finally made a profession of faith and was impatiently awaiting the pastor's return to be baptized.

"That's one I'll perform with pleasure," Dennison said heartily, also including Braden in the conversation.

The latter found a strange pleasure in this easy acceptance by the obviously close pair.

"Senor Cantavas is a kind of patriarch in the village. I've been witnessing to him for years. It's just like him to wait until I'm gone to make his decision." But there was no rancor in the words. Rather, Braden sensed a deep, abiding joy.

"Where are you from, Eric?" Cristina caught his eye in the rearview mirror as she asked.

"Our Eric is a man of mystery," Dennison said, stepping in quickly, to Braden's relief. "He's got a mysterious past that we're not privy to."

Apparently, even through the ironic tone of the words, Cristina caught some subtle inflection against further queries, for she didn't press the issue, but turned once more to affairs of the mission.

Braden listened to her voice, found himself studying the dark mane of her hair, marveling at the commitment he could sense in her tone and her words.

"Any medical crises?" Dennison asked her at one point.

"Nothing special. The usual cuts and scrapes. One snakebite."

"Cristina's an R.N.," the missionary explained to Braden. "She studied nursing in Texas. She has quite a ministry in some of the more remote villages, attending to their medical needs."

"Maybe Eric can go with me on some of my visits," she suggested. "That would give you more free time around the mission." Then to Eric: "Some of the villages really are remote—back up in the jungle. Howard doesn't like me traveling by myself. And actually, I don't feel too safe doing it myself."

"That's a good idea," Dennison agreed. "I told Eric there'd be plenty for him to do."

"Count on it." Cristina's dazzling smile flashed at Braden once again in the mirror, and to his own surprise, he returned it with interest.

14

Puerto Madero, in the wake of the collapse of the tourist industry which Dennison had described, was a boom town gone bust. Braden had seen the same air of apathetic defeat in an Oklahoma oil town following the demise of the oil boom and its frenetic drilling and commercial activity.

A gridwork of dirt roads was lined with shacks and houses constructed in varying degrees of palm fronds, bamboo-like wood, galvanized iron, and cinderblocks. Naked children played in the dust; indolent young men lounged in the shade of doorways and thatched overhangs, or prowled the streets. A few women moved about on their various errands, and older people sat as spectators, watching with tired eyes as they passed.

Bony dogs lay in the shade and slept as if dead, or followed the occasional street vendor hopefully, just beyond range of kicks and imprecations. Chickens and hogs wandered aimlessly or scratched and rooted through refuse which had been raked out of yards and houses and lay in decaying piles along the streets.

There were a number of bars which reminded Braden of the cantinas depicted in old Western movies, and the customers hanging around out front didn't look much different from some of the bit players hired to portray bandidos and pistoleros in the old flicks.

From a thriving tourist center, the town had deteriorated to the status of a crowded fishing village with a stagnating economy.

"But the people here are wonderful," Cristina told Braden. "Except for the riff-raff that hang around the bars, most of the people here are warm and more than willing to work. It's just that the economy is bad all over the country, and, in a way, they're trapped here."

Recalling the small crowd of people who had been waiting at the mission for Dennison's return, Braden had no cause to doubt her. The wave of warmth, friendship, and even love which had flowed from the waiting mission members had been almost tangible. Even Braden, an outsider, had been welcomed warmly into their midst.

The mission itself consisted of a cinderblock sanctuary with a tin roof. A screened expanse between the top of the wall and the roof allowed for free circulation of the tropical air. Two wings had been added onto the sanctuary, both serving as educational and administrative space. Dennison's simple frame home was across the road. Cristina's quarters were in one of the wings.

A large yard, shaded by coconut trees, stretched behind the mission. It was there at a sturdy hand-made wooden table that the trio sat for dinner following the hectic period of their arrival in the late afternoon.

Fish—baked almost black, but tender enough to fall from the bones—and tortillas were served by a cheerful middle-aged woman. Dennison addressed her as Inez. She served as his cook and housekeeper as well as organizer for church meals on special occasions.

"Cristina's right," Dennison agreed now. "These are good people caught up in bad times. The economy of Mexico is in a state of chaos. There aren't enough jobs or money to go around, and fishing can only support so many. But in spite of that, we don't have the problems you might expect. There's hardly any serious crime. Oh, we have our rough section of town, our trouble-makers, but they don't generally get too far out of line."

Remembering the hard-eyed men he had seen lounging in front of the bars, the ladrons, Braden suspected that Dennison's evangelical enthusiasm might make him tend to exaggerate a trifle.

A pleasant breeze nuzzled at the back of his neck, and the mild heat of the afternoon was beginning to diminish. As Cristina and Dennison chatted animatedly over some minor policy decision, Braden felt a curious sense of contentment creep over him. It would be easy to relax here, to drop his guard.

Dennison stretched, extending his long arms overhead. "It's good to be back," he commented to no one in particular. "Eric, Cristina tells me I've got some bookwork to catch up on—you can't get away from paper shuffling anywhere, it seems. I'll be busy with that most of the evening. Tomorrow I'll be going into Tapachula on business. You're welcome to come along if you like."

Braden hesitated. The less time he spent even in a backwater city like Tapachula the better off he was, he guessed. "You're the boss," he said. "But if you don't need me I'd just as soon stay around here. Surely there are some odd jobs that need to be done."

"Always," Cristina put in quickly.

"That's settled then. Eventually you can start doing some outreach with me, but there's plenty to do here. We've been thinking of adding on a section to serve as a kind of dorm for the children we take in. We've been boarding them with church members or at my house, but that's getting out of hand. We need a centralized location since that seems to be a growing ministry, thanks to Cristina's efforts."

"I've done some construction," Braden offered.

"Good! What did I tell you about having the resources available when the need arises? There are some townsmen—church members—who will help, but they need a coordinator."

"I'll be glad to act in that capacity if you think I'm qualified," Braden agreed.

"Great! Cristina can go over the details with you. In fact, she might even be willing to show you around a little bit before it gets dark."

"My pleasure," Cristina interjected. "I can show you the beach. And I really do need to go see one of my 'flock,' as Howard calls them. She's staying with a church family since her parents threw her out."

"Suits me." Somehow, even the idea of calling on an abandoned child in the company of this woman seemed strangely appealing.

"Come on." Cristina was already on her feet. "It's close enough so we can walk. Just let me get my Bible." She disappeared into the mission and Braden felt Dennison's eyes on him. He met the other man's gaze and was reminded of the almost antagonistic interrogation Dennison had subjected him to at their first meeting.

"She's like a daughter to me, Eric, or whatever your name is. You understand what I'm saying? I don't want to see her hurt in any way."

Braden kept his face expressionless. "You don't need to worry," he said flatly.

For another moment Dennison held his gaze. "All right," he said then. "Just thought I'd mention it."

Some of the tension went visibly out of him as he spoke.

Cristina's reappearance prevented the necessity of any reply from Braden.

"You ready?" she asked.

"Yeah, lead on."

She was wearing lightweight tan slacks and a simple white blouse buttoned modestly. She was, he thought, the kind of woman who would look good in almost anything she wore, and he enjoyed walking with her, their shoes kicking up little puffs of dust at each step.

Cristina carried a well-worn Bible with casual familiarity.

"We'll go by and see Carmelita first," she explained. "Maybe then we can catch the sunset over the water. It's gorgeous, and just about the best view Puerto Madero has to offer."

Braden glanced at her admiringly. "The view from here is pretty good as far as I'm concerned."

She froze up perceptibly, not replying, her lips tightening grimly.

"I'm sorry." Braden berated himself silently for being a fool.

"That's all right. Don't be." She gave him a brief strained smile. "But understand; I'm here to work at the mission. That's my life. I'm not interested in love or romance or an affair—that least of all." She hugged her Bible to her chest, her posture clearly defensive.

Braden groped for a safe topic. "Is Carmelita one of the children you, uh, minister to?" he finally asked awkwardly.

Visibly she relaxed, as if grateful to have a safer topic. "That's right."

"And her parents threw her out? How old is she?"

"Nine." At Braden's slightly startled look she went on quickly. "Child abandonment or mistreatment is almost an epidemic here. A lot of parents either force their children to do whatever work they can find to earn money—cleaning fish, farm labor—from practically the time they can walk, or they decide that the children are too much of an economic burden and simply turn them out on their own. That's what happened to Carmelita."

"And you took her in?"

"In a way. What I actually did was find a family who would take care of her for now. We at the church pay them a small amount for her board. We keep a few children ourselves at the mission, but we don't really have much room for that at this point."

"Are all the children of your 'flock' so young?" Braden asked.

"All ages. Some younger. Some teen-agers."

"What happens to them?"

She shrugged with resignation. "They grow up. They stay with us for a while until they're older; then they move on. Some remain here, others go to Mexico City. I wish I could say that they all grow up and have decent lives, but that just isn't true. Usually by the time we get them they're already so street-wise—most of them are liars, thieves, prostitutes by the time they're ten years old. But the ones that end up at the mission are the lucky ones. At least they have a chance to hear the Gospel and see that there's a different kind of life available if they choose to become Christians. But there are dozens, maybe even hundreds of children out there that we never see—that we'll never get a chance to minister to. Here we are."

They had reached a cinderblock structure with a thatched roof and a blanket hanging across the doorway. At Cristina's "Hola!" of greeting, they were admitted by a thin Mexican woman of indeterminate years who hugged Cristina happily and greeted Braden with embarrassing cordiality.

The floor was dirt, and a single low-wattage light bulb dangled from a wire overhead. Sleeping niches had been sectioned off by more hanging blankets or sheets. The furnishings were obviously handmade for the most part, the rest appearing to have been salvaged from a dump and partially restored. A scrawny dog, curled comfortably against one wall, blinked at the visitors.

A stocky man appeared from a bamboo kind of lean-to which had been tacked onto the rear of the structure. An elfin girl, with wide, dark eyes in a brown face beneath short, black hair and clad in a simple cotton dress, came eagerly from one of the sleeping niches and ran to Cristina's arms.

Cristina introduced the couple—the Santegos—before allowing Carmelita to pull her away to show her some new toy.

The couple greeted Braden graciously, then the three of them stood there awkwardly and looked at one another.

"The child seems well," Braden said at last in Spanish.

Realization that he spoke their tongue lit up their eyes simultaneously. The woman immediately began to chatter volubly about the little girl. The man hushed her after a moment. "You have come to work with Brother Dennison?" he asked.

"For a time," Braden answered.

The man gestured gravely toward the blanket behind which Cristina and the child had disappeared. "The little one is not much trouble for us. We are happy to take her in. But there are many others like her."

"Yes," Braden agreed with equal solemnity. And then, in inspiration, he added, "I plan to build a new section on the mission to house such children. I will need help."

The smile that lighted Santego's face gave Braden a curious feeling that was definitely not unpleasant. "I will help you!" he exclaimed, grasping Braden's hand in a crushing grip. "I farm and I fish, but all that can wait for this project."

By the time they left, Santego had promised to find addi-tional workers for the new wing. Braden made him promise to wait until he had a chance to draw up the plans and go over them with Dennison.

"But hurry," Santego urged. "The little ones need a place to stay."

"See what I mean?" Cristina asked him as they emerged out into the street. "You better get used to it."

"Get used to what?"

Her smile flashed. "Being an answer to prayer." She tossed her head in a way that had a gripping appeal to Braden. "It goes with the territory in this business. Santego has been wanting a dorm wing built for a long time now, but he doesn't have the skills to lay it out himself."

"I'm not sure I do," Braden admitted. He had done some makeshift construction over the years, but never anything this elaborate.

"Don't worry," Cristina quickly reassured him. "Howard

can help you with that part of it. He just never had enough time to see that it got done properly." Her words became more animated. "Once we get the wing built, I've always wanted to start a kind of school for our children—give them training in some kind of trade so they'll at least have a chance at a decent future. But we'd have to find instructors. Heaven knows I'm not qualified." Her voice took on a teasing tone. "What about you, Eric? What trades could you teach them?"

Assassination, guerrilla tactics, interrogation, Braden thought. Aloud, he said, "Not much, I'm afraid."

"Oh, I don't believe that. Come on, it's this way to the beach."

His brief feeling of depression could not stand before the growing fascination he felt for this unique woman. He found it easy to laugh at the whimsical story she told on herself and some of her young charges concerning a disastrous Christmas musical program. "Howard kept insisting we were excellent, but he never could lie very well at all."

The sun had just come to rest on the horizon as they came out onto the beach. "Oh, look at the sum!" Cristina exclaimed softly. then they both feel silent and watched as it seemed to slip beneath the surface of the sea.

Braden was extremely aware of her nearness, of the thawing toward him he had sensed in her since their visit with the Santegos and their foster child. He resisted the impulse to catch her hand in his. He had already almost spoiled things once by coming on like a libidinous teenager. He would not make the same mistake twice.

Besides, he knew the dangers of personal involvement for an operative, the vulnerability, the lack of concentration that inevitably grew out of any close personal relationship. Those same dangers were present with a vengeance for a man on the run. And he knew he must not let his growing sense of security and belonging here, in this village with these people, blind him to the dangers that stalked him.

"I see what Howard meant about the beach and its

undertow," he said because he did not trust either himself or his mood. "Those waves look mean." Was that a flicker of disappointment he saw on her face?

"It's very dangerous to swim here."

The waves, tall and ominous, broke in close to the sandy shore with a churning violence. They were the kind of waves to be expected on a rocky coast, not a smooth expanse of sandy beach. At intervals, fingers of jumbled stones had been built extending out into the water to break their force.

"Where's the naval base?" he asked. On general principles alone, he thought, it would be prudent for him to avoid any contact with the militia.

She pointed. "Down the beach that way. It's not much—just a dock and a few buildings."

As Braden opened his mouth to reply, a mournful wailing howl ululated out of the gathering dusk, rasping in his ears like the shriek of a demented wolf. It raised the hackles on his neck as it died away into silence.

"What was that?" he demanded.

"The brujo."

He realized she had drawn closer to him. "A sorceror? A warlock?" he asked, mentally translating the Spanish word.

She nodded. "Tobias. Our local witch doctor. He lives back up in the mountains, but every now and then he comes down to prowl around here and cause trouble. He hates the mission; he always tells his followers that they'll be cursed if they come to the mission."

"Black magic?" he queried. "Vodoun?"

She glanced at him, surprised at his proper pronunciation of the Haitian voodoo cult, but only shrugged. "He gets his deities all mixed up—Damballah, Quetzalcoatl, Beelzebub—by any name it's all satanic when you get right down to it." Her shiver in the warm air was visible. She hugged her Bible to her again. "Like I said, he comes down here to cause trouble."

"And howl," Braden added. He had not quite gotten over the icy chill which had touched his own spine.

15

"I need to go to Tapachula and pick up some groceries. I forgot to tell Howard to get them when he went this morning. Do you want to go with me, Eric?" Watching him as she asked the question, Cristina Rodriguez sensed the same reluctance she had detected in him the day before when Howard had made a similar offer. For some reason Eric—John McAllister—had no desire to go to the city. She waited for his answer and found herself absurdly eager for him to accept.

She had found him diligently at work with a tape measure on the site of the proposed new dorm wing. He appeared completely absorbed in what he was doing, and she had a moment to watch him before he was aware of her presence. She admired the smooth economy of his movements, which she had noticed before, as he rose now from where he knelt at a wooden stake driven in the dusty ground to mark the wing's corner. And he was handsome in a tired, rugged kind of way that had appealed to her from the first.

When he noticed her, she saw a flicker of irritation in his eyes at being caught, however briefly, unawares. In that moment he reminded her undeniably of some predator—a wolf, perhaps—scenting a hunter on its trail, and she felt touched by an awareness of the mysteries lurking in his background.

She summoned a smile—easily enough, to her surprise—and told him why she had sought him out.

For a moment longer he hesitated, his face unreadable. Then he grinned, and that vague air of danger and tension slipped away. "Sure," he said. "Give me a minute to change."

She almost told him that he looked fine just as he was, his T-shirt stretched tight across the muscles of his chest and arms, his hair pushed casually back from his forehead. She bit back the words, surprised at her own temerity in all but speaking the thought aloud. In another moment she would be sounding as hot-blooded as he had the night before on the beach.

That incident had bothered her, particularly coming as early as it had in their relationship. Not that she found him unattractive—if no one else, at least the Lord knew that was not the truth—but she didn't really know him at all, neither his background nor his intentions. She was unwilling to commit any part of herself to anything less than a serious relationship.

But she had been flattered by his attention and later that night had actually caught herself hoping for a repeated indication of it. Don't hold your breath on that one, girl, she thought with resignation. Not after the way you put him off.

Still, it was easy to toss her head at him now and tell him to hurry and change if he wanted dinner tonight. When he reappeared, clad in an open-necked shrit and casual slacks, his hair brushed, she had the quite unexpected thought that she would be proud to be seen with him anywhere at all, much less Tapachula. She guessed she was blushing and literally prayed that he would not notice.

At the Scout, she hesitated. Should she offer to let him drive? Would he be offended if she did not at least make the offer? She was used to doing the driving—Howard usually let her—and she realized with irritation that she was acting like a schoolgirl flirting with the football star.

But Eric was already moving easily to the passenger's

door with a total lack of hesitation which made her wonder if he had detected her own disquiet and chosen this way to alleviate it. If so, she was grateful.

She was aware of his eyes on her as she settled behind the wheel, and she wondered self-consciously how she looked to him. She was wearing her usual jeans and a white blouse that she knew flattered her figure. Had she been thinking of that subconciously when she donned it? Should she have worn something else? She fumbled a little getting the familiar vehicle started. Blast my unfaithful emotions anyway! she thought furiously. And blast Howard for bringing this man here to disrupt the peaceful, pleasant routine of her existence.

"Does Howard know we're going?" He might have sensed her flustration and broached the question to bridge the sudden awkwardness between them.

"I told him I was going and that I planned to ask you to go with me," she said with relief.

He kept his gaze on her. "Howard thinks a lot of you," he said finally.

"That's because he wouldn't know what to do without me." She gave him a quick grin to divert the conversation from any serious depth.

"I think you're right," he answered and smiled so that she took her eyes off the road to look at him for a moment and enjoy the warmth of that smile.

They both fell silent as she headed out of town on the blacktop. He seemed absorbed in the scenery and once he turned to look back behind them. A glance in the mirror showed her only an empty road and a receding Puerto Madero. Wordlessly he shifted back around and reached out the open window to adjust the side mirror so that, she assumed, he could see behind them without looking back. She felt a twinge of irritation. She had set the mirrors herself to suit her as the driver, and he did not apologize or explain making the change. It occurred to her, as he continued to glance frequently in the mirror, that he was behaving as if he thought someone might be following them.

When she pulled out to pass one of the lumbering old buses making the trek between Puerto Madero and Tapachula, he took his eyes away from the mirror and looked at the old vehicle in surprise. "That looks like the same bus I used to ride to school on as a kid," he said jokingly.

"It might be," she told him and enjoyed his attempt at humor. "That's what happens to old school buses that get too rundown to be used in the United States. They get sold here to be used as public transportation. We have some real antiques on the road."

"You mean I've stumbled on the mysterious School Bus Graveyard?"

She laughed and began to point out other things of interest on the drive. He listened, asking questions, joking a little bit with her, but she noticed that he kept glancing in that rearview mirror. Nothing overtook them, however, although at least one late-model American-made midsize car passed them going in the opposite direction. He commented on its presence.

"Oh, there's a thriving black market in stolen American cars down here," she told him. "Some car thief north of the border steals a car, drives it down here for the cost of gas, files off the ID number and sells it for two or three thousand dollars clear profit. Howard has always refused to buy a car like that, even through a third party, because he knows where they come from."

He seemed to grow thoughtful after that and little more was said until they reached the town. Negotiating the narrow streets, she drove past stucco facades fronting crowded tenements, emerging at last in the central square.

Numerous shops and vendors faced out on the little park with its carefully tended hedges and shrubs which occupied the center of the square. A fairly modern grocery store—their destination—fronted the square not too far from the bustling open-air market.

Cristina watched Eric sweep the whole area with a probing gaze as they stepped out of the Scout. "You want to look around some?" she offered.

"I'd like that," he answered, accepting her offer with a small smile that seemed somehow forced, and he continued to scan the plaza as they walked past the various foods and trinket vendors lining the sidewalks.

As they neared the market, a wave of multitudinous odors assaulted their nostrils and Cristina wrinkled her nose as she always did at the first whiff of the marketplace.

Braden saw her and grinned in sympathy. She guessed with sudden intuition that this was not the first time he had been a visitor to such an open-air market, common in the Third World countries. He was too casual in his ready acceptance of the panorama of sights and sounds and scents for it to be a first-time experience.

As they entered the market area, she felt his hand brush hers and felt a brief stab of disappointment at how quickly he withdrew from the contact. Your own fault, girl, she reminded herself firmly.

The stifling odorous atmosphere, trapped by the close conjunction of the covered stalls and the numerous sweating human bodies, closed over them. Cristina, despite the unpleasant aspects of the market, never tired of viewing the variety of goods and merchandise offered for sale or barter.

Foodstuffs predominated. In one stall fruits and vegetables were displayed in varying stages of ripeness. Next to it, enormous dead fish, two to three feet long, were awaiting a purchaser. Live chickens squawked protestingly from cramped cages. Nearby gutted possums were spread for inspection. The stench, intensified by the stifling air, made Cristina breathe through her mouth. Eric, she noticed did not seem affected.

As they stopped at her urging to examine some handwoven shawls and blankets, she saw him glance back the way they had come and continue to stare in that direction with a curious intentness.

Unreasonably irked at his continuing preoccupation, she chose one of the brightly colored shawls, and draped it around her shoulders, holding it in place at her neck. She turned then in a little pirouette. That got his attention, she was gratified to see, and she cheerfully accepted when he offered to purchase it for her.

They went deeper into the convuluted maze of the market, passing stands of knives and trinkets. Eric paused at one, examining the blades. After a moment, he selected an odd one, the hilt of which folded down in two sections to enclose the blade. He hefted it a moment then flicked his wrist around in a movement too fast for her eye to follow that ended with both sections of the hilt gripped in his big fist, with the gleaming six-inch blade exposed.

The owner of the stand was gaping at him wide-eyed. Cristina imagined her own eyes were wide as well. Absently he refolded the knife and seemed to ponder it, glancing back once over his shoulder. Finally he replaced it, almost reluctantly, she thought, and steered her wordlessly to the next stall.

In another man she would have classified the incident as showing off to impress her (it would not have succeeded). But there had been nothing of that nature to his almost unthinking manipulations of the blade. It had been, rather, like a craftsman evaluating a tool of his trade while contemplating its potential use. The thought sent a needle chill down her spine there in the heat.

He seemed to sense her reaction and made an effort to be more cheerful and attentive. When he saw a metal-worker using a hacksaw to cut names into rings of soft metal, he insisted on buying her one. The vendor protested that her name was too long, so they settled for Cris, and shortly she let him slide the ring onto her finger. His hands felt strong and firm as he adjusted the ring, and she recalled the easy familiarity with which they had flipped the folding knife open. She drew her hand back, then held it out for him to admire.

"Nice," he said. "Now I won't forget your name."

"Do I get a refund if it turns my finger green?" she retorted.

"No, I'll just buy you another ring for your other hand so your fingers will match."

Somehow, she reflected, their excursion, even with his strange preoccupation, had taken on the frivolous air of a date. Remotely it disturbed her, but she found herself enjoying his company too much to dwell on the fact.

As they moved on, the press of people pushed them briefly together and once again their hands brushed. For a moment she thought he was going to let his fingers intertwine with hers, and she felt as if the ground had dropped away beneath her feet because she did not know what she would do if he did. Then he drew his hand away, and she turned quickly to examine the handbags at a leathercraft stall.

He selected a hand-tooled Western-style belt and tried it experimentally around his lean waist. She had become so used to his alertness that she was expecting it when he turned slightly to study the faces of the people behind them.

She was not expecting him to speak. "Like it?" He moved so that she could see the belt. Without changing his tone, he kept talking. "In a minute look back at that fish stand and tell me if the fella with the black John Deere cap is still there."

She resisted the automatic impulse to turn and look immediately, but she knew her eyes got a little wide as she stared at him. He grinned encouragingly, then turned his attention back to the stall. After a moment, trying to keep her movement as casual as possible, she surveyed the stalls they had already passed. She had no trouble picking out the thin young Mexican loitering in front of the fish stand pretending to examine the merchandise from beneath the bill of his battered baseball cap.

"He's still there," she reported as she replaced the handbag she held. Automatically she had assumed a circumspect attitude, speaking out of the corner of her mouth, not looking directly at Eric as she did so. "Why? What's wrong?"

"He's been following us," Eric said. "He picked us up back in the square almost as soon as we got here."

"Are you sure?"

"Yes." His tone brooked no argument. "Do you know him?"

She risked another glance at the raggedly dressed youth. "I don't think so," she said. "But when I first got here, Tobias would have me followed sometimes. They followed Howard too at first. But they haven't done it lately. Maybe they're checking you out."

"What interest would the local witch doctor have in me?" Something in the way he asked the question, perhaps a certain underlying hardness to his voice, made her understand abruptly that when he had toyed with the folding knife it had not been an idle examination. He had been evaluating it as a weapon, and evaluating, too, the possible need for its use against their follower. The realization of his potential for violence frightened her, but, she told herself, he had put the knife back. He had chosen against violence. And she could not deny the innate goodness she sensed in him, the burgeoning of the Holy Spirit. Of a sudden she was glad of his nearness, glad of the security he seemed to offer.

"Tobias always keep tabs on the mission," she answered his question belatedly. "He hates us and everything we stand for, but he's never really offered to harm us. I'm sure he knows all about your joining us by now"—his eyes flashed strangely at her words—"and this is just his way of harrassing you and keeping tabs on you. He's got a few followers here in town. He must have either learned we were coming and alerted one of his followers, or else this one just chanced to see us and decided to follow us. He may even be from Puerto Madero and just happened to be in town when we arrived. Tobias would be pleased at anything done to bother us."

She thought he looked impressed at her appraisal of the situation. He glanced past her then and frowned. "Well, he's gone now. Maybe that's the last we'll see of him. But I think I would like to meet this Tobias."

"No," she said firmly, "I don't think you want to meet him at all."

16

Braden hefted the last of the concrete blocks out of the bed of the battered old pickup, and set it atop the stack which had grown up there behind the mission. He drew one muscular forearm across his brow and caught Luis Santego's grin thrown at him from across the pile of blocks. Automatically he returned it.

"Now we can start to build, eh, Eric?"

"That we can," Braden conceded and felt a simple pleasure in being able to make the statement.

In truth, things had moved with surprising speed in the past two days. Dennison, it developed, already had a rough plan for the new wing, and with Cristina's willing advice, Braden had been able to complete it and make an initial order of supplies. Luis Santego, true to his offer of assistance, had driven to Tapachula to pick up the load of concrete blocks. Together he and Braden had unloaded them in the Saturday afternoon heat.

"How's the construction crew?" Dennison had emerged from the mission. He was dressed casually and seemed as relaxed and at ease as Braden had ever seen him. "Remember, we've got a social tonight, and you're the guest of honor."

Braden's scowl was only half in jest. To his chagrin, Dennison and Cristina had arranged a pot-luck dinner among the church members to greet the new lay missionary.

All of Braden's protests had been brushed aside with good humor and the plans had gone forward.

Objectively, Braden was not happy about the dinner; it never made good sense as an agent to draw attention to yourself, and being the guest of honor at a function which the whole village would undoubtedly be aware of was not an ideal way to maintain a low profile. But he recognized, to his dismay, a sneaking anticipation for the affair.

"We better call it quits for today, Luis," he told the stocky villager now.

Santego grinned broadly. "Yes, we must rest so that we can eat tonight!" He clambered into the dilapidated pickup and backed it out onto the road. His laughter at his own jest followed him as he drove away.

Members were already beginning to arrive by the time Braden made use of the primitive shower facilities in Dennison's house. Pots and plates of food were already being placed on mismatched tables set up in the yard. There was much laughter and good spirits among the visitors. The mission, Braden had learned, served as the center of their social life, and a pot-luck dinner to welcome the new missionary was a highlight of the social season.

Cristina appeared in a simple, brightly colored dress. The straps stood out against her dark shoulders, and her long, black hair caught the glimmer of reflected light. She was stunning, and she curtsied prettily to Braden as he approached. "Our guest of honor," she greeted him.

"*Reluctant* guest of honor," he reminded her. "Do I get into trouble if I compliment you tonight on looking absolutely gorgeous?"

She smiled and tossed her head fetchingly. "I'd be disappointed if you didn't." Laughter sparkled in her eyes and he could tell she was pleased. "Come on," she said, catching his arm abruptly. "You have to meet everyone."

He made no effort to recall names, but the overwhelming surge of love, warmth, and gratitude for his very presence which he recieved from those he met made him distinctly uncomfortable.

Luis Santego, his wife, and little Carmelita showed up, neatly dressed in spotlessly clean clothes which belied the squalor in which they lived. Luis took it upon himself to assist Cristina in the introductions, and Braden was feeling quite desperate by the time he managed to extricate himself from the crowd.

He left Cristina chattering with a half-dozen children while Luis elaborated upon the virtues of the proposed dormitory to two of his cronies. Ducking into the sanctuary, Braden found it deserted and breathed a sigh of relief.

Despite himself he had enjoyed all the attention and fellowship, he had to admit. But he could not quite escape the nagging ache of conscience which insisted that he was hopelessly inadequate for this role he was being asked to play.

He stood in the open doorway looking out on the road, and his eye was caught by the movements of a young man opposite him. As he watched, the man whirled through a series of turns, lashing out with naked hands and feet as if engaged in a battle with unseen enemies.

He was, Braden realized with quickening interest, going through some kind of regimen of martial arts exercise or training. It was not one of the formal training sequences, or *katas*, he was certain. As he watched, the young man ended the sequence with a high leaping kick, flinging himself into the air, twisting to drive one foot through the skull of an imagined opponent, coming back down on flexed legs.

Frowning, Braden turned as he heard someone enter the sanctuary behind him. He relaxed as he recognized Dennison. The missionary approached him, seemed about to speak, until he saw what had caught Braden's attention.

"Who's that?" Braden nodded toward the martial artist who had started into another routine.

Dennison grinned slightly. "That's Jorge. He grew up here, but was kicked out by his parents and ended up running with the street gangs in Mexico City. He came back to Puerto Madero about a year ago. He likes to hang around here and show off, brag about how tough he is, all the fights he's had."

"Church member?"

Dennison shook his head almost sadly. "No. I've invited him plenty of times, but he always gets uptight, insists he doesn't need anyone but himself."

"But he keeps coming back," Braden made it more of a statement than a question.

Dennison's glance held a flicker of shrewd appraisal. "That's right, just about every time we have a service or fellowship. I think down deep he wants to but won't admit it, even to himself."

"Isn't that what they call being under the conviction of the Holy Spirit?" Braden asked blandly.

Dennison laughed and clapped him on the shoulder. "You're learning."

"We'll see," Braden murmured and went out into the street. As he crossed toward the young man, he had time to appraise the naked muscular torso, the muscles flexing and relaxing in smooth symmetry as he moved through his sequence of kicks and strikes.

He did not pause as Braden drew near, but the latter had no doubt that the young man was aware of his presence. He watched without expression as Jorge snapped out a crisp reverse punch, pivoted on the ball of his left foot to flick his right leg up and around in a roundhouse kick, spinning on around with the momentum to shoot out a back kick with his left foot, coming out of it into a defensive stance. For the first time his dark eyes snapped to his spectator.

Braden nodded toward the church. "There's plenty of room and plenty of food if you want to join us." He could not have told where the words came from.

Jorge spat into the dust between them. "You are the new gringo missionary," he snarled. "I do not need your church or your God." His arms blurred in a flurry of straight-arm punches, then he moved into another sequence. It was street-fighting stuff, the basic techniques of karate perhaps picked up at a dojo, but corrupted by street tactics learned secondhand or in drunken brawls, and accentuated by undisciplined workouts.

"You think because you can fight you do not need God?" Braden asked mildly.

Jorge spun toward him. "I do not need anybody!" His face was savage. "When I was in Mexico City I led my own gang! I was the best! Here" — he indicated the white line of a scar beneath his rib cage — "I was stabbed, but I beat him, even then, took his knife away from him and broke his ribs, like this!" He demonstrated with a thrusting kick. "And here, over my eye, I was hit by a pipe, but it did not stop me!" His muscular shoulders heaved.

"Only a fool brags of his scars," Braden said, "or boasts he cannot be beaten."

He saw the rage suffuse the handsome face, and before the younger man could act or speak Braden coiled back into a stance and swept into a sequence of his own, using one of the higher *katas*, flowing through the prearranged set of blocks and kicks and strikes with smooth, powerful precision. His feet seemed barely to disturb the dust as they shifted, his hands blurred as they struck. He whipped through the last sequence of blocks, then snapped into a rigid stance.

He relaxed and turned to the wide-eyed Jorge. "The thing about fighting, about karate, about any of the martial arts, is that there's always somebody somewhere better than you or tougher than you, or somebody with a gun or a lot of friends to back him up."

Jorge continued to stare at him.

"And if you concentrate on your fighting, on making yourself the best, you lose sight of other things, like God," Braden concluded almost gently.

Jorge's surprise did not last over a moment. He appeared not to have heard anything Braden said. "You think you are better, gringo? You think because you can dance that you can beat me?"

"Look," Braden said, the words coming to him as he spoke, "I'm twenty years older than you. I can do everything you can do in the way of karate and I can do it better and then some. But it doesn't prove a thing."

"It will prove that I am better than you! A gringo missionary who talks of fighting!" Jorge's voice was scornful, savage. "I will show you how to fight!" He snapped into a stance, hands lifted, feet set.

"You're out of your league, boy." Braden's voice had gone very cold.

"Haii!" With a shout, Jorge came, punching kicking, kicking again, foolishly using the same sequence he had demonstrated earlier.

Braden retreated automatically, gauging speed and balance, a sickness growing down in his gut. He had not wanted this absurd contest, not wanted it at all. But now was no time for self-recrimination. Jorge was not playing; he meant business.

As the back kick rammed at his middle, he stood his ground, left foot advanced. His arm swept down and across, the edge of his fist hammering against Jorge's ankle, the force of the block spinning the young man around. In that instant, Braden snapped his right foot forward and neatly kicked Jorge's anchor leg out from under him.

The kick could have crippled, as indeed could the block also, but he had pulled both blows and Jorge went down hard but unhurt.

He came up fast, however, scrambling in a cloud of dust.

"Leave it," Braden said.

Jorge spat out a foul epithet and flung himself at Braden in the same high, leaping kick he used in his practice, expelling his breath in a barking grunt as he attacked. Braden stepped sidewise and shot out a hand as Jorge hurtled past him. Again he could have broken bones, but he turned the blow into a straight-armed shove that disrupted Jorge's balance and brought him crashing to the ground on his side.

Instantly Braden was over him, and his powering fist stopped just brushing Jorge's temple. Staring down into those dark eyes, Braden saw the awareness of defeat. Jorge knew that, had Braden wished it, he would be dead.

Braden straightened, careful of renewed hostilities. He stepped back and away, standing loosely, waiting. Jorge scrambled to his feet then and Braden tensed. The twisted look the young man flung at him was equal parts rage and humiliation. He seemed to try to speak, then spun abruptly and fled, disappearing between two of the shacks.

Tiredly, Braden watched him go. It had all been so worthless. He had turned an attempt at spreading the Word into a common brawl. Some missionary, he thought bitterly.

He turned as Dennison approached. He had all but forgotten the other's presence as a spectator. "I blew it," Braden admitted flatly.

Dennison studied his face for a moment, then looked in the direction Jorge had fled. "I don't know," he said at last. "Maybe it helped to have it put to him on his own level. If he gets over being mad long enough to think about what you said, it may sink in. At any rate, your results with him can't be any worse than mine have been."

Braden shook his head in mute negation. The sense of failure had settled on him like a massive weight. The brightness and gaiety of the social seemed distant and unapproachable.

Dennison read his look. "You didn't start it," he reminded Braden. "You just defended yourself. There's nothing wrong with that. When Christ said 'turn the other cheek,' he was talking about responding to what amounted to an insult, not an actual physical attack. And you defended yourself almost passively from what I saw. You could have hurt that boy, I know." His look was gauging. "You're darned good at that stuff."

Braden shrugged. "It's not hard to look good against an amateur."

"And you're a pro, aren't you?"

Braden gave a mental scowl at his own carelessness. "I'm better than he is, at any rate," he said. He was aware of Dennison's eyes on him as he turned to cross the road back to the mission and its repellent merriment.

17

Cristina noticed Eric's absence from the pot-luck supper when she looked for him to introduce him to yet another member of the mission. He had disappeared, she realized, and recalled the unease she had sensed in his manner at being the focal point of so much attention. She should have been more considerate of him, she thought with a touch of guilt. At the very least she should seek him out to make amends. Perhaps Howard had kept track of him.

But Dennison, too, seemed to have vanished, which was unusual. She scanned the crowd again, wondering if she had just overlooked either or both of the men. But, no, they were not present. Where would they have gone? By nature an outgoing person herself, that aspect of her character only heightened by her life's calling, she was unable, quite, to understand Eric's reticence and reluctance to associate with other people.

He had relaxed some around her, she reflected, particularly since their excursion to Tapachula and the marketplace. Some discreet inquires among members by Howard had elicited the fact that their mysterious follower had indeed been a disciple of Tobias. Eric had said little when informed of this, but had seemed curiously relieved.

And Cristina, almost despite her best intentions, had found herself looking forward with a secret thrill to the time she could spend with Eric, to the prospect of them working together. She was happy too to finally have someone to accompany her on her regular visits to the mountain villages. She was glad Howard had agreed so readily that Eric should go with her.

The routine daily tasks involved in running the mission in Howard's absence had kept her from her usual medical rounds, and she knew the needs of the villagers—medical and spiritual—would be great. The idea of working with Eric to meet those needs was enticing.

"Hermana Cristina!" The excited greeting drew her back from her pleasant reverie.

She returned the smile of the pretty, dark-haired young woman—more of a girl actually—who hurried up to her, cradling a tiny baby in her arms. "Hola, Rosa," she said with genuine pleasure.

Rosa Enrique, still in her teens, was a member of the mission and something of a protege and friend of Cristina's. She was a recent mother, her child having arrived during Howard's trip to the States. Pablo, Rosa's husband, had ended a night of celebrating his new fatherhood in the jail of Tapachula with stitches in his scalp. Cristina had, she recalled, told Howard of the events on the way home from the airport when he had returned with Eric.

Cristina reached now to take the baby lovingly from his mother's arms. She held him gently, feeling that curious peace that always stole over her when she held a child. The Lord had blessed her with an affinity for children, and they seemed to be just as drawn to her.

"He is a good baby," Rosa reported proudly. "He cries only when I am late feeding him. And he is already very strong, like his father..." her voice trailed off and a shadow passed over her pretty features at this last statement.

Cristina looked at her inquiringly. "What's wrong?" Instinctively she had pressed the child more firmly against herself. "Has Pablo been drinking again already?"

Rosa's expression was one of distress. "He was good for a few days after he got out of jail," she said hesitantly. "He was so proud of little Pedro, so happy to be a father." Her face lit up with the memory. "But then lately, when I had to spend so much time with the little one, Pablo became angry with me. He has been staying gone much of the time now. I do not know where he is tonight." Her dark eyes, so recently happy, had suddenly filled with tears.

Balancing the baby in one arm, Cristina reached out with the other to hug Rosa to her, so that the two women and the baby clung for a moment in close embrace. "I'm sorry, Rosa," Cristina murmured. "I know how much you hoped it would be better after the baby was born."

Why was it, she wondered, that so often the genuinely nice girls ended up married to reprobates and losers? But Rosa had married Pablo, a non-Christian, against both her and Howard's advice. It had been the only major rift to occur between the two women since Cristina had first met Rosa, who at the time had been only a child herself.

"You were right, Cristina," Rosa said. "I should not have married him."

"Hush," Cristina cut her off before she could go further with her regrets. "The Lord can handle this. Come on, let's go over here and pray."

She led the younger woman to a deserted corner of the yard, and afterwards Rosa smiled weakly and brushed tears away from her eyes. "I feel better now." She reached to accept the infant back into her own arms.

"We'll keep praying for all three of you," Cristina assured her. She wondered with sudden brutal pessimism if in another ten years little Pedro might end up as one of her flock. *Please, God, no.* But Rosa appeared pensive.

"What is it, Hermana?" Cristina prompted.

"I was wondering if maybe Hermano Dennison and—the new hermano could come sometime and see Pablo, visit with him. Maybe they could..."

"Of course. They'll be happy to," Cristina promised. Howard, she knew, had already visited with Rosa's errant husband on several occasions with no discernible results. But there was no harm in another try. And maybe the Lord could use Eric somehow in the situation.

Together they moved to the tables and filled plates from the variety of food available. As she ate, Cristina looked for Eric again and finally spotted him engaged in conversation with Howard and several male villagers, apparently concerning the new dorm. Eric looked grim and seemed to be letting the other men do most of the talking.

She had deliberately worn the brightly colored dress to impress him — no question this time — and she felt a warm glow as she remembered his compliment. She wondered again where he and Dennison had disappeared to earlier.

"The new Hermano," Rosa said with a mischievous little grin, "you like him, don't you? I can tell. Ah, you are right, he is very much of a man."

"Don't be silly, Rosa!" Cristina was sure that she was blushing, and a smile came to her lips even as she made the denial.

"Oh, do not lie," Rosa scolded. "You will spoil your witness to me."

Then Cristina could contain herself no longer, and the smile became laughter that was joined in immediately by Rosa. And now it was the younger woman's turn to hug Cristina to her.

"I am so happy for you, Hermana. I know how lonely you have been, and he is a good man."

"Now, hush, Rosa," Cristina tried in vain to make her voice firm. "There's nothing between us. Really. And I don't want you telling stories to everyone in town, either!"

Rosa's smile was knowing. "Oh, I will not tell, but I will pray for you." She laughed merrily, then managed to repress her laughter as little Carmelita scurried up to the pair.

"We are looking for you," she announced, and Cristina

looked past her to see her foster parents, Luis Santego and his wife, approaching.

"Of course, darling," she answered, bending to receive the customary hug. "What is it?"

But Carmelita's attention was distracted by the infant Pedro, and it fell to Santego to explain that they were heading home and that Carmelita wanted Hermana Cristina to go with them to tuck her in bed.

Cristina searched Santego's impassive features for a clue. Seeing Carmelita to bed was an old ritual, but one which, of late, Carmelita seemed to have outgrown, disdaining Cristina's last offer to perform it. She wondered what had brought about this minor relapse.

Santego shrugged expressively, somehow managing to convey that he probably knew the answer, but did not want to speak within earshot of Carmelita.

Frustrated, Cristina glanced around the yard. A few of the guests had already left, and it was growing dark. She did not see Eric or Howard. Never mind; it should not take long to accompany the Santegos back to their house and see what was bothering Carmelita.

Rosa departed with Pedro, casting one last conspiratorial grin at Cristina as she left. Cristina scowled back in mock warning, then she turned to Carmelita and her foster parents.

Once the four of them had left the mission and were walking down the darkened street, Carmelita's high spirits seemed to evaporate. She clung tightly to Cristina's hand and kept looking about as if expecting something awful to spring out of the encroaching shadows.

At their house, while Carmelita made hurried preparations for bed, Cristina drew Santego aside. "She is frightened of the brujo, Hermana," he explained.

"Tobias?" Cristina asked, startled. The witch doctor, of late, seemed to have become something of a nemesis, she thought.

Santego nodded somberly. "Si, she saw him the other

evening lurking in an alley nearby. You know how he looks, and apparently he saw her and deliberately tried to frighten her."

"Blast him!" Cristina hissed sharply, and Santego looked surprised.

"We have told her not to be scared of him, but she thinks he will come back in the night and carry her off. She wanted you to come and see her to bed."

"The poor child," Cristina said with sympathy. "I'll talk to her."

Carmelita, in an old T-shirt that served as a nightgown, led Cristina to the niche which was her sleeping quarters. Cristina drew aside the hanging blanket and arranged the bedclothes once Carmelita was under the sheet.

"Have you said your prayers?" she asked.

Carmelita shook her head and Cristina took one of her hands. "Go ahead," she urged. "You pray first and then I will."

She closed her eyes as Carmelita haltingly prayed for the Santegos, and the mission, and brother Howard, and sister Cristina, and the new brother, and all her friends, and then thanked God for her home. "And please protect me, Jesus. Amen," she finished at last.

Cristina squeezed her hand and began to pray aloud herself, asking the Lord's blessing on this family and asking that He encircle each member of the family with angels to protect them from whatever would harm them. When she was through, she smiled down at Carmelita, who looked up at her with wide, trusting eyes.

"Is there something that frightens you, Carmelita?" she asked gently.

Carmelita's eyes got even wider and genuine fear stirred in them as she nodded. Hesitantly, then with mounting emotion, she told Cristina of the incident Santego had described.

"I am scared," she finished. "He will come back one night and get me."

Cristina gave her a comforting hug then caught her gaze. "Listen to me, Carmelita," she said softly. "You don't need to be afraid of Tobias. He can't hurt you if you stay away from him. And he won't come and get you."

"But yes he will!" Carmelita protested with masterful illogic.

"No," Cristina told her firmly. "He won't. Do you remember when I prayed, I asked Jesus to send down angels to protect you?" At the child's nod she continued. "Well, he really does that. Once there was a man named John Paton. He was a missionary just like brother Howard, except that where he lived there was a tribe of natives who wanted to kill him."

She had Carmelita's full attention now, she saw, and she went on. "Well, one night the natives came to kill the missionary and his wife. They got all around their house and were going to burn it down with them inside. All that night the missionary and his wife prayed to God for protection, at any moment expecting the natives to set their house on fire. But in the morning, the natives were gone. They had disappeared into the jungle and left the missionary and his wife unharmed.

"A year later, the chief of the natives became a Christian, just like you did. The missionary hadn't been afraid to go and tell him about Jesus even when he knew the chief hated him. And the chief accepted Jesus into his heart, the same way as you. After that happened, the missionary asked the chief why he and his warriors had not killed them on that night a year before.

" 'We could not,' the chief answered, 'because of all those men you had with you protecting you.' The missionary told him that there had not been any other men—only himself and his wife. The chief shook his head and argued that he and his warriors had seen hundreds of big men in shining robes with drawn swords in a circle around the house, protecting it from harm."

Cristina paused in her narrative. Her audience of one

was listening with rapt attention. "The missionary realized then that God had answered his prayers and sent an entire army of angels to protect them, just like I asked Him to do for you."

"There are really angels protecting me?" Carmelita's tone still held a trace a doubt.

Cristina nodded emphatically. "That's right. They may not protect you if you do something foolish like going swimming on the beach, but Jesus is always with you when you are trying to obey Him and live as He wants you to."

Carmelita considered this thoughtfully, then finally nodded gravely. "Okay," she decided. "I won't be scared of Tobias any more."

Cristina heaved a sign of relief. She kissed the little girl good night, then emerged from the sleeping niche to reassure the Santegos. They were grateful and Luis offered to walk her back to the mission.

"That's all right," she declined. "It's just barely dark. I'll be okay."

Brushing aside any further protests, she took her leave. It was dark now, and she regretted not having brought a flashlight. The only illumination came from lighted windows and an occasional low-wattage outside light. She found herself walking a little more quickly, glancing nervously about in the darkness.

Remember, girl, she told herself resolutely, angels are protecting you.

She had first heard the true story about the Reverend John Paton and the hostile natives of the New Hebrides from Howard, who said he had read it in a book by Billy Graham. She had forgotten the story until the imagery of the protective angels had come to her while she prayed for Carmelita. Apparently the story had satisfied the little girl.

But it was not hard to understand why the child had become frightened of Tobias, particularly if the brujo had made a deliberate effort to scare her.

Recalling the hideous appearance of the witch doctor, she could well imagine Carmelita's terror. *He knows she's one of my flock,* she reflected with a surge of anger. *He's just doing this to harrass the mission, blast him.*

She wondered disquietingly what other twisted plans the sorcerer might have in store for them. It was not a pleasant thought, and it seemed to her that the darkness between the houses she passed had grown even more dense, that it now harbored grotesque lurking shapes waiting to seize body and soul at the earliest chance.

A skeletal dog faded back into the shadows like a ghost and a cat yowled unnervingly. She suddenly regretted turning down Santego's offer to accompany her. But the mission was just ahead there. She could see the comforting glow from the floodlights Howard had installed.

She hurried to reach it.

18

Braden saw the naked hatred in the fiery eyes of the tall, sinewy man in the grotesque reptilian headdress and felt the almost physical impact of the other's enmity. It made the violent anger of Jorge, the street-fighter, seem mild and innocuous by contrast. Remembering that violence, Braden tensed as the stranger recoiled from the obviously unexpected presence of himself and Dennison there in the road outside the fenced enclave.

But the costumed man made no overt hostile movements. Still, Braden could feel the tension in Dennison's big form beside him. The man that confronted them with such latent threatening violence had a gaunt body across which ropes and cables of muscle writhed sinuously as he moved. His face was elongated, its thick lips and high cheekbones betraying obvious Indian and Negro blood somewhere in his background. Three short, horizontal scars marred each copper cheek. The parallel ridges of scar tissue were too precise to be other than intentionally inflicted.

With the exception of the bizarre headdress, his clothes—tattered cut-offs and faded shirt—were not unusual for Puerto Madero. But it was the headpiece which lent the final unnerving touch to his appearance. The top half of the mummified head of a caiman, South America's crocodile, not known in these climes, was set atop his head like some ancient demonic helmet, the toothed upper jaw jutting out to overhang his scarred features, leaving them in partial shadows as if he peered out from the gut of the saurian. The stench of the thing, mingled with the odor of its wearer's unwashed body, was almost nauseating.

A sheathed machete hung from a rope belt at his waist.

"Go!" Dennison uttered the one word, his voice hard.

The man hissed like a snake, the sound all the more chilling, seeming to issue as it did from the jaws of the reptilian headdress. Slowly then its author straightened to his full height, assuming a kind of savage dignity in his stance, although the feral aura of him was still strong. He jerked his head imperiously toward the fenced enclave of huts. "They do not want you here, missionary," he said with a strong voice.

Dennison was unyielding. "Let them tell me that. Now, go!"

Braden detected a faint movement of one wiry hand toward the hilt of the machete, but the stranger did not complete the motion. His eyes raked over Braden. "This is the gringo dog who follows you," he sneered.

"He does not follow me," Dennison corrected him. "He follows Jesus Christ, who died for all men, including you, Tobias."

So this was the infamous brujo, the sorcerer whose unnerving howl Braden had heard that first night. Having seen him now, Braden could easily picture him as the author of that unearthly sound.

The man's obsidian eyes were still fixed on him. "I have called down the curses of the demons on you, gringo. You will never rest here, for Quetzalcoatl himself seeks your soul!"

"Jesus Christ has my soul," Braden replied, meeting that gaze. "Get out of here."

For a moment Tobias seemed intent on prolonging the confrontation. Then his eyes shuttled back and forth between the two big men facing him. He lifted his head so that it seemed as if the dead caiman opened threatening jaws to them. Then he brushed past Braden, the foul stench of him passing by like a wave, and stalked off.

Dennison shook his head as if to dispel an unpleasant thought. "Tobias," he said by way of explanation. "Our local witch doctor."

Braden nodded. "So I gathered. He certainly lives up to his reputation. I heard him howl the first night I was here. Cristina mentioned his name."

"He's bad," Dennison said. "Evil. Come on, let's see what harm he's been up to."

They had come from the mission following the noon meal after the Sunday morning services. Dennison's sermon had been on going out to spread the Word, and Braden was again the reluctant center of attention. He was only grateful Dennison hadn't asked him to speak.

Afterwards, Dennison had recruited him to accompany him on some calls in the village. "You're the big drawing card," the missionary had told him cheerfully. "Everybody wants to see the new gringo."

Cristina's sympathetic smile had made it only a little easier. Braden kept recalling his abortive efforts with Jorge and Chandler. Every time I try to share my faith with someone, he thought dismally, they try to kill me. It was not an encouraging thought.

Dennison led the way through the gap which served as a gateway in the sagging bamboo fence. Inside was a rabbit warren of ramshackle huts, rotting piles of garbage, rooting hogs and dogs, and villagers clad in rags.

Here, Braden realized, were some of the real poor of Puerto Madero. The slovenly hovels made the Santegos' dwelling seem palatial by comparison. In an area not much over fifteen yards square were, he estimated, over a hundred people subsisting side by side with animals, which roamed at will in their midst.

As Braden watched, an enormous hog shoved under a

lopsided table, toppling a bowl of unidentifiable foodstuffs into the dirt.

The woman who had been preparing it shrieked in outrage, and a small, naked boy darted from the nearest hovel to set upon the happily chomping hog with a heavy stick. The porker retreated in grunting protest, and, at the woman's command, a tiny girl in a filthy dress scooped the food from the ground back into its wooden bowl, undoubtedly with a liberal sprinkling of the powdery dirt as well, and set it back on the table.

Elsewhere, a young woman leaned in the doorway of a hut, the naked child she held clamped under one arm, nursing at her breast. The mother's eyes watched them without expression.

Dennison nodded toward an emaciated old man who ambled in their direction, grinning toothlessly beneath an old baseball cap with a logo so faded as to be undecipherable. This worthy seemed to be the head man of this village within a village.

He led them back deeper into the maze of makeshift dwellings. Scrawny chickens scattered from in front of them. A few of the inhabitants called out to Dennison or came to greet them. Others watched with indifference but little hostility, Braden noted.

"We met Tobias," Dennison said as they made the rounds.

The oldster spat contemptuously. "That one! Yes, he was here. Viejo—the Old One—is ill. The family wanted the brujo." He spat again, leaving no doubt as to his stand on the issue. "Come, I will show you."

He hobbled on calloused feet to a lean-to—little more than a large sheet of rotting cardboard punctured by upright stakes—which had been erected next to a thatched shack. Under the shade of the lean-to, Braden detected a frail figure lying as still as death on a pallet of palm fronds.

As they drew nearer, stooping to step under the roof of

the lean-to, he detected the slow rise and fall of the hollow chest beneath the tattered shirt. The man was old, aged by the burden of his pitiful life as much as by his years. If Braden was any judge, the oldster was dying, perhaps not today, or even the next, but dying nonetheless, as his old, mistreated body finally gave out on him.

A crude image freshly carved from a stick of wood had been set next to the pallet. Some form of incense, harshly sweet, burned in a clay bowl, its fumes stinging Braden's eyes.

Denninson made a wordless sound of disgust. He snatched up the idol and with a single convulsive effort snapped the carved stick in two over his knee. He booted the bowl over and ground the small cone of incense out beneath his booted foot. Then, gently, he knelt by the old man.

"Viejo," he said softly, and then repeated the word more loudly.

The old man's eyes fluttered open. They were pale and shrunken and he seemed to have to strain to make out Dennison's features. Then his bloodless lips parted in a feeble grin. "You have come." His voice was a hoarse whisper.

Dennison nodded. "I am here. I did not know you were so ill or I would have come sooner."

"I told my daughter to call you, but she only sent for the brujo."

Braden had to strain to catch the old man's words.

"He has gone now." Dennison's tone was reassuring. "I destroyed the evil things he left."

The old man nodded. "I did not want him here. I tried to tell him to leave, but he would not." He broke off and collapsed into a series of gasping coughs that threatened to break his frail body like a twig.

When the attack had subsided, Dennison reached to clasp one fleshless hand in his own. "The Lord has sent me to you, my friend. Is there something you wish to settle now?"

"Yes, yes. Many times you have spoken to me, and I have always listened, but have never done what you asked."

Dennison nodded. "I know."

"I am dying," the old man went on with an effort. "I can feel it. And I know that you were right. I have always known, but I was too stubborn, too proud, to ever admit it." He fell briefly silent. Dennison did not prompt him. "But now, I want to do as you said. I want to commit myself to Jesus Christ." He raised himself up slightly, reaching to grasp at Dennison with a desperate clawlike hand. "Tell me I have not waited too long."

Gently Dennison pressed him back down on the pallet. He still held the other's hand in his own. "You know it is not too late, my friend. And you do not need me to do what you ask; you know that, too. You have heard me explain it often enough. It is between you and God."

Again the clawlike hand reached. "But you will help me?"

"Yes, I will help you."

The sound of voices outside in the cluttered courtyard made Braden turn away from the strangely gripping scene. The elderly headman who had first welcomed them was trying with little success to placate a heavyset woman in a sack-like dress who with determination was making her way in the direction of the lean-to. As she approached, Braden stepped out to meet her. The headman drew gratefully back.

"Let me in!" the woman demanded. She might have once been pretty, but her body was now bloated and overweight. "He is my father! He does not want that one in there!"

"I think he does."

She grunted, for all the world like a hog, and tried to step around Braden. He interposed himself between her bulk and the lean-to. She drew back and glared hatefully. A number of other residents of the enclave had gathered to watch the proceedings. They did not seem disposed to take sides. The fat woman was obviously a figure of some authority in the group.

Again she tried to bypass Braden and again he thwarted her. For a moment he thought she would try to physically move him aside, so great was her rage. But she stared at him and drew back slightly.

"He does not need your Christian God!" she cried.

"He does need Him. So do you. And it is not your place to decide for him."

She looked angrily about as if seeking support from the spectators. None was forthcoming, however, and after a moment, a young woman stepped forward. "Leave them be!" she called out to the older woman. "Brother Dennison is a good man, a man of God." There were murmurs of approval for her statement. Braden thought he recognized the speaker from the church dinner of two nights before.

The older woman glared angrily, but some of the fervor drained out of her at this open opposition. Reluctantly she drew back. Braden maintained his place in front of the lean-to. The sound of Dennison's voice came to him. He could not hear the old man's replies.

After a moment, the heavy woman turned and waddled awkwardly out of sight behind one of the huts. She did not look back. Braden caught the eye of the girl who had spoken and smiled. Her return smile was shy, but the sense of unspoken camaraderie warmed him pleasantly.

The headman approached him then; others of the spectators gradually followed. By the time Dennison emerged from the lean-to, a small crowd had gathered to await him.

He led them in a short prayer and they dispersed, many of them lingering to visit with Dennison and the new gringo. The old man's daughter did not reappear.

"You did all right back there," Dennison commented once they had left the rabbit warren of huts. "I knew his daughter would be lurking around somewhere. She's a big fan of Tobias."

Braden recalled the evil malignancy of the sorcerer. "Just how much influence does he have?"

Dennison shrugged. "Not so much any more. A lot of his followers have become Christians over the years. He blames me for that, and he hates the mission and anything associated with it."

"Was that fat woman typical of his followers?"

"No, not really. She's an extreme example and there aren't many left here in Puerto Madero. He comes down every so often, prowls around at night and howls like a banshee, then calls on his followers to dispense charms or spells or cures. Not many of the villagers will actually stand up to him. Mostly they just try to ignore him." Dennison paused thoughtfully. "It's different up in the mountains, though. He has quite a following in some of the villages back up in the brush."

"He looked ready to try that machete on us," Braden commented.

Dennison nodded. "I've heard that he has used it on occasion. Just rumors, but I'm prone to believe them."

Recalling that deliberately disfigured countenance beneath the mummified saurian skull, Braden tended to agree with the assessment.

"He'll really be mad when he hears about the old man. Funny, I don't even know the old fellow's real name—he always just been El Viejo, the Old One."

"He's dying," Braden said.

Dennison frowned. "I know; he won't last much longer. But at least he got things straight about where he'll end up."

"Amen." Braden spoke it with unexpected feeling.

They walked on past a giant concrete tower which, Dennison explained, had been part of some kind of defense system set up during the Kennedy years as part of a mutual aid treaty between the two countries. Long since abandoned by the United States government, the giant structure served now as a bizarre home for several families. It towered in huge incongruity above the other village structures.

Nearby was the home of Senor Cantavas, the prominent

citizen who had accepted Christ in Dennison's absence. The latter had baptized him that morning.

They stopped and were eagerly admitted by Cantavas, a widower. Dennison was on good terms with the new convert, as indeed he seemed to be with almost everyone they encountered in the village, with, of course, the glaring exception of Tobias and his acolyte.

Listening to Dennison visit easily with this man from such a totally different background, Braden wondered at the missionary's seemingly casual ability to relate and interact with others.

The majority of his own significant contacts with the villagers seemed to have been on the order of confrontations—violent or nearly so. It was, he thought, listening to Dennison, not a record he was proud of.

19

"Wonderful!" Cristina's eyes sparkled with pleasure. "Marvelous! I'd love to have been there to see that—Eric backing down that old cow in front of everyone!"

"'Old cow'?" Dennison echoed. "Where's your Christian love?"

"Oh, hush," Cristina refused to be baited. "Everyone will be talking about you now, Eric. Just watch how our attendance will pick up! Praise the Lord!"

Braden felt absurdly pleased at her happiness over his dubious accomplishments. He and Dennison had just returned from their visits. Cristina had stopped her busy preparations for the evening service to listen raptly as Dennison recounted their adventures.

"You must go with me into the mountains tomorrow," she declared to Braden now. "I'm overdue to visit some of the villages. They'll be wondering what's happened to me."

"Santego will be upset," Braden protested mildly. "He's all set to start work on the dormitory wing. He promised to show up bright and early Monday morning with plenty of help." Actually the idea of accompanying this exciting woman on a mission trip into the mountains was not unappealing at all.

And, thankfully, Cristina was not to be dissuaded. "You can get them started in the morning before we leave," she overrode him, then added with a mischievous grin, "I'll supervise."

She did too, showing up to give directions to Santego and the two cohorts who accompanied him and to field their objections to Braden's absence.

The latter stood bemusedly by as she put the three men to work with specific goals which, she told them, she fully expected them to have achieved by her return on the morrow.

"Now," she said, turning breathlessly to Braden, "are you ready?"

Braden caught Santego's look of mock appeal to heaven and suppressed a grin. "Just a minute."

"Well, hurry."

"I promise."

In his room in Dennison's house, he stood for a long moment hefting the .38 in his hand. He had reassembled the weapon at the first opportunity upon arriving at the village, but had left it concealed in the room. Now he weighed it thoughtfully, debating whether or not to take it.

The gun seemed more heavy and awkward in his hand then he remembered, and he recalled the similar feelings he had experienced during his target practice with Chandler back at Operation headquarters. He found himself wondering how he could have ever carried the thing concealed on his person with such little discomfort. Still, it could be worse than stupid to go into the jungle without a gun.

From outside came the impatient blast of the International Scout's horn. Somehow the sound made him decide, and he slipped the gun back under his mattress where he had concealed it. He went out feeling as if a weight had been lifted from him. Somehow he did not think he would regret his decision.

With Cristina at the wheel, they headed north out of the village toward Tapachula. She handled the heavy vehicle well, manipulating the stick shift with an easy dexterity.

Dennison had seen them off with a hug for Cristina and a

firm handclasp for Braden. "You keep each other out of trouble," he warned with a grin. "If you get into a jam, you're on your own. I'm too busy here to come up there and bail you out."

"Listen to this," Cristina had protested to Braden. "He'll just use our being gone as an excuse not to do any work. But I visited with Senor Cantavas, and he promised to make sure our pastor doesn't shirk things too much."

"Heaven forbid! I really will have to work!" Dennison had laughed.

Now, as they left the village behind them, Braden looked on both sides of the road. For as far as he could see stretched a jungle of scrub brush. The plants weren't tall, but they were interwoven in what seemed an impenetrable mass.

"It goes on like that for miles along the coast," Cristina said, following his gaze. "You almost need a machete to get through it at all."

As she spoke, Braden thought he detected movement back in the tangled mass of verdure. "Anything live back there?" he queried.

"Wild pigs, some feral dog packs. Every now and then they get to be a problem in the village. Some wild dogs even attacked a man on the beach once, during a drought when wild game was scarce and he was chasing them away from his pigs."

Braden peered closely, but could detect no further sign of movement, and within a couple of miles they had driven out of the inimical brush and were crossing arid, almost desert-like terrain.

"There," Cristina pointed to the dim blue shapes of the low mountains in the distance. "That's where we're going. We'll be practically right on the Guatemalan border. The villages are really primitive. There are usually a lot of medical needs. More than I can handle."

"You went to nursing school in Texas?" Braden recalled Dennison's thumbnail sketch of Cristina's background. Of a sudden, he found himself wanting to know more about her, how she had ended up doing mission work in Puerto Madero.

"That's right," she answered his question, then glanced at him quickly as if debating with herself. "My family lived in Nuevo Laredo, on the Texas border. I worked to put myself through school when I got old enough." She hesitated again. "That's where I met my husband."

Of sorts, her decision to share this with him was a commitment, Braden realized, a revealing of a private part of herself to him. He met her brief glance, and some of what he felt must have shown in his eyes, for she looked quickly back at the road and continued.

"He was a medical student from Houston. I helped put him through medical school. He had just set up his practice when we were in an automobile accident. A drunk driver crossed the center line and hit our car head on. I was just slightly injured," she shook her head slowly. "James was killed almost instantly."

"I'm sorry."

"I've gotten over it, as much as you can get over something like that. Looking back now, I don't know if it ever could have worked anyway. Neither of us were Christians." She fell silent, then tossed her head in that fetching way as she looked over at him. "Were you ever married, Eric?"

Alarm bells went off in his mind. Instantly his defenses went up. He caught himself as he saw the slight startlement in her expression and realized that this own face had gone tight and hard and cold. With an effort he forced a reply. "No, I never was."

"I'm sorry. I didn't mean to pry."

"Forget it." Braden regretted the episode. She had shared with him, and when she had given him an opportunity to open up to her, he had cut her off cold. But what other option did he have? he asked himself angrily.

Aloud, he said, "I'm a confirmed paranoiac."

She smiled at the weak joke, and he felt a quick sense of

gratitude. "How did you end up at the mission?" he asked.

"After James' death, I was working as a nurse in Austin when Howard visited my church—I was a Christian by then. I was impressed by him, and when a lay mission group offered an opportunity to come down to this part of Mexico, I jumped at it. I even requested Puerto Madero. Once I got down here and saw the needs and worked with Howard, I couldn't forget it, even when the mission trip was over and I went back to the States. I spent a whole year waiting for my vacation just so I could come down here again. That second time, I think I knew deep down that I was going to stay if he'd have me. And I did!" She said the last with triumph.

"How long have you been here?"

"A little over five years now."

"Any regrets?"

"None." she answered firmly. "If I had it to do over, I'd do it again, only I wouldn't wait that extra year before coming for good." She looked at him directly and her face seemed almost to glow. He was struck by her beauty. "I love it down here. I love the people, and the challenge, and being able to use my training to do the Lord's work."

She was so vibrant, so lovely in that moment, that Braden's dismay showed in a grin.

"What's so funny?" she matched his grin.

"You're just not what I would have ever pictured in my wildest dreams as a widow missionary lady."

Her grin widened. "There was a time when I couldn't have pictured it either."

With Tapachula behind them, the road snaked gradually up into the mountains. The countryside was greener now, the verdure more plentiful. They passed an area of restored Aztec ruins, and Cristina stopped so that Braden could see them. Two small pyramids had been partially reconstructed and Cristina pointed out the massive stone which had once served as the sacrificial altar.

"Sometimes I think the people in these villages aren't

too far removed from the old Aztecs," she said as they pulled back out onto the road.

"No human sacrifices, I hope."

"Not that. It's just that they're more resistant to the Gospel, more steeped in old pagan traditions."

Braden remembered the ugly little idol Dennison had destroyed in the old man's lean-to. "Tobias cursed me in the name of Quetzalcoatl," he told her.

She nodded. "The feathered serpent god of the Aztecs. Some of the people up here still worship him. Mostly it's harmless, except for the barriers they erect to their own salvation. All those pagan religions are evil."

Somehow the shadows in the slowly thickening forest seemed a little darker to Braden. Eventually the road deteriorated to a rutted track. Cristina down-shifted and kept it there, the engine laboring as they ascended. Once they passed a man and a burro, the former's face obscured by a ragged sombrero. A basket, loaded with some unidentifiable cargo, weighted down the burro's back.

Cristina smiled cheerfully and called a greeting from the open window of the truck, eliciting no discernible response.

The village itself, when they finally reached it, consisted of a collection of huts and shacks of varying modes of construction set in a clearing at the edge of a steep slope. A couple of dilapidated old vehicles of indeterminate vintage were visible. Braden was reminded of the rabbit-warren enclave where Dennison had witnessed to the old man.

A small crowd of perhaps twenty individuals gathered to greet them; others watched impassively from the huts. Cristina was obviously a big favorite with at least a section of the populace. There was much clamoring to greet her, and a number of the villagers were eager to discuss their ailments with her.

She handled it all with diplomatic aplomb and introduced Braden, whereupon a portion of the group transferred their attentions to him. He had his hand gripped by hard calloused palms and was hugged by villagers of both sexes. Cristina caught his trapped look once and gave him a grin in support. It helped.

As in Puerto Madero, he enjoyed the attention, but felt quite inadequate to deal with it. Most of these people who had greeted them were, he guessed, Christians. They welcomed him as a brother with much gratitude for his willingness to leave the luxuries of "Los Estados Unidos" to come here to their poor village. He envied Cristina her poise and equanimity.

Eventually they were seated as the guests of honor for a noonday meal that took on some of the attributes of a celebration. There were bananas, a coarse bread, and a kind of stew, the contents of which Braden did not wish to examine too closely. He also decided, after glimpsing the interior of the hut where it had been prepared, that he did not want to inspect those premises either.

Still, it was filling, and afterwards, while Cristina began her examination of some of her patients, he was given a tour of the village by a middle-aged man named Jose, who obviously wielded some authority, official or otherwise, in the village.

The villagers farmed in small tracts carved out of the surrounding forest. They were on, Braden realized, a kind of plateau. Behind the huts, the ground sloped steeply away to heavy brush some fifty feet below the level of the village. The air was warmer and more humid at this altitude, and the heavier rainfall was evidenced by the luxurious plant growth and the nearly muddy condition of the cleared land.

Braden was sweating slightly when they returned to the hut which had been established as Cristina's medical center.

"Good, you're back," she said glancing over her shoulder with a quick smile. She was seated in a rickety chair in front of a young man with a hugely swollen arm. "You can help."

"Snakebite," Braden remarked as he got a better look at the swollen limb.

Cristina glanced at him in surprise. "That's right. Rattlesnake. Happened a week ago. He made an incision and tried to suck the venom out. He got most of it, I think, but some of it was left in there. And the incision he made got infected. That's real common with the way these people live. Here, hold his arm like this so I can clean the cuts."

As he followed her instruction, he observed her from the corner of his vision with a kind a pride. She was efficient—cleaning the cuts and adminstering antibiotics from a bulky comprehensive first-aid kit she had produced earlier from the Scout.

She completed her ministrations and smiled at the young man. "Here." She handed him a small container of pills. "Take one of these morning and night. And wash those cuts with soap. The pills should take care of the infection, and you're strong enough to throw off the effects of whatever venom is left." Her patient seemed expectant, as if waiting for some additional phase of treatment. "Now, let's pray," she added. "That's something else you can do and hopefully have been doing all along. It's the best treatment there is."

The young man smiled gratefully and bowed his head. This was the additional treatment he had been awaiting, Braden realized. Belatedly he bowed his own head.

Her prayer, like her work, was efficient and compassionate. She offered thanks to God for sparing the man's life and a request for his healing that he might serve the Lord in all aspects of his life.

As the youth left, the next patient, an elderly woman, entered the hut, bobbing her head obsequiously. Cristina greeted her warmly by name and inquired as to her arthritis. Braden saw that a short line of patients had formed outside the hut, patiently awaiting their turns with her.

He felt a quick stab of humility. He had spent years perfecting his expertise in the sciences of mayhem and destruction. How worthless such accomplishments seemed when weighed against the compassion of this woman.

Through the afternoon Braden worked with her on ailments ranging from a sprained ankle to a nearly completed pregnancy. Cristina finally assigned Braden to occupy the hovering, overly protective expectant father while she conducted her examination.

"There," she said when there was no longer a line. "That's the last of them." She was wearing jeans and a T-shirt, her dark hair pulled back in a pony-tail. She shoved her arms out straight in front of her where she sat and stretched luxuriously. Braden was struck again by her loveliness.

She twisted around in the chair and tossed her head at him with a tired smile that was quite bewitching. "You make a good assistant." Her tone was teasing.

"Yes, ma'am," Braden said humbly.

"Howard always gets jumpy. He wants to go out and witness and preach when he sees a group gathering."

"I think I'll stick to playing candy-striper."

"We've got two more villages to stop by tomorrow, but we'll stay here tonight and lead a prayer meeting. That's Howard's area, I'm afraid. I always feel awkward." She stretched again.

On impulse Braden stepped forward and began to massage her shoulders, his fingers working expertly. He could feel her firm flesh beneath the T-shirt.

She relaxed after a moment. "Ah, that feels good." Her voice was a murmur.

Braden placed his fingertips against the nape of her neck, pressing gently against her warm flesh. She tilted her head a little, almost pressing it against the back of his other hand on her shoulder. A wisp of her hair brushed his knuckles like a fleeting caress.

"You better stop before I go to sleep," she whispered drowsily. Braden lifted his hands and she made a little sound of protest before straightening slightly in the chair.

Abruptly she stood up as if summoning all of her energy

for the effort, turning toward the door as she did so. For a moment they were very close there in the warm confines of the hut. Braden was extremely aware of her femininity, of the exciting scent of her.

Awkwardly he stepped back out of her way, pulling the blanket back from the doorway as he did so. "After you."

"Thank you, kind sir." She seemed slightly breathless.

As they emerged, blinking into the afternoon sunlight, Braden felt what seemed like a slight wave pass beneath his feet. Cristina let out a little exclamation and bumped into him. He caught her as, simultaneously, several cries and screams rang out across the village.

"An earth tremor," Cristina said, drawing away from him a bit with seeming reluctance. She swung her head back and forth almost expectantly. Braden could feel her tension.

"All right," she said after a moment and visibly relaxed. "It's over."

20

The humid afternoon air had grown still, but electricity seemed to crackle in it. The surrounding forest had taken on a hush, and Braden's vision seemed obscured, distorted.

A breathless silence fell over the villagers dining with him and Cristina in the central plaza of the village as they sensed the eerie stasis of the atmosphere.

At Braden's feet a gaunt dog whined. He glanced at Cristina and saw her eyes wide in a face gone suddenly pale.

"Oh, my God," she whispered. It was not an oath; it was a prayer.

And the ground heaved up beneath Braden's feet as if some gargantuan beast in the bowels of the earth struggled to burst up to freedom. He felt himself flung backwards, aware of the heavy table and all its foodstuffs toppling over in the opposite direction, of the terrified dog scrambling frantically for safety.

Earthquake! he thought, and raw, primeval fear clawed at him: fear for Cristina, for himself. Then he was rolling, coming up onto his feet on ground that pitched sickeningly beneath him like the deck of a ship on a storm-tossed sea.

He had a fleeting panoramic vision of the terrified villagers being cast to the ground, of collapsing huts, of the treetops tossing wildly. He went down again, scrambling in the moist earth. He had lost track of Cristina.

He tried to find footing, irrationally terrified at the inability of his trained reflexes to serve him in the nightmare of shuddering earth.

It seemed he was pushed flat, and a six-foot-deep ditch opened up in front of him as if the supports beneath the area of the ground had been abruptly snatched away.

Lying there he saw the whole back line of village huts disappear, sloughing away down the steep slope in a welter of mud and debris. He heard screams, the howl of an anguished dog, the rasping shriek of some jungle bird. Thunder seemed to roll in his ears.

He spotted Cristina, across the ditch, lying prone, spread-eagled. He rose and forced his trembling limbs and spasming muscles to obey him. He half fell down into the ditch and scrambled up its far side, fearing that, like the jaws of a monster, it might close and swallow him up.

As he reached her, the ground beneath him seemed to steady, to grow firm under his weight. Cristina must have sensed it too, for she jerked her head up abruptly, staring about her. Braden realized she had assumed the prone spread-eagled position deliberately as a safety precaution.

"You all right?" he demanded.

She nodded dazedly. The ground was indeed ceasing its undulation. A final ripple fluttered under him and then there was only stillness, broken by cries and screams.

Braden helped Cristina to her feet. "Come on." He ran toward the back of the village where he had seen the huts dis-appear. She drew sharply up at his side as he halted at the newly defined edge of the slope and looked down.

Beside him he heard her gasp. They stared down on a chaotic tangle of mud and debris from the devastated huts. The whole edge of the plateau seemed to have sloughed away in a massive mudslide carrying with it a good portion of the hapless village and at least some of the occupants.

Braden saw a body sprawled like a broken doll half under a pile of wreckage. Farther down, a woman was trying to scale the slippery mud of the slope with the mindless dedication of an automoton. Her eyes held the glassy stare of severe shock.

Movement closer up caught his eye and he felt a thrill of horror as he beheld a groping hand extending up from the mud. The rest of the hand's owner was invisible, buried be-neath the slide. The fingers clenched into a fist, opened, closed, opened...

Braden wheeled to Cristina. "Get somebody to see if you can get one of those vehicles started. Send someone to a phone to call for help," he said crisply.

She didn't argue, but hurried away. Some other villagers had materialized to stand staring in numb awe at the destruction below them.

"You and you!" Braden barked. "Go and get some shovels, tools, anything to dig with. The rest of you come with me. Now!" He plunged down the slope toward that groping, desperate hand.

As he reached it, skidding past it before he could halt himself on the steep slope, it gave a last despairing tremor, the fingers outspread, stretching fruitlessly upward. It went limp.

Braden snatched up a splintered fragment of planking and attacked the mud, wielding the makeshift shovel with desperate strength. Then some of the villagers, men and women, were around him, scrabbling at the dirt with debris, fingers anything that came to hand.

There were too many of them for the one victim. They were getting in one another's way, impeding the progress. "You two stay here," he snapped indicating two strong men. "The rest of you go on and help the others farther down."

He was aware of them moving off down the slope. He dug the plank into the mud and heaved. His two helpers clawed at the stuff with grimy hands. He reached the shoulder of the entombed victim and discarded the plank to use his own hands. In seconds they had uncovered the lifeless form of a middle-aged man.

Braden did not waste time checking for a pulse or breathing. The man's nose and mouth were plugged with mud. He used his fingers to clear the nostrils and mouth, tilted the man's head back as well as he could on the slope and, pinching the nose shut, jammed his mouth over that of the man's, forcing his own breath into the victim's lungs.

Four times he did this before lifting his head. His two assistants were watching him with wide eyes. "Go on! Help the others," he panted, then lowered his ear to his patient's lips, watching the chest for any sign of life. Nothing. He pressed two fingers against the dirty neck, there was no pulse.

Immediately he straightened and, still on his knees, placed the heel of one palm against the man's sternum, just above the V of the ribs. He put his other hand atop that one and, lifting his own shoulders and torso, came down hard on the sternum, keeping his elbows straight, bending from the hips.

"One thousand," he counted aloud and repeated the maneuver. "Two thousand." Ideally the victim was supposed to be on a flat surface for cardiopulmonary resuscitation, but present circumstances were far from ideal.

At fifteen thousand he stopped and forced more air between the parted lips. "One thousand," he started all over again, oblivious of his surroundings, of everything save this seemingly lifeless man before him. "Fourteen thousand, fifteen thousand..."

"I'll take over."

He looked up to see Cristina beside him. He didn't know how long she had been there. "I sent one of the men for help," she reported. "Here," she bent over the prone man and Braden drew back to give her room.

But even as she lowered her mouth to his lips, there came a sudden convulsive gasp. The man coughed, choked, then began to breathe on his own.

"Praise the Lord!" she cried, and her smile lit up her dirt-streaked face. Braden knew that his matched it.

He called up to two spectators who had not joined the rescue effort, but were gaping dumbly. "Get this man up there! Come on! Move!"

His tone broke through their paralysis. They started down and he caught Cristina's hand without thinking, and together, half on their feet, half sliding, they made their way on down to where the other villagers were working.

Braden spotted Jose, who had given him the tour of the village, in the center of a group of men and women working to shift what had once been a hut. He caught the villager by the arm. "Start a head count," he ordered. Jose stared at him blankly. "See who you can account for," Braden explained quickly. "Make a list. See who is missing. That way we'll know how many there are to look for."

Understanding came into Jose's eyes. "Si!" he agreed excitedly, and began to count those nearby. Braden left him to his task.

The villagers he had sent for shovels had returned. It was early evening and darkness would be upon them soon. They would need lights. And they would need other things as well if they were to have a chance at reaching the remaining victims in time.

As night fell, they worked by flashlight and torches mounted on poles and stuck into the muddy slope. Braden had organized the villagers into teams of searchers and workers to scour the slope for victims and, where necessary, to extricate them from the mud and wreckage.

Cristina he had placed in charge of the field hospital atop the slope. She worked in the illumination of torches and the Scout's headlights on the victims that her assistants transported up the slope by use of ropes and travois-like stretchers.

They found two dead, suffocated and crushed by mud. A dozen others, with injuries of varying degrees and severity, they found and excavated. Jose had ascertained what villagers were unaccounted for, and Braden had him keep a tally of those located as they worked.

He recalled that, following the terrible earthquake which had devastated Mexico City, victims had been found alive in the ruins for days afterwards. There, as here, minutes and organization could make a difference.

When at last Jose reported that all the villagers were accounted for, Braden was too tired to do much more than grin and clap the man on the shoulder in a shared sense of accomplishment.

He left the remaining workers trying to salvage goods and possessions from the wreckage, and slogged tiredly back up the slope, using one of the ropes of Cristina's assistants to pull himself up the last few yards.

A good percentage of the inhabitants had been in the central square area where they had been dining when the quake struck. This had greatly reduced the number of injured and dead.

He found Cristina working to set a man's dislocated knee. As she took the leg in her hands, its owner moaned in agony and began to thrash wildly until she released him. Her assistants, Braden realized, were occupied elsewhere.

She looked up at him helplessly. Her face was lined with dirt, the muscles lax in exhaustion. He thought she looked wonderful there in the torchlight.

"It's no use," she said with resignation. "He won't hold still enough to let me help him."

Braden knelt and gripped her patient's shoulders. The man was in shock, mostly delirious. "Go ahead," Braden said to her and bore down hard. Beneath his grip the man writhed.

"There," she said triumphantly after a moment. The man relaxed and Braden released him.

"We've got them all accounted for," he reported as they rose to their feet.

It took a moment for the words to register, and then some of the exhaustion in Cristina's face disappeared beneath an exultant smile. "Thank God!" She hugged him and he returned it, pressing her to him for a moment, sharing her joy. Tiredly they moved to the open tailgate of the Scout, and he drank thirstily from the large water thermos there. "Let's go check the rest of the damage," he said after a moment.

Their steps weary from exhaustion, they walked back through the village, away from the light and turmoil of the rescue operation. Braden used a flashlight from the Scout to survey the collapsed huts. There were surprisingly few damaged. Although flimsy, the structures, by their nature, were flexible and had stood up well beneath the quake.

They stopped once, and their hands brushed, then automatically entwined. She leaned her head briefly against his shoulder then as they walked.

Ahead of them the cleared area ended and the dark wall of the forest loomed. They halted, and self-consciously he released her hand. A deep tiredness was in him, but there was satisfaction too. He felt Cristina's eyes on him.

"You were wonderful back there," she said softly. "If it hadn't been for you organizing things the way you did, a lot of people would have died."

He felt suddenly embarrassed. "You weren't bad yourself." She smiled slightly.

"Yeah, we make a pretty good team."

He turned to her then, and she came into his arms, all firmness and softness and woman scent, and he just held her, marveling at this moment, savoring it. She raised her head from against his shoulder, and he lowered his mouth to hers, tasting her, feeling the warmth of her lips.

Finally she leaned back in the circle of his arms. "I must look a sight," she said a little ruefully.

"You're beautiful." He kissed her again, and then the ululant keening shriek ripped through the night and tore them apart. They stood frozen as it died away. Braden thought it had come from back near the Scout.

Cristina's eyes were wide in revulsion and fright. "Tobias," she breathed.

21

They ran back through the village toward the lighted area. Braden slowed as they neared it, pulling Cristina back in line with him. "Go slow," he cautioned her softly.

She was impatient, but obeyed him, and they went forward vigilantly. The injured had been placed on makeshift pallets in the central square. The flickering torches and the glaring beams of the Scout's headlights shed a shifting, unnatural illumination over the scene.

Those who had acted as Cristina's assistants and some of the rescuers stood back in a huddled group. Behind them, like corpses rising from the grave, the begrimed faces of other workers appeared as they ascended the slope to see what was going on.

In the center of the square—a demon stalking among his victims on the floor of hell—the grotesquely headdressed figure of the sorcerer Tobias minced from one pallet to the next. Save for a ragged cape, he was clad as he had been on Braden's earlier encounter with him, the caiman headdress giving him a bizarre otherworldly appearance that sent a chill down Braden's spine.

In the unnatural light, his scarred face, in shadow, was a distorted visage. The sheathed machete dangled at his waist and in one hand he wielded some kind of short, carved stick, passing it through the air over the victims, as he mumbled in sibilant tones.

Even as they watched, he knelt fluidly before one of the unconscious accident victims. Braden saw that it was the first man he had freed from entombment and breathed life back into. Tobias vibrated the stick and reached one clawed hand out toward the unconscious face in some pagan ritual.

"No!" Cristina cried in vehement protest. She wrenched loose from Braden's grasp with frantic strength and darted forward into the light.

Tobias heard or sensed her coming, for he rose and swung toward her with frightening speed. To Braden it seemed that she rushed barehanded to grapple with a grinning reptilian demon. One long arm swept her sprawling past him to fall on the ground, and he turned, the ragged cape swirling blackly, to loom over her prostrate figure.

Braden came out of the darkness and reached him in three long strides. There were a dozen ways of killing a man barehanded from behind. He did not use them. He reached and caught a bony elbow—only a fool or an amateur came up behind an enemy and caught him by the shoulder. He set himself and snapped his own arm out from him like a whip, whirling Tobias away, his cloak flying.

The brujo came out of the spin facing him, and immediately hunched his sinewy body into a question mark. A serpentine hiss issued from the dragon jaws. Braden crouched, anticipating a rush.

But Tobias held back, straightening slightly. "Gringo." The word was a curse.

"Get out of here!" Braden was dimly aware of Cristina regaining her feet beside him. He did not look at her. He concentrated on the man before him. He remembered Dennison's and his own evaluation of Tobias. The witch doctor was dangerous. And here, confronted by interlopers in his own territory, he would be doubly so.

"Quetzalcoatl lusts for your soul, gringo." Tobias pointed the carved stick at him like a gun. "You cannot escape."

Words came to Braden. "I have already escaped. Satan,

by whatever name you call him, has no power over me. But my God has power over you in the name of Jesus Christ."

"Your Christ was a weakling! And your God could not protect Him from his enemies!" Tobias wheeled toward the growing crowd of spectators. "Hear me, my children," he spread his arms wide, his figure etched grotesquely by the firelight. "I have warned you! See what has happened to your homes, to your families. You have allowed the Christ-woman and her lover into your midst and listened to their lies, and Quetzalcoatl has poured out his wrath upon your village!"

The villagers were staring at the sorcerer as if entranced. To a certain extent they were still in shock from the quake, and were faced now by a crowd manipulator whose beliefs had influenced their lives for generations. There was no telling how they might react. Braden found himself wishing for Dennison's calm pressence and assurance. This was the missionary's field of battle and he himself was hopelessly outmatched.

"No!" Cristina's voice rang out strongly. She too faced the crowd. Braden guessed that by now almost the full hundred-odd population of the village had gathered in the plaza. "You know me. You know the things I have done here in the Lord's name! How many of you have I treated? Prayed with? Some of you have accepted Christ as your Savior. You know the evil of this brujo. Where has he been this night when you needed help? When this brother in Christ and I worked side by side with you to save your loved ones?"

"Do not listen to her, my children," Tobias cut her off. "She is the whore priestess of a weakling God. Look at this man she calls her brother. She speaks for him because he has no words. Quetzalcoatl has gripped his soul!"

Tobias whipped his wand through the air in a pattern too complex for the eye to follow. Braden felt the eyes of the villagers upon him. Tobias had scored neatly. It was always the man who took the lead in the Spanish culture; the whole convoluted doctrine of machismo, of male dominance, spoke to these people across the centuries.

And he stood there helplessly while Cristina fought the good fight.

"In the name of my Savior, Jesus Christ. I command you to go!" Cristina flung the words at Tobias.

The reptilian head tilted back and inhuman laughter gobbled from it. "She calls upon her weakling God, and I defy him!" Tobias' face was lost now in the shadow of his headdress, but somehow his eyes seemed to glow with an evil light.

"Look what they have brought upon you!" The sweeping wand took in the carnage left by the earthquake. "The old gods are displeased." The wand came back and encompassed Braden and Cristina in a single gesture. "Take them, my children! Take the followers of the weakling God. Take them!"

Cristina had spun back toward the crowd. There was a murmuring there, an uneasy shifting movement. One man stepped forward, his face savage in unholy fervor. The earthquake, the generations of pagan beliefs, the manipulative power of the sorcerer, were working the passionate nature of the people into a killing frenzy. Another man stepped forward, his eyes wild, then another.

Astonishingly, Cristina dropped to one knee and began to pray. The restless motion of the crowd slowed, then froze. Kneeling there, her voice a murmur, Cristina seemed illumined, caught somehow in a pure, white light.

Braden tore his glance away from the vision and looked at Tobias. Cristina had her back to the witch doctor, her head bowed. Kneeling thus, she looked like some pagan sacrifice before him. Apparently the same simile occurred to Tobias. Braden thought he saw the glowing eyes beneath the headdress light up with ungodly fervor. One bony hand flashed to the hilt of the sheathed machete.

My kind of game now, Braden thought, and moved.

Even before the heavy, gleaming blade could clear its sheath, Braden's hand clamped on the hard wrist, fingers digging into the sensitive area on the underside of it, locking the man's arm rigid in mid-movement. Tobias strained against that pressure.

For an eternity of seconds the two men stared into one another's eyes. Braden saw hate and madness and damnation in that grotesque, scarred visage beneath the caiman mask. He felt the wiry, sinewy strength of the sorcerer, and, had Tobias moved against him with the wand held in his other hand, Braden would have gladly killed him.

The ropy muscles stood out and writhed in the gaunt torso and arms. Braden gripped with all his strength, gouging his fingers cruelly into the muscle, working them deeper until it seemed to him they must meet through the other's flesh. The stench of Tobias was in his nostrils, the horror of him etched into his brain.

For long straining seconds the tableau held, and then slowly, slowly, Braden forced the machete back down, into its sheath. Pain had contorted the savagery on Tobias' face now, but still he strained. Braden tightened his grip, tightened it, and saw Tobias' legs begin to buckle.

Braden grinned coldly, savagely into the man's face. Inexorably he forced Tobias down onto his knees in the mud.

He held him there for a moment longer until the villagers could have no doubt of his dominion. Then, with a snap of his wrist, he sent the brujo sprawling.

Briefly Tobias lay there, limbs moving ineffectually. Then he scrambled to his feet, his headdress askew, and fled, disappearing into the darkness.

Braden was panting, his muscles trembling from exertion. With an effort, he slowed his breathing, and turned toward the crowd. Cristina had risen, and he realized she had seen at least some of the contest. He could not read the expression on her face.

"Your brujo is defeated, beaten by this man of God," her voice rang out as she addressed the villagers. "Such evil as his cannot stand before the strength and righteousness of the Savior, Jesus Christ."

Braden felt a sudden deep wave of self-loathing wash over him, banishing the triumph of only moments before. He did not hear the rest of what Cristina said. He turned and walked away, sick to the very depths of his soul. Her voice seemed to follow him into the night.

She found him at the same spot where earlier he had held her in his arms. The stars overhead were sharp bright diamonds. A light breeze played through the brush.

He heard her step as she approached, but did not turn to face her. She stopped close beside him, but now it seemed to him there was an insurmountable barrier between them.

"You left. Why?" Her voice was soft, questioning.

"Is the crisis over with the villagers?" he asked, to change the subject.

"Yes, I prayed with them and they dispersed. There wasn't much left to say. You..."

"I screwed it up!" He was unable to hold it in any longer.

"What do you mean?" She started to grab his arm, then hesitated. He would not look at her. "I saw what you did. You were magnificent!"

"I was a weakling," Braden said lamely. "Tobias was right. I couldn't face him on spiritual terms. You did that. All I could do was meet violence with more violence, while you fought the real fight."

"That's not true," she protested. "You prevented violence. It was both of us who were fighting, and it was because we fought for Christ that He gave us the victory. That's why I prayed, because I knew that things were beyond our control. Ultimately things are always beyond our control. That's why we have to rely on Christ."

"I didn't even think of praying," Braden said angrily. "You did it automatically."

"Next time you *will* think of it, and it will become automatic to you too, once you realize that you can rely on Him for everything, not just for your salvation."

"You said it yourself." His tone was dogged. "You said

evil cannot stand before the Lord. Well, I'm evil." He could not have looked at her now had he wanted to. "You think Tobias is evil, but you don't know the things I've done. I'm not worthy to be used by the Lord. There's no way He could want me. I saw that clearly back there. All of this—my conversion, my thinking I could come down here and play missionary, it was all a fool's game, a farce."

"No!" This time she did grab his arm, forcing him to turn toward her. Tears streaked her face; her expression was desperate, yearning. "I was evil too, before I came to know the Lord. Everyone is. The Scriptures say so. 'For all have sinned'; 'There is none righteous, no, not one.' "

When he didn't respond, she continued. "I may not have done anything so awful by some standards, but I've done lots of things I'm not proud of, things the Lord would have no part in. That would make me unworthy too, don't you see?

"The Bible says you are a new creation in Christ," she rushed on, "that when you accept Him, you become like new, that all your sins, no matter what they were, are put aside and are forgotten by God. What you used to be doesn't matter. You're new and cleansed of sin and given a brand-new start. That's why Christ let himself be nailed on that cross and hung there and suffered until He died. He died in your place and my place as a sacrifice for our sins, to make us worthy!"

Her words reached down inside Braden, made some adjustment, opened a door he had not known was there, and let him see himself in some inner mirror.

She was right. Whatever his past sins — and they had been legion — he had been given a new start, cleansed by the blood of a Man who was much more than a man, who had died two thousand years ago for this very moment, this revelation.

"It really doesn't matter, does it?" he asked in quiet wonder. "No matter what I've done before, when I committed myself to Him, it stopped mattering."

"That's right," she said softly. "If He has forgiven you

for what you've done, why don't you forgive yourself?"

Braden looked down into her uplifted face, then raised his eyes to the stars overhead. A sense of deep gratitude welled up in him, abolishing the last of the self-contempt and pity. "Thank you, Lord," he mouthed the words and felt Cristina move closer to him.

He looked down at her again. She was lovely there in the starlight, and he drew her to him.

Nothing interrupted them this time, and when at last they drew apart, the words came quite naturally to him. "I love you," he told her.

She closed her eyes for a long moment, and when she opened them, they seemed to shine with a warm light. "God be with us," she whispered. "I love you too."

22

"There isn't as much damage here," Cristina commented, surveying the tiny village in which she had just alighted from the mud-splattered Scout. She could see some collapsed huts and scattered debris as indications of the earthquake, but nowhere was there the wide-scale destruction which the larger village in the lower altitudes had experienced. She felt a surge of relief. On the laborious drive up here, she had tortured herself by imagining what awaited them at their destination.

"They're positioned a little better here," Eric commented from the other side of the vehicle. "They don't have the side of the plateau to slide down."

Villagers were appearing from the huts to meet them. Cristina shrugged off the tiredness and went forward to return their greetings. She had gotten little sleep in the past twenty-four hours and she suspected that Eric had gotten even less. They had been given cots in two of the surviving huts, but she had not been able to leave her patients until the early hours of the morning, and then for only a few hours of fitful dozing. Somehow, though, Eric seemed little the worse for it, having apparently thrown off the effects of the exhausting rescue efforts and the dramatic showdown with Tobias.

The belated arrival of units of the Mexican army to aid in rescue and cleanup had roused her from sleep this morning.

Realizing that there was little more to be done there, she had suggested to Eric that they go on to this tiny enclave of humanity located even higher in the remote mountains.

The drive had been an ordeal. The track, never much more than passable, had been all but destroyed in places by the earthquake. Even the Scout's four-wheel-drive capabilities had not prevented her from getting it stuck on two occasions, necessitating sweating efforts by Eric to push and lever it clear while she manipulated the wheel. He had borne it all with good humor, seeming actually to enjoy the minor episodes. Watching him, being in his presence, she had made a silent reaffirmation of her vows of love the night before. The intensity of her feelings was at once pleasant and a little frightening.

There were a few injuries at the village, they learned, and one death—an elderly man unable to move fast enough to escape a falling tree. The body had already been buried. In the ever present heat and humidity, delay of interment was both dangerous and impractical.

They set up their makeshift clinic in an undamaged hut, and Cristina went to work. The majority of the injuries were minor, although one man had what she painfully diagnosed as a broken back. She gave him a sedative and explained to his wife that he would need to be transported to a hospital by the army rescue crews when they arrived. There was little she could do to comfort the woman. Even if her husband lived, he would most likely be handicapped. Doggedly, she returned to her work.

Again, Eric willingly took on the role of medical assistant. "Candy-striper," as he called it. And they did work well together, she thought. Even as they labored, she recalled with admiration his heroic efforts following the earthquake and his courage in opposing Tobias. She had seen in action now that potential for violence she had sensed in him from the first. But it had been violence in the name of the Lord, if that was not a contradiction of terms, and awareness of his abilities gave her a feeling of comfort rather than apprehension.

He looked around now at the sound of a vehicle's engine from outside the hut. She noticed the caution with which Eric peered out the door. "The army has finally made it," he reported.

Cristina finished tying the sling she had prepared for the young girl's sprained arm and went to stand by his side. "I hope they can get that one man to a hospital soon," she remarked. "I can't keep him sedated indefinitely."

He glanced at her, then stepped aside to let her pass, following her once she did so.

A mud-caked jeep had just pulled to a halt beside their Scout. The Mexican Army, Cristina noted with satisfaction, also appeared to have had its share of problems making the trek.

Two uniformed men, one of them an officer, climbed from the jeep. Cristina recognized the handsome officer as the one who had directed the official rescue effort at the larger village. She waved in greeting, then glanced around for Eric. He was nowhere in sight.

She blinked, bewildered at his abrupt disappearance. He had, she recalled then, had very little to do with the soldiers when they had arrived at the first village. But now was not the time to ponder his behavioral quirks. Erasing the momentary frown from her features, she went forward to meet the officer.

"Senorita, you have arrived ahead of us again," he greeted her graciously. "Since you are here first, there is probably little for my men to do when they arrive."

"Unfortunately that's not true," Cristina replied. "We have a badly injured man who needs to be transported to the hospital." Quickly she explained the man's condition.

The officer did not question her diagnosis. He turned to his driver and gave quick orders to summon another vehicle. Then he accompanied Cristina to view the other injured villagers. Eric, she noticed briefly, had joined several men working to remove what was left of a collapsed hut. He seemed determined to keep a low profile around the military.

"You and your associate have done a great deal of good," the officer complimented her when he had seen the casualties. "You have saved a number of lives in these villages almost certainly. Where is your friend, by the way?"

Cristina hoped her hesitation was imperceptible. "Over there helping with the work." She pointed.

The officer looked in that direction for a moment, then turned back to her with a broad smile that just failed to relieve her anxiety. "And what is his name again?"

"John McAllister." She had almost used his nickname. Or was that his real name? she wondered.

The officer nodded. "Yes, now I remember. And were there any other serious injuries here?"

He had adroitly changed the subject, leaving her wondering if his question had only been out of simple courtesy, or if he harbored some other more sinister motive.

Who was Eric, really? she asked herself as she continued to chat on a superficial level with the inquisitive officer. Howard had told her that Eric had denied being a fugitive from the law, and she could not, in her heart, believe that he could be a wanted man.

But what secret in his background was he concealing? She knew very little—nothing really—about this man to whom she had given her love. Should she ask him? Force the issue? No, she vowed to herself. What was love without trust? She would place the matter in the Lord's hands as she had advised Eric to do. When Eric felt the need to confide in her, he would do so. To press him now would be a betrayal of sorts.

"You are tired, Senorita?" the officer's solicitous voice intruded.

"What? I'm sorry." She realized her preoccupation had become noticeable to her companion. "Yes, I am tired; it has been a long two days."

"I understand," he nodded. "My men will be here shortly

to coordinate cleanup operations and to transport the injured man to the hospital."

"Thank you," she told him sincerely.

"No, it is I who should thank you. You have been of immeasurable service to these communities. But we will take care of things now. You can rest."

"There is one other village a little east of here," she told him. "I think we might try to reach it tonight since you are in charge here." Why did she feel the need to be away from this obsequious man and his subtle interrogatives?

"Ah, my men may have already reached there. I sent two of them to check on the state of affairs there. But I am sure your presence will be appreciated. I may see you there myself tomorrow."

"I will look forward to it," she responded.

"Thank you, Senorita. Oh, there is one thing more..."

"Yes?"

Again that charming smile. "Be sure to tell Mr. McAllister that I appreciate all his efforts also."

"Of course." She left him there and went toward where Eric was working. He had no objection to leaving immediately. Indeed, she thought, he seemed almost eager to do so.

As she jockeyed the Scout onto the rutted track, he glanced back once, then turned his attention to the road in front of them. "Did you and the officer have a pleasant visit?" he asked. His tone was casual.

"Yes. He was very polite." She hesitated. "He asked about you."

Eric did not look in her direction. "What did he want to know?"

She shrugged. "Your name, mostly."

He nodded, but remained silent and thoughtful for most of the next half hour. She concentrated on driving, noticing, nonetheless, that he glanced in his mirror frequently. The road was not as bad, although it still required the four-wheel drive at times. They saw a few freshly toppled trees, and numerous broken branches and limbs. Even though the road had mostly been spared, this area had not entirely escaped the ravages of the quake.

The soldiers had indeed reached the final village before their arrival. One of them, apparently a trained paramedic, had already begun seeing to the injured, but he welcomed Cristina's presence and assistance eagerly.

Again Eric remained somewhat aloof from the military personnel. She saw him assisting with the cleanup efforts as it grew dark, and had time to notice that he seemed to be enjoying himself.

The evening meal was something of a communal affair and by that time Cristina was feeling the weight of her labors over the past two days. At one point, as she sat beside Eric on a crude wooden bench at the edge of the gathering listening to the headman give a rambling speech about the earthquake, she felt Eric's elbow poke her gently in the side.

"Wake up," he urged. "He's just getting to the good part."

She smiled up at him tiredly, and he grinned and then, unexpectedly, slid an arm around her shoulders and pulled her briefly to him. She relaxed against him with a little sigh of satisfaction.

He held her like that for a time, then murmured in her ear, "Come on, I'm about played out, too. I think the head man has reserved a couple of rooms in the executive suite."

No one appeared to notice as they slipped away from the gathering.

Cristina leaned her head against Eric's shoulder as they walked. The head man's house was the nicest in the village—a frame structure that once, years before, had actually had a coat of paint. Only a few flakes of indeterminate color still adhered to the weathered wood.

Their "rooms" consisted of a single area partitioned by a hanging blanket. Eric, she realized, had unloaded her things from the Scout at some point, but Cristina was too exhausted to do much more than give Eric a sleepy kiss and retire to her side of their quarters.

Drowsily, relaxing on the makeshift pallet which had been prepared for her, she imagined Eric lying so close to her on the other side of the suspended blanket. From afar, it seemed, came the sounds of the communal dinner. More closely, a night bird called eerily.

"Good night, love," came Eric's voice from out of the darkness.

On impulse she extended her hand under the edge of the blanket, knowing, somehow, that his would be there to take it. Clinging to his strong hand she drifted to sleep.

Sunlight coming through the cracked window and the morning sounds of the village awakened her. Eric was already gone, and she spotted him conversing with several of the men when she emerged from the house. He seemed to be giving advice or instruction, but he spotted her after a moment and left his audience to come over to her. She smiled at his approach and tossed her head at him. He brushed her cheek with his lips. He had somehow managed to shave, she noticed.

"I think we're about done here," he informed her. The military is supposed to send in a few more men, and the locals seem to have everything pretty well in hand."

He accompanied her as she checked on the patients. The paramedic, she learned, had already departed. She led a prayer, and Eric, surprising her a little, added a few simple closing lines.

They left before noon, and Cristina willingly accepted Eric's offer to drive. He did it, as he seemed to do almost everything, with a restrained competence. She was a little chagrined that he did not get the boxlike vehicle stuck even once during their return to the large village.

She sensed a relaxation in him, a lessening of the coiled tension which seemed to brood over him. Again she resisted the urge to question him concerning his enigmatic background. Just keep it cool, girl, she told herself. Don't blow it now.

The progress that had been made in the first village was enough to make him purse his lips in a silent whistle of appreciation. "They've been busy," he commented.

Indeed, a great amount of wreckage left by the earthquake had been cleared away. Token efforts had even been made to start rebuilding some of the demolished huts, thankfully, Cristina saw, well away from the edge of the plateau. The air of exhaustion, defeat, and death which had hung over the little town seemed to have lifted.

As they stepped down out of the Scout a number of the villagers approached eagerly. In their forefront, Cristina recognized Jose, the man Eric had put in charge of the census immediately following the earthquake.

He was grinning broadly. "I called Senor Dennison as you requested, Hermana," he reported. "I went on foot to the nearest phone to call him."

"Is he all right?" Cristina demanded. "What about the mission?" She had not had any time to consider the possible impact of the earthquake on other parts of the state.

"He is fine," Jose reassured her. "And the mission was not hurt. There was no damage there."

"Thank God," Cristina said with deep feeling.

Jose began an excited recitation of their endeavors in her and Eric's absence. The Army had now left them to their own resources, he reported. Cristina glanced sidewise at Eric. His face showed no emotion at this news, but she noticed that he slackened his relentless scanning of the village.

"What about Tobias?" he cut into Jose's monolgue abruptly. "Have you seen him again?"

"No, Hermano. He has not returned. He is in hiding, they say, humiliated by the way you beat him." Jose grinned confidently. "Do not fear that he will return. We will not allow him back into our village." There was a murmur of agreement from his companions.

Cristina hoped it worked out like that, but she did not know if Tobias, particularly smarting from his defeat, could be so easily dismissed. Glancing again at Eric, she guessed he shared her thoughts.

"We are planning a prayer meeting for tomorrow night," Jose was hurrying on. "People from the other villages will come," he promised. "We have sent messengers. And—" he paused, his eyes sparkling as he looked at Eric, "—we want Hermano Eric to lead the prayer meeting! To preach to us on how he defeated the brujo!"

Eric actually looked like he wanted to break and run. Cristina bit her lip to repress her mirth. "I think that's a wonderful idea!" she exclaimed.

Eric gave her the frantic look of one betrayed. She tossed her hair back in a motion of her head and grinned.

"No way!" Eric blurted at last. "There's no way in the world I'm going to preach a sermon!"

Despite herself, Cristina could not stop grinning.

23

Howard Dennison hung up the phone and sat quite motionless for a moment before offering up a silent heartfelt prayer of thanksgiving. They were all right. Praise the Lord. Not only had Cristina and Eric come through the quake un-scathed, but, according to Jose, the man who had called, they had played a heroic role in rescuing victims of the upheaval.

And an upheaval it had certainly been, said the reports now beginning to filter out of the area of the quake. Puerto Madero had escaped damage—another blessing to be thankful for. As in the case of the devastating Mexico City earthquake, Dennison himself had not felt much more than a tremor underfoot. We have our hurricanes here, he thought with feeling. God spare us from earthquakes.

He got up from behind his desk where he had been engaged in some largely pointless but necessary paperwork, and had a sudden mental image of Cristina and Eric together there in the mountain village. He felt a curious satisfaction with the imagined scene, and recalled his blunt warning to Eric about Cristina early in his relationship with the other man. He had been trying to come across as tough to a past master of the game, he reflected ruefully. Now that approach seemed almost foolish to him, for despite the conundrum of his background, Eric seemed to be proving a worthy and dedicated servant of the Lord.

He had another sudden image of Alex and Sharon, the yuppie couple back in Tulsa, trying to deal with earthquake victims in the jungle or even ministering to the mission right here in Puerto Madero. He felt a little ashamed of the thought, but he could not quite suppress the grin that came to his lips.

He was still musing over the idea when the grumbling sound of an automobile engine reached him as it pulled to a halt in the dirt road in front of the mission. His first thought was that it might be the Scout. But that, of course, was ridiculous. He had just hung up from talking with the villager who said that Eric and Cristina were still up in the mountains. He had no reason to anticipate their arrival before tomorrow at the earliest. Still, the degree of his pleasure at the thought of having them back made him realize how much he missed them both.

Not waiting for his visitors—if such they were—to come looking for him, he went out of the mission and blinked in surprise. An olive-colored jeep of the Mexican Army had halted in front of the door and two men were just alighting. The tires and body of the jeep had a good coating of dried mud, evidencing some recent cross-country or heavy-terrain driving, he noted absently.

As the two soldiers approached, Dennison smiled and went forward to greet them. Generally he got on well with the military, but it was unusual for him to be singled out for attention. Somewhere in the back of his mind a faint warning bell began to ring.

The driver dropped back a little, leaving the handsome officer to introduce himself and shake hands politely. Somehow the soldier's erect presence in the background reminded Dennison of a guard.

"Come on into the mission, out of the sun," Howard invited after the introductions were out of the way.

The officer paused long enough to give a brief nod over his shoulder to the driver who, as if by prearranged signal, turned smartly back toward the jeep. Dennison ushered the officer into the mission and offered him a chair in his office.

"Thank you, Senor," the officer said graciously.

Seated behind his desk, vaguely glad for the physical barrier it placed between him and his guest, Howard studied the officer while the latter complimented Dennison on the mission and its work.

"In a way, that is why I am here," he said finally. "My driver and I have just recently returned from the mountains."

Dennison felt himself tense. "You have news?" he asked quickly.

The officer's smile was all white teeth and charm. "Oh, there is nothing to concern yourself about," he assured him. "I am very sorry if I gave that impression. I was in the mountains directing our initial rescue and support operations to assist the victims of the recent earthquake in that area. While there, I had the opportunity to meet your assistants, and I am here merely to advise you of their safety."

Dennison relaxed somewhat. "Thank you."

The officer waved a deprecatory hand. "It is nothing. Actually, it is I who should thank you for the work your assistants have done for the people in the villages that were most heavily damaged. By the time we arrived at the first village—the one most severely struck—matters were already well in hand." He went on in this complimentary vein for a few moments. "And Senorita Rodriguez is most lovely and charming," he concluded at last. "And your other assistant, he is very skilled and efficient in these matters. What was his name? I don't seem to recall it."

The alarm bells set up a deafening clamor in Dennison's mind. He was fairly certain, however, that he kept his features immobile. "John McAllister," he answered evenly.

"Yes, that is correct. Thank you. He is a new worker here at your mission, I understand?"

Dennison nodded. "He volunteered to come down here from the States and do volunteer work for a time. I don't know much about his background." May as well be as

205

cooperative as possible, he reflected, although his instinctive reaction to all this was to defend Eric against this man. But, even cooperating, there was really very little he could tell the officer.

"Ah, then you have not known him for long?"

"No, not long. Tell me," Dennison ventured, "why do you ask?"

Again the deprecatory wave of the hand. "No reason. Just curious. This Senor McAllister apparently engineered a heroic rescue operation. We are naturally pleased that he would respond so ably to a crisis."

"Jesus told his followers to serve others. That's what mission work is all about."

A quick nod. "Of course."

As Dennison had half hoped it would, bringing the Gospel openly into the conversation had made his guest more than a little uneasy. Dennison smiled benignly. "I've been very pleased with Senor McAllister's work also," he went on. "He is a dedicated Christian and I feel blessed to have him here." And that, certainly, was not a lie.

The officer had had enough. "Yes, I am sure. Well, thank you for your time, Senor." He got abruptly to his feet.

Dennison rose also. "Any time. And you're welcome to come to one of our services here." He gave the times.

The officer nodded his thanks, but his polite smile was a little forced now. "One thing—for my records, do you, perhaps, have Senor McAllister's passport? I neglected to check and see if he had it in his possession in the mountains."

"I don't know where it is," Dennison told him truthfully. "He may have it with him for all I know. Perhaps if you come to one of our services when he has returned, you can ask him yourself."

"No, it is really not important. Thank you again."

Dennison followed his hurried retreat out of the mission. As they emerged, he looked past the officer and saw the driver striding rapidly toward the jeep from the direction of the small frame parsonage across the street. Something—the man's rapid pace, perhaps the slightly nervous air to his movements—made Dennison frown. Where had the man been? Had he tried to sneak a quick drink at one of the cantinas and now feared being caught in his indiscretion? But no, he seemed to be returning from Dennison's house.

He watched the two leave. The officer apparently was speaking sharply to his subordinate, but the words were lost in the sound of the engine. When they were out of sight, Dennison crossed to his house. The doors were unlocked, as always, and he could find no evidence to verify his suspicion that the driver, presumably under orders, had taken the opportunity to search the house while his superior kept Dennison occupied.

Had McAllister—Eric—been the object of their peculiar visit? He did not know, but the incident cast a pall on the rest of the day as he went about his work. Nor had the pall entirely lifted on the following morning. At intervals throughout the day, he found himself praying for Cristina's and Eric's safe and prompt return.

He saw nothing more of the army officer, and preparations for the Wednesday evening prayer meeting that night, particularly in Cristina's absence, kept him occupied until it was nearly time for the service.

There was a good turnout, better, proportionately, he guessed with a little pride, than that of the Wednesday night service at the Tulsa church where he had preached. The prayer meeting was just that. Following a hymn and a Scripture reading, he would open the floor for prayer requests, leading the prayers himself or asking specific members to do so. There was a closeness to the meeting, a unity in the Spirit that was often lacking in the more structured Sunday services. He really enjoyed the more intimate sharing.

As always, standing at the pulpit, he took the opportunity to unobtrusively scan those present for new visitors or irregular comers whose presence might indicate a crisis—

spiritual or otherwise—in their lives. As he completed the Scripture reading, he saw a figure slip quickly into the back of the sanctuary, and the shock almost made him stumble over his words. The newcomer was Jorge, the former street gang member whom Eric had fought to a humiliating standstill the other night.

Recovering, he continued with the service, keeping an eye, however, on the young man who remained lurking at the back of the room. More than once during the course of the service, he thought that Jorge would cut and run. The boy stayed on his feet much of the time as if comtemplating just that. When he did sit, it was perched on the edge of the pew closest to the door, his eyes darting about like those of an animal caught unawares in a trap.

But he stayed, perhaps in answer to Dennison's silent prayer that he would do so.

As Dennison closed the service, he saw Jorge all but bolt out of the door. He himself hurried out through the door at the front of the sanctuary, coming out into the warm darkness of the evening in time to see the young man heading away down the street. Jorge's pace had slowed following his abrupt departure from the church, and the hands jammed in the pockets of his ragged jeans bespoke a certain dejection.

"Jorge, wait," Dennison called.

For a moment it seemed that the boy had not heard, or, hearing, was prepared to simply ignore the request. Then his pace slowed even more, and he finally halted, although he did not turn around until Dennison overtook him.

When Jorge did turn, it was with an aggressive pivot on the ball of his foot as if turning to confront an opponent. Which, perhaps in a way, Dennison thought, he was. The boy's sullen, almost angry expression struck him as forced. He halted and confronted the young man, careful not to take on any kind of posture himself that might be interpreted as hostile. "I'm glad you came tonight," he said at last.

Jorge shrugged his powerful shoulders and didn't answer.

At least he didn't spit on the ground or lash out at him with a karate kick, Dennison reflected, and felt a little encouraged. "Some of our members would like to meet you," he tried again. "Why not come back and visit for a few minutes?"

A mistake, he saw immediately. Jorge almost turned away. Whatever his stage of spiritual questing, Jorge was not ready to be subjected to the attentions of well-meaning mission members. Sudden inspiration came to Dennison. "Did you come to see Senor McAllister?"

The dark eyes flashed with quickened interest. "Where is he?" Jorge's first words came out as a demand.

"He and Cristina—my assistant—were in the mountains when the earthquake hit. They stayed to help the villagers."

Jorge's gaze appeared skeptical. "He—they will be back?"

Dennison nodded. "Yes. Eric will be sorry he missed you. Perhaps when he returns he could come to see you."

Briefly Jorge's resolve seemed to waver. Then he did spit on the ground. "I do not want to see him!" he exclaimed. "Why should I? He is nothing but a weak gringo!"

Dennison stared the obvious answer at him.

"He was lucky!" Jorge snapped. "I can beat him! But that is not why I came here tonight."

"Then why?" Dennison prodded.

"I was bored! This town has nothing but pigs and gringos! I should go back to the city. There I was respected, admired, a leader!"

"You left that to come here," Dennison reminded him. "It would be a mistake to go back."

"You cannot stop me!"

Jorge had shifted sidewise a bit into what could be the beginnings of a martial arts stance. His hands were out of his pockets and clenched into fists at his sides.

Dennison realized it was best to drop the matter for the time being. "No, Jorge," he responded gently to the other's boast. "I cannot stop you."

Jorge appeared somewhat mollified. Slowly his fists unclenched. His anger did not seem as deep or as violent as on the other occasions Dennison had been near him. He hesitated now, as if wanting to say something further. But he finally performed another of those quick pivots and started wordlessly on his way.

"I'll tell Senor McAllister you were here," Dennison said to his retreating back. Jorge did not respond.

Tiredly Dennison looked back toward the mission. The whole brief confrontation with Jorge had not lasted more than a few minutes, and the congregation was still issuing from the mission, a number of them clustered in groups outside the door. Among the sparse social options of Puerto Madero, church activities constituted the recreational highlights of many citizens. Dennison knew from experience that it would probably be some time before the last of them dispersed.

Rosa, little Pedro cradled in her arms, came to meet him. During the prayer meeting she had requested prayers for Pablo, her husband. She bustled anxiously up to Dennison now. "You do not know when Hermana Cristina and her ...Hermano Eric will return?" she inquired.

Dennison shook his head. "No, I don't. You heard just about everything I know during the service." He had reported the contents of his phone conversation with Jose to the congregation and then they had lifted Eric and Cristina to the Lord in prayer, committing their safety into His hands.

"I will pray for them," Rosa promised. There was a sparkle in her eyes that hinted at some happy secret, Dennison noted. But she was rushing quickly on. "When they return would it be possible for you and Hermano Eric to come and speak to my Pablo?"

"Of course we will," Dennison assured her. Cristina had told him of Rosa's request at the supper, but Eric had been gone most of the time since then. "We will come as soon as we can after they return."

"Oh, thank you." She tiptoed to brush his cheek with her lips. "I must go now."

When the last of the congregation had departed, Dennison wandered back through the sanctuary, straightening things some. An enormous black toad had made it into the room, probably through one of the large drainage holes drilled at the base of the wall. He prodded it back out through the hole with the toe of his shoe, although it would probably return as soon as he left. A tiny lizard scuttled along the wall near the ceiling, searching for insect prey.

At last he turned out the lights in the empty sanctuary and headed to his house. It was lonely with Cristina and Eric both gone. How quickly and naturally Eric had seemed to fit into the scheme of things here. And, if nothing else, he thought, remembering Rosa and Jorge, Eric's presence had enlivened things. Yes, it would be good to have them both back. They should certainly have a story to tell.

24

"Quite a story." Dennison grinned in wonderment and leaned back in the straight-backed chair behind the desk in his simple mission office. "Earthquakes, rescue operations, showdown with the witch doctor." He shook his head, but he seemed pleased, Braden thought.

"Oh, hush," Cristina said. "It was fantastic. We had a prayer meeting last night in that first village and more than fifty people accepted Christ. That means there's work for you to do. There are a lot of little babies in Christ up there just waiting to be nurtured by the Word. Eric led the meeting."

Dennison's eyebrows went up in surprised inquiry.

"Yes," Cristina continued in the same teasing tone. "You should have heard him." She flashed a laughing smile at Braden. "He kept telling me he couldn't possibly speak, so I wrote down some basic things for him to say. And then, when he got up there in front of an audience—I've never seen a bigger ham! He didn't use a single thing I wrote. He stood up there and told them that a test of strength with a brujo didn't mean anything. That Jesus had already won a greater victory over sin and Satan, and that through that victory they could become new people. Most of them who came down didn't even wait for him to give the invitation."

Dennison's smile was wide and genuine. "I knew you had the makings of an evangelist," he said to Braden. "When can I count on you to preach this marvelous sermon here at the mission? It would probably do our members here a lot of good to hear such a message."

"I think I'll pass," Braden said firmly, but he really was pleased. The time spent in the mountains with Cristina, ministering to the people there, working with them to repair the damage to their homes, beginning to discover the depths of his feelings for Cristina, had been a hectic yet satisfying interlude that he would always treasure. In a way he was sorry to see it end.

Preaching to the villagers—he did not think of it in those terms—had left him physically drained yet spiritually fulfilled in a way that not even his conversion could match. It had been with a certain reluctance that he had parted from new friends this morning to return to the mission.

"I figured you would stay awhile," Dennison was saying. "We felt the quake here, but they say it was centered in those mountains. Of course, I'm probably telling you things you already know. Did you have any warnings before the big quake hit?"

"There was a tremor about an hour before the big one," Cristina said, "but we still weren't prepared for the big one. The devastation was unbelievable."

"I'm sorry you had to go through it," Dennison said, "but I know the Lord had you there for a purpose. When Jose called me on Tuesday, he told me of all the people you two had helped. He assured me you were both all right, but not to expect you back for a couple of days. He seemed quite sold on both of you."

"I sent him to the nearest phone to call you after everything had settled down," Cristina acknowledged.

"And you had it out with Tobias on his home ground and sent him running," Dennison said wonderingly to Braden.

"It wasn't me," Braden replied.

Dennison nodded, sobering some. "I'm glad you see that. The Lord used you in a mighty way up there, Eric."

213

"He used Cristina and me both. I couldn't have done anything if it hadn't been for her setting me straight about a few things and then being there to prop me up when I needed her."

"It sounds like you made quite a team," Dennison commented innocently.

Braden didn't have to look at Cristina to know she was blushing. He thought he was successful in keeping his own expression straight, although he was reminded with poignant pleasure of that night when Cristina had spoken almost the same words as Dennison had just said. By mutual, if unspoken, agreement, they had not told Dennison of the newly awakened feelings they had found for one another.

The missionary's eyes shuttled back and forth between them, lingering the longest on Cristina. "Quite a team," he repeated after a moment as if unable to summon any new words. Then, recovering, he went on, "Well, maybe we've seen the last of Tobias at any rate."

Remembering the implacable malevolence of the brujo, Braden was prone to doubt it. Humiliated, Tobias might be more dangerous than ever. He realized Dennison had continued to speak. "What?" he asked.

"I said, that even as bad as Tobias is, God still loves him. That's something to remember. Oh, by the way, your sparring partner of the other evening showed up for prayer meeting last night."

It took Braden a moment to get it. "Jorge?"

Dennison grinned slightly at his surprise. "That's right. I told you that once he calmed down he might remember some of the things you said to him. The fact that a missionary can beat him at karate and then tell him that none of it means anything had to have made an impression on him."

"And he actually came to church?"

"Well, he hung around the back of the sanctuary, on his feet half the time and acting like he'd bolt any minute. He did finally, but it was after the service was over. I tried to talk to him, but it was plain he was looking for you. I think he'll be back. Come on, let's look at the progress on the dorm."

Braden and Cristina followed him out into the back courtyard. They had taken time to clean up when they had arrived, but had not looked around. It was mid-afternoon.

Where there had been nothing only a few days ago, cinderblock walls had risen some three feet around a roughly poured slab floor. The fourth side of the rectangle was a side of the existing mission building.

From where he worked with a trowel, Santego climbed to his feet, grinning broadly. "Hola, Hermano!" he exclaimed, and came forward to grip Braden's hand. Three other villagers of varying ages also halted in their labors. "I heard you and Hermana Cristina were in the mountains when the earthquake hit. But you are all right, I see."

"We're both fine," Braden assured him. "And you have done well without me." He was impressed with the progress.

"We did not want sister Cristina mad at us when she returned," he chuckled. "To avoid that, we have worked hard." He winked conspiratorily at Braden as Cristina gave him a mock glare. "We have built well, to withstand even an earthquake!"

"I'll be back with you tomorrow," Braden promised.

"I think you both deserve the afternoon off," Dennison told them as they reentered the mission.

"Oh, good," Cristina turned eagerly to Braden. "How about a swim?"

"In the deadly killer surf?" Braden objected.

"No. There's a cove down the beach where it's still safe to swim. Today would be perfect for it."

She was right. The sky was that clear blue which seemed only to exist in tropical climates, the sun a brilliant yellow against the azure background, its heat dissipated by the gentle breeze that played with strands of Cristina's dark hair and blew coolly over Braden's naked chest when they arrived at the beach.

The cove was a large circle of shallow blue water surrounded by a sandy strip marked by piles of massive boulders that extended out into the waves. A bridge had once spanned the cove, but, gradually undercut by erosion, it had finally fallen victim to hurricane winds, and the road came to an abrupt end at a sheer drop of some twenty feet.

A number of people were scattered about the beach, but Cristina chose an isolated spot to park the Scout. She was wearing a light jacket over her swimsuit, but she shrugged it quickly off once she was out of the vehicle.

Her suit was a modest one-piece affair of jade green, probably out of date by current American fashion standards. But it showed off her statuesque figure admirably and emphasized the long tanned lengths of her legs.

She ran lightly to the water's edge, then looked back over her shoulder to give her head that fetching toss and throw Braden a challenging grin. "Let's go," she said. "I'll race you."

She plunged out into the light surf, then dove cleanly. Braden held back for the sheer pleasure of watching her lithe form knife through the water. She was an excellent swimmer.

Braden raced after her then, hitting the water in a long, flat dive. He swam hard, using an efficient crawl that sent him churning through the water in her wake. For thirty yards out into the cove, they swam, and Braden slowly narrowed the gap between them.

She glanced back once, saw him closing, started to laugh, then choked as she swallowed water. Braden's reaching hand grazed her ankle before she jackknifed and dove like a porpoise.

It became a game with her, daring him to catch her, then slipping gracefully away from his efforts. Braden prolonged it, enjoying her laughter, the sight of her, her tantalizing nearness. When at last he extended himself and encircled her from behind with his arms, she twisted deftly to face him and he kissed her radiant face. She tasted of the sea, and the sleek smoothness of her legs slid against his. They tried to swim back to shore holding hands, but only succeeded in almost managing to drown one another. She was laughing and breathless when he turned to give her a hand up out of the surf.

He thought she looked wonderful with the dark mane of her hair wet from the sea, and the swimsuit molded to her full body. Her laughter was infectious.

She got a beach towel from the Scout and spread it on the sand for them, sinking gracefully down onto it as she used her hands to fluff her hair. Braden settled beside her, and watched until she grinned provacatively and brought a laugh from him.

"What's funny now?" she demanded playfully leaning toward him.

"I still can't get used to your being a missionary. I pictured a middle-aged old maid."

"Sorry to disappoint you," she said archly. "Anyway, you're not quite like any lay missionary I've ever met either." She seemed about to speak further, but thought better of it. Her expression sobered.

Braden knew what her unasked question had been. He studied her, the strong lines of her face, the dark eyes that could flash with laughter. He felt a stab of guilt, deep and bitter. This woman had declared her love for him, shared of herself, and asked nothing in return from a man who was, even yet, virtually a stranger to her.

"You're right," he said heavily at last, "I'm *not* like any lay missionary you've ever met." She drew back slightly, her expression expectant. Braden groped for words. "Howard brought me back with him on faith. And you accepted me on faith, not knowing anything about me or my past."

"Eric..." she began, lifting one hand as if to reach for him.

"No," he cut her off. "Listen to me. You have a right to know as much as I can tell you. I want you to know." She remained silent, and he told her about the Operation, of his time as an agent, but sketching the story in broad strokes.

He told her of his training, of the nature of his assignments, of the ruthless amorality it had instilled in him. "I was the best they had," he said simply, "with but one possible exception."

He told her of living life on the dagger's edge of danger, of the incipient paranoia of knowing you might any time, any place be the victim of an assassin's bullet. He told her of loves lost, of betrayals by and against him, of pressure, mental and physical, to never slip, to never let down his guard, of comrades-in-arms who had slipped for one brief moment and paid with their lives. He spoke of danger and violence, which had grown to become an ingrained part of him that, he felt now, could never be eradicated.

"That's why I was able to handle Jorge and Tobias. They were amateurs playing against a pro. They never had a chance—neither of them." He paused reflectively. "I know some of the things I did for the Operation were justifiable; they had to be done for the good of the country, the Free World, if you will. But some of the other things I knew were wrong, morally wrong by almost any standards, even when I did them. But I didn't question them too much. Maybe that was my mistake...just going along with what others decided was right or best."

He could not read Cristina's face, but she listened to him with rapt attention. He told her of his conversion, of his accepting Christ and the resultant upheaval of his life.

"I began to see everything differently, to question what I had not questioned before, to apply different standards that seemed somehow to have just become a part of me. I realized gradually that I couldn't continue to work for them, that I had to take some kind of a stand or my conversion didn't mean anything at all."

"Amen," Cristina said softly and reached to lay one hand on his knee. "What did you do?"

Her touch strengthened him. "I quit. I resigned."

"And that's why you came here? To try to forget?" she asked gently.

"No. I came down here to escape."

"Escape?"

"They're trying to kill me," he said flatly.

Her eyes widened in disbelief and he rushed quickly on, recounting his flight in general terms, the seemingly omnipotent powers of his pursuers to anticipate his moves.

"So when I heard Howard give that invitation it just seemd like the Lord told me to accept it. And when Howard accepted me in faith, I felt like it had to be the Lord's will that I come."

"Of course it was." Her tone was reassuring. "After all that's happened you can't really doubt that, can you?"

"I guess not," he conceded, "but the longer I'm here, and the more I—I care about you, the more afraid I am that they'll find me even here, and that you and Howard will be in danger because of me. I don't like that; I don't like it at all."

"The Lord will protect us," she said dismissing his fears. "Christians have been aiding other Christians in times of persecution for two thousand years."

"But this time there is only one Christian being persecuted."

Her eyes snapped with sudden fire. "Christ said that whatever was done to the least of His children was done also to Him. Do you think that we would turn you out, that I *could* turn you out now?"

He shook his head. "All right, but I don't want you hurt."

"And I don't want you dead." She frowned in thought. "Can't you just turn yourself in to the F.B.I. or something?"

"I haven't committed any crime, not really," he said. "There's nothing they could prosecute me for, and the Operation doesn't want me prosecuted. They want me dead."

She shuddered. "What about some kind of protective custody or something?"

"It's no good. If I was in any sort of custody, they could

get to me eventually. And even if I could make a deal with some branch of the government and get the dogs called off, I don't think I'd be safe even then. It's become kind of a personal vendetta with one of the Operation's agents."

"Who is it?"

"His name is Bob Chandler," he told her after a moment. "He was a kind of protege of mine. I trained him."

"And now he wants to kill you?" she asked in disbelief.

"That's right." Braden was saddened by the revulsion he saw in her eyes.

"But why?"

He shrugged. "Orders, pride, honor, jealousy. Maybe just the fact that I'm a Christian."

She looked thoughtful. "Sometimes when people are under conviction, when the Lord is working on them, they react like that—with hostility, even with violence, toward Christians."

"The only conviction Chandler is under is the conviction of his need to kill me."

"Don't be too sure of that."

Braden shook his head. "Chandler is even more of a lost cause than Tobias, as far as the Lord is concerned. He's an assassin, a professional killer."

She shivered as if a cold breeze had touched her there in the warm sunlight. Briefly she shut her eyes, and he realized with a sense of humility that she was praying.

She opened her eyes and they were bright with moisture. "You can't just keep running."

"Maybe I'm safe. But if he ever does show up here, I'll either have to kill him or keep running. It's as simple as that. And even if I kill him, they might just send someone else like him."

"We have to tell Howard," she said after a moment.

Braden nodded. The time for secrecy was past.

"John McAllister," she said finally, "that's not your real name, is it?"

"No."
"What is it?"
He told her.

25

"The latest news from stateside, dateline two days ago." Dennison casually tossed the newspaper onto the table behind the mission where he had found Eric seated, poring over plans for the dorm.

Eric looked up from the plans and idly spun the newspaper to where he could see the headlines on the lower part of the front page. Dennison saw his face go hard and cold, and Eric abruptly abandoned the dorm plans, his eyes flickering over the newsprint.

Something on the page had struck a nerve, Dennison thought. He himself had glanced at the front page, and he strained to recall what news items had been headlined there. A local murder in Houston, the city of the paper's origin. The Russians stepping up their ineffective efforts in Afghanistan. A popular young Senator announcing plans for an upcoming junket to Central America. Had there been something else? What had caused that sudden hardness to lock into place in Eric's eyes?

He tilted his head to get a better view of the story that had claimed the younger man's attention, but Eric abruptly shoved the paper away from him, as if, by that act, physically and mentally dissociating himself from whatever had emerged to haunt him. He looked around at Dennison, and his grin seemed forced. "I'll pass on two-day-old news," he said drily.

"It doesn't make very pleasant reading," Dennison agreed. "You up to a little visitation?"

Eric looked past him to where Luis Santego directed the current work crew. Dennison could actually see his eyes lose some of their hardness.

"Sure," Eric said after a moment. "I think our construction crew can get along without me for a while. Who did you want to visit?"

"Cristina set us up," Dennison said loudly enough to carry to Cristina who had just emerged from the mission. "She promised Rosa we would go and talk to her reprobate husband."

"I heard that," Cristina said sternly as she approached.

She had never looked more radiant than in the last couple of days, Dennison reflected. Her face positively shone, and he noticed her gaze catch that of Eric and hold it for a moment before sliding away. He darted a covert glance at Eric, who seemed momentarily to have forgotten not only his own presence, but the workmen, and the dorm plans, and the newspaper story as well. Dennison recalled imagining the two of them together in the mountains, and the essential rightness he had felt about the scene.

But whatever had transpired between his two assistants had united them on many levels. In addition to the happiness he had sensed in the pair, there was an additional element almost of strain, as of a second, not-so-pleasant truth lurking beneath the surface of their smiles.

Have faith, he chided himself silently. Cristina's a big girl; she knows what she's doing. And Eric, whatever the enigma of his background, has proven himself a friend as well as a dedicated servant of the Lord.

"Rosa will be thrilled," Cristina was saying. "She really does want you to talk to Pablo, especially since they've be-come parents."

"Don't get your hopes up," Dennison felt obligated to caution her. "I've talked to him before. You know that."

"Where do we find this scoundrel?" Eric asked, rising. He seemed, Dennison thought, to be making an effort to avoid even glancing again at the newspaper. Whatever he had read had really upset him.

"He'll be down along the beach, most likely," Dennison answered the question. "When Pablo does work, it's as a fisherman. There's a whole group of them that hang out down along one section of beach on the edge of town. Pretty rough bunch."

Eric absorbed this without visible emotion. "Well, let's get going."

"Be careful." Cristina's gaze lingered on Eric.

A morning breeze was coming off the ocean as they negotiated the dusty streets. Eric seemed thoughtful, almost moody, like he had been when he had first come to the mission. Dennison had hoped this dark side of his personality was gone for good. There had been a subtle change in Eric since the earthquake and the prayer meeting that had become a revival.

Dennison had detected a new strength. Eric seemed to have a new confidence in his role as a Christian. It was something more than the almost arrogant self-assurance he had radiated when dealing with secular affairs. Now there was the genesis of a different, more humble confidence in his ability to serve the Lord. Dennison had seen it before and knew that the potential for even greater growth was there. Eric still had some lessons to learn. This newfound confidence was, as yet, a fragile thing, and given Eric's inherent character and nature, could easily become conceit.

"Tell me about Jorge's visit to the prayer meeting," Eric requested as they walked.

Dennison repeated the story. "He's another one we need to call on," he concluded.

At the edge of the village they made their way down to the beach. Fishing nets had been hung from posts for mending, although none of the group of men congregated there appeared to have any great interest in doing the job.

As he and Eric approached, Dennison saw one man make a rapid throwing motion. A glitter of metal spun in the sunlight, followed by an audible thwack of sound. An appreciative murmur went up from the other bare-chested men clustered around the thrower. Dennison looked more closely and saw four knives embedded in a twelve-inch-square piece of wood nailed to a post. Knife throwing. A little competition, most likely with some devalued pesos riding on the outcome.

The knives were retrieved; money changed hands, and the apparent victor took up a position in line with the post, balancing some kind of heavy combat knife in his hand. Dennison caught Eric's attention and nodded at the thrower. "That's Pablo," he said.

They stopped a short distance from the group and watched in silence. Eric's gaze, Dennison noted, was intent as he studied the young man preparing to throw. Pablo was of medium height with good shoulders and well-muscled arms. His physique was marred, however by the definite beginnings of what promised to be a formidable beer gut in the not-too-distant future. His features were likewise beginning to show a certain softness.

His companions were cut from the same cloth. Young, cocky in their strength and masculinity. Most of them were barefoot and shirtless, and a number of them held bottles or cans from which they partook liberally. A rough crew, Dennison had told Eric. And he saw nothing to make him revise that description.

Pablo flipped the heavy knife in the air and caught it deftly by the blade, showing off now. It was not a blade designed for throwing, Dennison knew. Pablo lined it up carefully with the post, grinned, and threw. The knife spun across the intervening twenty feet and sank into the square block just off center. A good throw, and Pablo's strutting arrogance as he turned away showed that he knew it.

Another man took his place, measured the distance and

threw. His knife—it appeared to be a hunting blade—struck the target low and to the side. He scowled at the jeers of his comrades and reached for a proffered bottle.

Two more competitors followed in quick succession, neither of them quite matching Pablo's performance. As the victor turned with outstretched palm to collect his winnings, he spied the two spectators and said something to his companions. They all turned, and after a moment it was Pablo himself who stepped foward. "What do you want here, gringos?" He put both hands on his hips and waited for an answer.

"You throw the knife well," Dennison said, and let a moment go by. "Perhaps it is something you can teach your son one day."

"And what do you know of knives, preacher?" Pablo demanded.

"I know there are many things you can teach your son as he grows into a man," Dennison parried. "Some of them good, some bad."

"I will worry about my son, and I can teach him all that he needs to know! And, yes, I will show him how to use the *cuchillo*. Could you show him as much, gringo preacher?"

"Maybe he could; maybe he couldn't," Eric broke into the exchange. "But I can show you a few things."

He went forward with an easy confidence in his movements and approached the makeshift target. Watching him, Dennison noted almost absently that he did it in such a way that his back was never offered completely to the group of fisherman. Almost effortlessly, it seemed, he withdrew the embedded blades from the target and returned, the hilts of two of the knives gripped in each hand.

Studying those knives, Dennison experienced a sinking unease. He was not unfamiliar with blades. In the dark period of his youth and early manhood—his lost years, he called them now—he had been more than proficient with a switchblade. He was a veteran of encounters with similarly armed opponents—slash and stab in a darkened alley with the whole affair over in moments. He recognized that if Eric intended some kind of exhibition to show up Pablo and his cronies then he was almost certainly doomed to failure.

The art of knife throwing required knives especially balanced for just that purpose, or, lacking such specialized equipment, long practice and familiarity with a specific knife. In his hands Eric carrried four mismatched weapons—Pablo's combat knife, another similar weapon, the hunting knife, and what appeared to be an actual balanced throwing blade—none of which he had ever handled before. For him to expect to achieve any kind of success in a throwing competition was all but absurd.

Dennison had only a moment to contemplate this, because Eric had reached the line from which the others had thrown. And then, with no warning, he was turning fast—*fast*—his right arm snapping back, then forward, with a speed that defied Dennison's vision to track it. And Pablo's heavy combat knife was cartwheeling to drive home dead center in the scarred target. Already another blade flew in its wake. Eric's arm blurred and a third, then a fourth knife cleft the air.

Another bullseye was impossible. Eric's first throw had accomplished that feat. But the other knives buried themselves so close to it that they all could have been encompassed by a two-inch circle.

A stunned silence struck the onlookers. Dennison realized that he himself was gaping in disbelief. He shut his mouth as Eric turned casually to his spectators.

"I can show you a few things about knives," he repeated. "But this man has taught me about things that are more important than tricks with knives, things that you need to tell your children. Listen to him."

He had his audience now, Dennison thought. Eric had bought him the chance, by whatever dubious means, and he would not waste it. He spoke crisply, decisively, keeping it short and basic. And, after a few last glances at Eric and his handiwork, they listened. Eric came and stood to one side, silent and motionless.

When Dennison stopped speaking, the group of men contined to stare at him. After a moment, it was again Pablo who stepped forward and regarded them both. "You are dif-ferent from what I thought," he said gravely. "I did not think a man of God could do the things that this man has done." He nodded at Eric.

"Jesus does not take away your manhood when you ask Him into your life," Dennison told him. "He gives you a new strength and confidence. He makes you more of a man."

"Rosa has tried to talk to me about these things," Pablo admitted. "And now that I am a father, I know that there are things I *should* change..." His tone seemed to indicate that he was not sure just how happy these changes would make him. Dennison remembered Cristina telling him that, according to Rosa, Pablo was actually growing jealous of the time his wife spent with their new son.

"You have a big responsibility now to both your wife and your son," Dennison said.

Pablo glanced around as if fearful his companions would overhear him. But they had begun to disperse, some of them approaching the target to study the knives embedded there. "I have been thinking about this responsibility," Pablo said. "I am not sure I know how to be a good father."

Quite an admission coming from a man nurtured by the precepts of machismo, Dennison knew. Rosa and, of course, the Holy Spirit had indeed been doing some talking to Pablo. "The Bible can tell you how to be a good father," Dennison said. "The Bible tells us about God. It teaches us His rules, but more important, it tells us how much He loves us—as only a father can love his children. God wants to be your Father, Pablo."

Pablo's gaze was at once both anguished and gauging. "Maybe," he said, "Maybe I will come to your mission and hear what you have to say."

Wordlessly Dennison extended his hand. Pablo gripped it once firmly. A commitment. His eyes flickered briefly to Eric, then he turned back to his comrades and their discussion of Eric's prowess.

Dennison waited until he and Eric were some distance down the beach before he glanced sidewise at his companion in a wry, wordless comment.

Eric's mouth pulled up in an almost reluctant grin. "Well," he said defensively, "it worked on Jorge. I figured why not try it on Pablo too."

They both laughed then in a moment of mutual understanding and encouragement. "Where in the world," Dennison said when they stopped, "did you learn to throw knives like that?"

The question had been asked without thought, and he almost regretted it as he saw Eric's features stiffen. "Picked it up here and there," he answered, but without the tightness Dennison expected.

Cristina hurried to meet them as they neared the mission. She blocked their path, hands on her hips. "Well?"

Dennison and Eric exchanged glances, and it was the former who answered. "Well, I think there's a good chance we'll see Pablo sitting beside Rosa and little Pedro in church within the next couple of weeks."

Cristina's smile was radiant. She caught each of them by an arm, and, walking between them, insisted Dennison give her the details of their visit. "You are both wonderful," she said when he was finished. He noticed her hug Eric's arm tightly against her and look up at his face.

Tactfully he disengaged himself as they entered the mission. He glanced back as he headed for his office and saw the two of them standing very close together engaged in conversation. Eric looked up and for a moment their gazes met before Dennison looked away. He wondered what Eric had been able to read in his eyes.

It had become obvious to him in that moment that his

earlier fleeting suspicions were correct. Cristina and Eric were much more now than co-workers or friends. He remembered telling Eric that she was like a daughter to him, and he experienced a moment of bittersweet pleasure that he guessed must come to all parents, even pseudo ones, at one time or another.

He liked Eric, trusted him, loved him as a Christian brother, but he could not shake a lingering doubt as to whether he was the man for Cristina. Where had Eric learned to use knives with such proficiency, and to fight with the skill of a trained master? In Eric's past lurked demons of secrecy and mistrust; Dennison could sense them there and knew that he could never fully sanction Eric's new relationship with Cristina as long as those demons remained unexorcised.

And something else—threatening and ominous—hovered over Eric like a brooding, relentless stalker. John McAllister—Eric, or whatever his name was—carried with him the air of a man at once hunted and haunted by his enigmatic past.

He looked up from his desk as Eric and Cristina entered his office. They stood close to one another and their hands seemed to strain to come together, but did not quite touch. Cristina glanced up at Eric. His hard face was unreadable.

Dennison waited.

"I think," Eric said at last, "that it's about time you had a little biographical information on your assistant."

Cristina was smiling softly, and Dennison could not help but return the smile. "I think so too," he said with relief.

26

The new dormitory wing of the mission had progressed remarkably in a week, Braden thought, pausing in his work to take stock. The exterior was almost completed; the interior needed to be divided to separate the boys from the girls. The sanitation facilities, as were almost all those in Puerto Madero, would be primitive.

He looked to where Dennison himself worked alongside one of the half dozen or so villagers who had swelled the original work force. Dennison had joined them that morning and thrown himself into the labor with a passion. Clad in old canvas pants and a T-shirt, he looked fit and rugged.

Now he paused too, feeling Braden's gaze and glancing to catch it. He grinned. "Don't look so surprised. I've done plenty of this sort of work in my time. Besides, there's nothing else quite as satisfying. I told you this morning I wanted to get in on the blessing all you fellas are getting out here working."

And a blessing it had been, Braden reflected. The progress on the dorm and the easy camaraderie that had grown up between him and the villagers involved in the project had given him a deep sense of satisfaction. He was almost sorry to see the structure nearing completion.

"I thought you two were supposed to be working."

Braden turned at the sound of Cristina's voice. She had emerged from the mission, accompanied by two of her flock, one of them the elfin Carmelita who was in the charge of the Santegos.

The little girl left Cristina to scamper over to Santego, who swept her up laughingly into his arms.

Braden, glancing at Cristina, caught a ghost of sadness in her smile. In an ideal world, Carmelita would be expressing that kind of happiness over seeing her real parents.

"I think it's your turn to get out here and get your hands dirty," Dennison told her.

"Uh uh, not me. That's men's work." She wore jeans and a faded man's work shirt. Her makeup was minimal and her hair looked black and glossy in the sun. Braden had a sudden image of her, tired and dirty, working side by side with him in the mud after the earthquake. He felt an unexpected surge of love for her.

They had returned to the mountains once for a day during the ensuing week to minister to the new Christians there. Dennison had accompanied them, and Braden had been impressed anew with the missionary's abilities in that regard. In a sermon/lecture, Dennison had sketched in what it meant to be a Christian and what obligations and blessings were theirs. It was something Braden had never heard except on a piecemeal basis, and he found himself listening as raptly as the new converts.

Afterwards, they had visited with the new Christians on an individual basis and worked briefly with the older Christians to establish an ongoing system of Bible study.

"We can't just lead them to the Lord and then forget about them," Dennison explained to Braden. "It's too easy for them to never really understand what they've been given and what's expected of them." Recalling his own experiences, Braden had to agree. He himself had acted as counselor to a number of converts, incuding the man he had revived following the earthquake. He had come to Christ following Braden's impromptu sermon.

There were others as well, who came to him seeking

counsel. Braden ministered to them as best he could, at times having to turn to Dennison or Cristina for advice or answers. Surprisingly to him, the times he needed help were few, and he found a new confidence in his ability to share the Gospel.

Cristina was a constant pleasure to him, and the time spent together, whether in work or play, was always something to be treasured. He found her warm and humorous, but steadfast in her dedication to serving the Lord.

Dennison, with the evidence obviously before him, had come to understand the nature of the new commitment between his two assistants. Tactfully, he said nothing, and seemed outwardly to approve of the relationship, although on more than one occasion Braden had felt the other man's eyes evaluating him shrewdly when he was with Cristina. He had not repeated the veiled warning concerning Cristina that he had given Braden early upon their arrival at the mission.

Perhaps Cristina's obvious happiness in the new relationship and Braden's own growth as a Christian had persuaded him to lend at least acquiescent support to the couple.

His reaction to Braden's revelation of his dubious past had been guarded. He had listened with little expression while Braden spoke, his eyes moving occasionally to Cristina where she stood behind Braden's chair, leaving no doubt as to her loyalties. Braden had been grateful for her presence there, the fleeting touch of her fingers on his shoulder as he spoke. He did not think he could have done it without her.

"I like to use the story of my past when I preach," Dennison had said when he had finished. "You heard me do that back in Cromwell, Eric. It usually shocks a few people when they hear it. But next to your story"—he shook his head—"mine stacks up as a tale for children."

He was silent for a while longer. Braden waited, aware of Cristina's nearness. He was committed; if Dennison wanted to oust him now, it was in the Lord's hands. Somehow there was relief in the thought.

"I'm glad you told me," Dennison had said at last. "I've

been hoping you would. I knew you were hiding something, but I didn't expect anything quite so bizarre. They actually kill agents rather than let them resign?"

"They've tried three times on me so far."

"Do you think this Chandler can find you here?"

"I don't know. I think I've covered my tracks, but I've been wrong about it before."

Dennison's eyes had shifted to Cristina. He had grinned slightly. "I can see where you stand."

Cristina had not replied and Braden had not been able to see her expression. "I'll leave today if you want," Braden had said. They were some of the hardest words he had ever spoken, but he had felt obligated to say them.

"I know you would," Dennison had replied almost immediately. "But I'm not asking you to. You told me once you needed a second chance just like I did years ago. Well, the Lord sent you here, and I'm not the one to turn you away. Besides," he had grinned broadly, "I've gotten used to having you around to handle witch doctors and street fighters." He had paused, then gone on more seriously. "Now that we know, we'll just have to be careful not to advertise your presence here in the wrong quarters. And there's one thing we can do right now. Let's pray and commit this whole matter to God."

Remembering that prayer, Cristina's hand resting lightly on his shoulder, Braden felt again that sense of overwhelming gratitude, of profound thankfulness.

"We're going down to the store for soda pop," Cristina said now, looking at Braden. "You want to go with us?"

"I think I will play hooky," Braden answered, glancing cunningly at his co-workers.

"I heard that," Dennison objected. "You have our permission to go, but only if you bring us back some of that soda pop."

"Why, I think the mission budget can afford that," Braden said expansively.

"Mission budget, my eye. This is your treat."

"Okay, but it comes out of my tithe."

"You're good for Howard," Cristina told him as they left with the two children. "I haven't seen him so up in a long time."

"He's good for me," Braden admitted. "The last person I had whom I could call a friend is doing his best to kill me."

She shuddered and he was immediately sorry he had brought up the subject.

There were a number of tiny stores in the village, specializing in candy bars, soft drinks and a few staples and canned goods. The inescapable dust coated their shoes and lower legs of their pants as they walked to the nearest one.

Cristina smiled a greeting at an elderly man selling fresh bread from a small wooden cart. A whiff of the aroma made Braden's stomach growl, but the bread was almost as dusty as his shoes.

A bony dog erupted from inside a hut to bear down with a cacophony of barking on an enormous hog lumbering stol-idly past in the street. The porker looked askance at the oncoming canine, then abruptly let out an echoing snort and turned to meet the attack. The dog, his prey having suddenly turned hostile, did a flailing, skidding turn that raised a cloud of dust.

Through the dust charged the hog, grunting in righteous rage. The dog streaked for the refuge of the hut, disppearing inside. The hog, apparently content with his victory, drew up short of entering the hut. With a series of self-satisfied grunts and snorts, he backed away, then resumed his lumbering progress down the road.

All of them burst out laughing. The dog cautiously stuck his head out of the hut and gave a low face-saving bark in the wake of his triumphant foe.

Braden caught Cristina's hand as they continued, and after a moment he felt a tugging of his other hand and looked down into the smiling pixie face of Carmelita.

"She's jealous," Cristina said. "She wants somebody to hold her hand too. Go on, take it."

Reluctantly Braden took the tiny hand in his, and Carmelita's smile doubled in wattage. I don't even like kids, Braden thought. How did I end up here?

But it was kind of nice.

In the tiny store, the two children began an excited survey of the treats displayed. Cristina grinned mischievously at Braden. "You've made another conquest. Maybe *I* should be jealous."

Braden shook his head helplessly. He felt the impact of eyes on him and turned in time to catch the gaze of a youngish bare-chested man who had just entered the store. The fellow was well-built, but there was a sense of dissolution about him. Braden typed him as one of the indolent sorts who frequented the rough cantinas in the town—a ladron.

He thought he detected a flicker of surprise in the man's eyes before he turned abruptly and left the store.

Cristina read Braden's frown. "What's wrong?"

"I'm not sure. That fellow acted like he knew me, and like he wasn't too happy about running into me." Braden stepped to the door and looked out. The man had vanished, and Braden mentally chastised himself for not moving faster to check the man's route. He was getting slow.

"Forget it," Cristina said lightly at his shoulder. "You're a celebrity around here, remember? And a missionary can make enemies of people he's never even seen. That might have been one of Tobias' local followers who's afraid you'll start on him next."

Reluctantly Braden turned back to the store and helped in the selection of treats and soft drinks. But the incident rankled, and as they returned to the mission, he kept his eyes open and several times checked behind them. He did not hold Cristina's hand, although Carmelita still clung to his other one. He felt better with at least one hand free. If Cristina noticed this lapse or his uneasiness, she made no comment.

As they relaxed with their soft drinks under the palms behind the mission, Dennison studied the incomplete dormitory thoughtfully. "We're getting spread thin," he commented. "With this wing completed and the response we've had in the mountains, we'll have our hands full."

"That's a good kind a problem to have, though," Cristina reminded him.

"I suppose. But we need to establish some kind of permanent presence in the mountains. If we're not careful, Tobias or someone like him could regain a lot of lost ground before we could prevent it."

One of the workers, a muscular youth, addressed himself to one of the coconut trees and went up it, gripping the rough bark with hands and feet. Once at the top he sent several of the large nuts thudding to the ground before descending.

He produced a machete and cut the husks from the nuts and punctured the ends. Braden took one of the nuts and sipped the milk. He was no stranger to it, and after a few swallows, he opted for the soft drink.

Once the milk was gone, the nuts were cut open. Braden took a large piece of meat and bit into it with relish. The two children were chasing one another, their laughter loud and uninhibited. For some reason, he thought of the mountains.

"Are there many brujos like Tobias?" he asked Dennison.

"There aren't many that extreme, I don't suppose, although most small towns have their folk doctor or fortune teller who dispenses charms and arcane wisdom. The old religions, as well as perverted forms of Christianity, have had a strong hold on these people for centuries. Most of them have been exposed to Christianity, but many times it has been watered down by various pagan elements. But the very fact that they have been exposed to it makes the people open to hearing the Word."

"Does the government frown on rabble rousers like Tobias?"

Dennison shrugged. "The government has other worries

these days." He paused, studying Braden. "Were you concerned that there might be some official inquiry into what happened between you and Tobias?"

"The thought had crossed my mind. I'd hate to draw official attention to myself. There are too many ways something like that could end up in the hands of the Operation. You told me the military was asking about me."

"Forget it," Dennison advised. "The government is too worried about the economy collapsing or the American banks calling their loans to pay much attention to what lay missionaries are up to."

"Glad to hear it." Braden used the last of his soft drink to wash down the coconut meat.

Dennison was still studying him thoughtfully. "You worried they might find you down here?" he asked finally.

"I always worry."

Dennison let out his breath in a long sigh. None of the others were within earshot of them. "What's this Chandler like?"

"Young, amoral, usually cold-blooded except when it comes to me."

"Why do you think that is?"

Braden shrugged. Cristina had asked him almost the same question, and he hadn't had a good answer for her either.

"What does he look like?"

Braden described him briefly. "He moves like a cat," he finished. "And he's good, very good." Now it was his turn to study the other man. "Why do you want to know?"

"So I'll recognize him if he shows up here." There was an unfamiliar edge of hardness to Dennison's voice.

"If he does show up, don't get in his way. Just leave him to me."

"I won't stand by and see any of my people hurt," Dennison vowed. "And if it comes down to it, I can take care of myself."

"Not against Chandler, you can't," Braden told him. "Don't even think about it. On the best day you ever had, you couldn't take him on his worst."

Dennison's expression was unreadable. The children's laughter seemed to have grown distant.

27

The massive waves curled out of the night, alarmingly close to the shore, breaking almost immediately with pounding violence. The surf rushed in to lap near his feet before receding back out into the darkness. The near-white sand made the beach pale and ghostly.

None of the lights from the village reached the water's edge, although the moon and stars cast a wan illumination. The disturbing beat of discordant music came to Braden from the cantina at the beach's edge behind him. He stood staring out into the violent sea.

He remembered Dennison's questions about Chandler that afternoon, the note of grim determination he had read in his friend's voice. And he thought of Cristina. He had told her good night, and then come here to the beach alone. The thought of either his friend or his love coming to harm because of his presence in their lives was a gnawing torture to him.

Perhaps he should slip away even now, leave Puerto Madero and the mission and Dennison and Cristina and all the rest, before, like a lightning rod, he drew down fire upon them. He turned and walked slowly along the beach. Ahead loomed one of the massive stone breakwaters extending out into the surf.

He heard the whisper of feet on the sand behind him, the muffled grunting voices, and turned, nerves shrieking in alarm.

There were three of them, thugs, ladrons from the local bars, and they slowed a bit in their rush as he turned to face them. The moonlight glinted off their nearly naked torsos, their wild dark eyes, the machetes they gripped in their fists.

They were almost upon him, but he saw that their rush was not concerted, that they would not reach him at the same time.

The foremost one emitted a stifled cry as he charged, machete uplifted to begin its downward slash. Braden dropped low to the sand and whirled across it, one leg extended to scythe his attacker's legs from under him in a single sweep. That one went down with a grunt of surprise, limbs and blade flailing. Braden spun up onto his feet.

The next one was almost upon him, within arm's reach, the machete cutting down from overhead. In that clock-tick instant, Braden recognized the thug from the store that afternoon, saw the dilated pupils of his eyes in the moonlight, and knew that he dealt with at least one hop-head, maybe more. The drugs would hype these men, churn their violence to a deadly high.

The heavy blade slashed down. Braden blocked, forearm to descending wrist. The villager's arm bounced back, and Braden had an opening for a killing blow. He did not take it. Instead, he thrust the flat of his other palm against the sweating chest and shoved with all his strength.

The ladron went staggering back, almost into the arc of his remaining comrade's sweeping blade. But that one avoided the collision with the deft movement of one high on some upper. Still, it slowed him, and Braden pivoted ninety degrees to the left, skipped sidewise and drove his right leg out, pulling it so that the impact was more of a shove than the gut-splitting kick it could have been.

Even pulled, it was enough to force the air out of the

man's lungs, drive him backwards. The awkward slash of his machete missed Braden's retracting leg by inches.

The first attacker was scrambling to his feet in the yielding sand. The one he had recognized from the store was already coming back at him.

The dark face radiated all the savagery of his pagan ancestors who had offered human sacrifices to their demonic gods. But the man's technique was wild, undisciplined, and Braden blocked again, catching the descending arm in the raised V of his own crossed forearms. Immediately he curled his left hand around to clasp the thick wrist in the same painful grip he had used on Tobias. He pulled as if to yank his foe past him, at the same time stepping in with his left foot. As his attacker was hauled off-balance toward him, Braden swung his right leg forward and past as if he were kicking a ball, then brought it reaping back behind the machete-man's leg.

The judo move slammed the villager to the sand on his back and Braden arched in a kick that sent the machete cart-wheeling away into the night.

This could not go on. He was playing defensive games with men who were trying to kill him, and sooner or later he would make a slip and one of those heavy blades would slash home.

But there was no time for thought. The one he had first felled was coming back, his machete sweeping around as if it were an ax aimed to fell a tree. Braden dived headfirst over that slashing blade, sucking in his gut, landing on his shoulder and rolling smoothly up onto his feet, facing back toward his opponents. The startled thug was just beginning to turn. Beyond him Braden could see the third man moving to rejoin the action. Braden dug his feet in and flung himself forward.

As the ladron completed his turn, Braden clamped onto his arm with both hands and twisted in opposite directions as if wringing a dish rag. Nothing broke, but the man gasped shrilly in pain and his fingers opened convulsively. The machete dropped to the sand. Even as it fell, Braden set his feet and pivoted, swinging the lighter man around in a complete circle before releasing him.

Momentum sent the disarmed villager reeling into his charging cohort. As the two of them went down in a welter of arms and legs, Braden turned and ran. Ahead of him was the bulk of the breakwater extending across the beach and down into the surf. He heard their cries behind him, the crunch of feet on sand in his wake, and knew that one of them was close on his heels.

He clambered up the massive stones of the breakwater with hardly a pause. At its summit, some ten feet above the beach, he wheeled. His pursuer was close behind him, scrambling up the stones, hampered by the machete he still gripped in one fist.

As his head came level with the summit, Braden put a foot in his snarling face and shoved. With a cry the man went backwards hard to the sand below. Braden turned and leaped, flexing his legs to take the impact. The breakwater now separated him, however briefly, from his attackers.

He heard what at first he thought was an echo of their cries, then in front of him a figure materialized and another. Their shouts had brought reinforcements. He spotted two more between him and the shacks at the beach's edge. Four newcomers in all. The others would even now be coming over the breakwater after him. He was cut off, cornered.

The new assailants did not appear to be armed with machetes, but he saw moonlight reflected off a piece of pipe, the gleam of a hand knife. And they were not as eager as the machete-wielders, content to hold him at bay for the moment. Perhaps they had not anticipated taking part, but had joined the action in response to their compadres' cries.

There might be even more lurking among the flimsy structures of the village, Braden thought. Unless he wanted to stop fooling around and start playing for keeps, he did not have a chance against them.

Turning, he sprinted into the surf.

He cleft the first curling wave in a smooth dive, but still he felt its power slam down on him, drive him flat against the sand for one frantic instant. Then he was through it, surfacing as the next wave loomed hugely over him.

He ducked under, avoiding the worst of it, but the rush of water threatened to suck him back to the beach. He stroked hard against it, kicking desperately. He surfaced and struck out in a crawl, trying to get beyond the breaking surf.

The next incoming wave was only a swell that lifted him momentarily as it passed. He was not far from the shore, but the brutal waves broke close in, and they had eroded the bottom until the depth was already well over his head.

He had a moment to remember Dennison's tales of drownings in this water, of how the construction of the naval base had altered the whole nature of the surf, transformed it from a gentle wash to a brutal and unpredictable killer.

He slowed his rate long enough to cast a glance back over his shoulder. His pursuers predictably had not followed him, but he could see them gathering and hear their voices.

The water was numbingly cold, and he could feel the drag of his clothing. He wore only jeans, a T-shirt, and sneakers, but was reluctant to discard them, not knowing what might await him when he came ashore. *If* he came ashore, he amended the thought as he sensed the dangerous latent strength of the water.

He began to angle to his left. He estimated he was far enough out so that it would be difficult for his opponents to detect him now. He wanted to parallel the beach until he was safely beyond them before going ashore, which might not be so easy.

He could still hear their voices raised in anger and excitement, and they seemed to be splitting up, some of them going in each direction as if they planned to spread out and intercept him when he came ashore.

He swam harder, feeling the first faint ache in his

muscles. His conditioning and training, plus a healthy dose of adrenalin, had carried him this far. He tasted salt water as he turned his head to breathe in rhythm with his strokes.

Then a demonic force gripped him around chest and legs and sucked him down under the black water. He was thrust foward and down, tumbled end over end, his lungs screaming, his limbs thrashing futilely.

His equilibrium was gone, lost in the chaotic rush, but he forced his arms and legs to move in synchronization, to try to thrust him clear. Then a vagary of the maniacal current pushed him to the surface long enough for him to gasp in a lungful of air before it drew him relentlessly back down.

But his orientation was restored now, and that first gasping rip of fear had passed. An expert swimmer, he quit fighting the freak current and began to swim with it, angling up through the black water toward the surface.

His lungs were straining and redness tinged his vision when he finally made it, and he sucked in great draughts of air. He was still being carried along at an alarming rate, and he had completely lost track of his pursuers. Surely they would not have come this far along the beach.

He swam, allowing the current to carry him, but working to angle clear of it. Salt water stung his eyes; his clothes felt like leaden weights. He kept swimming, aware that he was being carried further and further. But he could at least be thankful that he was not being swept out to sea.

His breath was rasping his lungs from the effort of opposing the current even indirectly when at last he felt its power ebbing and realized that he had won free of it. He felt a brief surge of renewed strength. Tiredly he headed into shore.

He had a glimpse of the beach as an ingoing swell lifted him. The village was long gone. He thought he caught the glimmer of its lights back to his left.

Ahead of him the beach was empty, and just a little farther to his right the dark mass of the ominous scrub jungle reached almost to the water's edge.

He felt another wave starting and he flogged his body to greater effort, trying to stay with it and body surf to the shore. The next moment it was lifting him, and he was stroking one last time before flattening himself, arms extended before him.

He didn't quite catch it. For a moment he rode it, then it tumbled him, rolling him along the bottom. He gagged on sand and salt water as he was washed at last onto the beach.

It was easier to crawl than to regain his feet in the re-ceding surf. He made it up past the waterline and let himself collapse, his cheek pressed against the gritty sand.

He wasn't sure how long he lay there letting his breathing return to normal, his limbs begining to regain their strength. Something—a whisper of sound, a grunt of exhaled breath, the rush of displaced air—warned him, and he rolled instinctively so the machete chopped into the sand where his head had rested a heartheat before.

The blow would have split his skull like one of the coconuts he and the others had eaten that afternoon. He rolled again and made it crouching to his feet in a single coordinated surge of motion.

His attacker, one of the ladrons, drew up short in his rush, waving his blade menacingly before him. He opened his mouth and let out a loud yell of summons that split the night, skipping back as he did so to avoid Braden's aborted rush.

Braden recognized him as the one from the store. Maybe the death of the gringo had become a matter of honor to him. Certainly none of his cohorts had searched this far down the beach.

But they were on their way. Braden heard an answering shout and knew that his opponent would soon have reinforcements. And this time, knowing how he fought, they would be more careful. He did not know if he would be able to get by again on defensive tactics alone.

Perhaps he would not get by at all.

"Venga, ladron," he hissed in Spanish. "Come on, punk. I have seen women who fight more skillfully than you."

The broad features twisted in rage. Remembering his wild technique from the earlier struggle, Braden was not prepared for his unorthodox attack. The ladron lunged like a fencer, thrusting the machete out to impale rather than to cut or slash.

At the last moment Braden swayed sidewise, lifting his left arm so that the heavy blade passed between it and his body. Instantly then he dropped his arm, clamping the thug's extended arm against his side. He rotated his own forearm up and over the imprisoned arm, entangling it in an arm bar. Then he heaved cruelly.

The ladron was lifted up onto his toes by the pressure, air escaping from him in a gasp of painful surprise. Braden felt the arm muscles relax their grip, heard the machete thud to the sand. From down the beach came the cries of the other pursuers. They were close now.

Braden jerked his own arm free from that of the ladron and shoved him staggering back. He snatched up the fallen machete and plunged headlong into the scrub jungle.

28

They were behind him. He could hear their cries and curses as they battled through the tangled undergrowth. A thorned branch seemed to pluck at his eyes out of the night. Deftly he avoided it, the thorns raking across his scalp as he passed.

After the first few frantic yards he had stopped relying so heavily on the machete to clear his path. The scrub brush formed a tangled, matted jungle that defied travel in a straight line, but Braden was able to weave silently through the growth with the skill of a trained jungle fighter, using the machete only when the growth was too thick for passage and no alternative presented itself.

The sound of the voices behind him diminished, but he did not pause. He had already underestimated this pack once—he did not want to do so again.

In the darkness, he moved in an evil fantasy world of ghostly branches and grasping limbs that seemed to intertwine cunningly to bar his passage. Sweat soaked him. Thorns and branches tore his clothing, raked his flesh. The tallest of the growth was just a few feet higher than his head, but that made no difference to the nearly impenetrable barrier it presented to him.

Still, progress was possible if he fought off the lurking claustrophobia and moved along the paths of least resistance, as often as not on hands and knees or crouching low to the ground.

The thought of Cristina entered his mind. In the survival mode into which he had lapsed, she seemed far away and alien. Would she miss his presence? She had been on her way to bed when he left her.

Dennison was more likely to note his absence, although the missionary generally was in bed early. Besides, even noting that Braden was gone, he would have no reason to attach any significance to it before morning.

Braden's Omega watch had survived hand-to-hand combat, saltwater immersion and jungle flight, but he did not really need it. A glimpse through the intervening branches of the moon and stars reeling in the heavens above told him it was past midnight.

He halted at last, the machete dangling in his fist. His breathing was regular, only a little heavier than usual. He strained his ears, but heard nothing of his followers. Had they given up the chase? Surely they did not have the motivation to penetrate very far into this cruel, relentless undergrowth.

He thought he was still fairly well oriented, although keeping a sense of direction at night in the brush could be tricky. The sea should be to his right, the village at his back. Going in either of those directions might well only take him back into the arms of his enemies.

Ahead, if he remembered Cristina's ad hoc topography lesson, the curious jungle ran along the beach for miles. He went left. Eventually he hoped to emerge into the arid flatland which stretched to the mountains. Once he was free of the scrub, he should be able to return on foot to the village with relative ease.

The going was slow, but he was in no hurry now. Let the blood lust of the thugs subside, then perhaps they would return to the bars and cantinas. He thought with brief longing of the .38 back in his room. But he had had the opportunity to kill his attackers with his hands, and he had not taken it.

Something writhed from underfoot and he stepped quickly away from it, jamming his back into an inconvenient limb.

Snakes would be prevalent in this environment. A quick image of the swollen arm of the snakebitten youth in the mountains came to his memory. Soggy tennis shoes would provide scant protection against the fangs of some venomous serpent.

Salt from the seawater and drying sweat irritated him. His clothing was stiff and uncomfortable. He used his fingers to shove his hair back off his forehead and kept moving.

He began to sense that he was being watched. The hair at the back of his neck prickled, and he kept wanting to spin around to see what was behind him. He did once, machete half-raised as if to meet an attack. Nothing. A shadowy vista of eldritch skeletal limbs.

The jungle seemed to close in upon him as he worked his way through it. The feeling of being watched would not go away. He thought he saw shapes out of the corners of his eyes—low, dark shadows that slipped along the jungle floor and disappeared when he looked at them directly.

He tried focusing on them with the edges of his sight where night vision was strongest. Elusive as ghosts, they evaded his efforts. Nerves, he thought.

Then one of the shadows, as it disappeared, broke a tiny branch with an audible snap.

Braden froze, the hilt of the machete suddenly sweaty in his hand. He lifted it, but there was nothing there to fight. He stood, probing into the brush with all his senses. The shadows skittered silently away from him.

He could feel it now; he was being stalked.

He pivoted in a slow circle, sensing the presence of—what?—all around him in he dense growth.

As he completed the circle, he saw his first one—a compact four-legged shape that crept silently out of the underbrush and confronted him with black, gleaming eyes.

Its movement had betrayed it, and as he stared at it, he became gradually aware of another presence motionless a few feet to its side. He jerked his head and found himself staring all the way through bestial yellow eyes and into the savage soul of a great, gaunt tawny wolf of a creature there before him.

It stood as motionless as a statue, lips drawn back from pale fangs in a frozen soundless snarl. And behind it lurked other shapes, emerging into the open now, some boldly, some slinking across the ground. A low growl sounded behind him. They were back there too.

Dogs. A pack of feral dogs such as Cristina had described, such as had attacked a man on the beach. Here he was a stranger, the interloper in their domain.

Most of them were smaller than the yellow one who was undeniably their leader. They were mid-sized and shorthaired — these were the optimum characteristics for the survival of a dog in the wild. That did not make them any less dangerous.

The motionless pack leader was the exception, a large animal with short, tawny fur and the blunt muzzle and massive jaws of a Rottweiler. Shoulders bowed, head lowered slightly to protect its throat, it blocked his path.

There were at least a half dozen in front of him, more behind him. And he was not fooling himself. They were as dangerous as almost any human opponent. Their instinctive animal fear of man had long since dissipated through generations spent in close proximity, their awe and reverence for humans lost in the savagery of their existence.

With the machete and his training, he might have a chance if they attacked. But even if he drove them away, he would not do so without a mauling that would leave him crippled and as good as dead. And inevitably they would return for a second attack.

He had not shown fear or they would already have attacked him. They could smell the blood from the myriad superficial scratches that covered his body. The smaller dogs were more uneasy, moving restlessly, snarling fiercely, but waiting upon their leader. That one stood stock still, eyes blazing with primeval ferocity. As if in slow motion, Braden watched the lip curl further back from the gleaming fangs. He saw the head sink a little lower, although the eyes flared with undaunted savagery.

A tremor rippled over the lean animal body; the shoulders hunched. Any instant the leader would attack now, and he would be pulled down like a stag by ravenous wolves.

Slowly Braden shifted, redistributing his weight into a defensive position. The wrong sudden move would trigger the attack. He slid his right foot forward, shifting his left gradually behind it, lifting the machete, so that he stood at last in an unarmed combat stance with the machete presented like a fencer's blade.

The big yellow dog recognized the antagonistic posture of the stance, but Braden's movement had been too gradual to provoke a rush. It bristled now and snarled aloud—the first sound it had made. There was something uncertain in the sound. Braden realized that the animal sensed in him the same willingness to kill that it knew in itself.

Braden opened his mouth and yelled—a *kiai*, the karate attack yell, designed to freeze the opponent, to focus maximum concentration and strength. The sound blasted out, Braden's body and the machete he gripped vibrating with the effort of it.

The dogs, even the yellow one, recoiled from the awesome sound and Braden moved smooth and fast toward them, whirling the machete overhead and slashing it down, deliberately short of the beasts, yelling again as he did so.

For a frozen moment he thought the yellow dog would stand firm, would meet his charge with slavering fangs. Then it broke, lurching back, almost falling in its efforts to escape, its feet scrabbling at the ground. And then it was gone, its followers disappearing in its wake like phantoms. Braden heard their progress through the brush for a moment and then there was silence. The ones behind him had vanished also.

He drew a shaky breath and lowered the machete, almost dropping it as his fingers twitched involuntarily.

He did not think they would return, but he wanted to be out of their territory as quickly as possible. He slipped away through the jungle.

The remaining hours of darkness were a nightmare that took him back to recon patrols in Nam. He pushed through brush, slid and crawled past and under it, hacked it away when there was no other choice. Once he became disoriented and had to freeze, forcing the clawing panic down until he was certain in which direction to go.

He kept expecting the lupine form of the big yellow dog to materialize and spring for his throat, or the evil face of the ladron from the store to appear out of the gloom, lunging at him with a machete. He was getting soft, he thought, to get this rattled by a bunch of feral dogs and hyped-up villagers. He forced his emotions under control.

He did not know how far he had come, but it was still dark when he emerged at last on the arid plain, circling past the few remaining clumps of scrub brush.

To the east, light was beginning to show on the horizon. He crouched behind a small thicket for a time, recovering his strength, grateful to be out of the jungle. Had he prayed at all during the night's ordeal? He did so now.

The old instincts were in play now. He had been the subject of an assassination attempt, crude but almost effective nonetheless. The attack by the villagers had not been a random mugging of a wealthy gringo. There had been too many of them, and they had been too well-organized. The presence of the reinforcements, the extent and tenacity of the search, all indicated a planned effort at killing him.

Who had masterminded it? Tobias? He wanted that to be the answer. It was possible that the brujo had goaded his followers into executing his vengeance on the man who had humiliated him. But Braden did not think that was the case, and the alternative left him cold. Had the Operation tracked him down even here in this remote place? Had all his running, his attempts to cover his trail, been fruitless? Please, God, he prayed, don't let it be so.

It occurred to him that he should avoid the mission, or at least approach it in a circumspect manner until he had some idea of what was going on back in the village.

There were few habitations in this barren area, and he did not see another person. The sun rose higher, warming him. He felt stiff and sore and gritty. He had sustained no serious injuries, but the scratches from the thorns had developed into angry red welts and burned irritatingly.

On the outskirts of town, he recognized the house of a mission family and approached the door. He offered vague excuses for his appearance and received permission to use the primitive shower facilities behind the house in a cinderblock shower stall with no drain, only a hole in the base of the wall.

He showered and donned the clothes they had insisted he take. The pants were baggy, and the shirt tight across the shoulders and loose at the waist. Still he felt better.

He stayed off the main roads in the village, and on those he travelled, keeping to the side, near the huts. He passed a group of nicer homes, built of the inevitable concrete blocks, each with its T.V. antenna. By the standards of most American cities they would have been lower class. Here they were the height of affluence.

He was cautious when he passed a bar, but most of them were still closed at this hour. A friendly dog followed him for a distance. He could not stop himself from casting occasional wary glances at it. After a time it lost interest and left him.

He was negotiating a rutted refuse-strewn track behind one of the rabbit-warren enclaves when he heard rapid footsteps behind him.

"Senor..."

He turned sharply and found himself facing Jorge, the youthful street fighter.

29

Unthinkingly Braden assumed a subtle defensive posture. Jorge's trained eyes detected it, and he halted, lifting one hand. His face went tense. Braden could see the powerful muscles of his arms stretching the sleeves of the threadbare knit shirt he wore.

"No, Senor," Jorge said. "I do not want to fight you this time." He grinned nervously.

"What do you want?" Braden did not relax his stance.

"I have been wanting to talk to you." The youth was standing open before him. There was no betraying tension in his body to indicate hostility or an impending attack.

Slowly Braden relaxed. The events of the past twelve hours had roused the old paranoia to its former levels. "Talk about what?" His voice was still gruff.

"About what you said when we fought," Jorge answered hesitantly. "I have been thinking about it a great deal."

"Good." Jorge did not seem to be surprised to see him in his present condition, and there was something more pressuring the youth. "What else did you want?" Not so gruff now.

"I have been waiting for you, watching for you," Jorge went on with more confidence. "I have heard about what happened last night on the beach. If I had known about it beforehand, I would have helped you."

His sincerity was not to be doubted. Braden felt a twinge of guilt at his own distrust of the young man. "That's all right," he said awkwardly.

Jorge's eyes lit up. "Si! I know that you did not need any help. They say you fought a dozen of them who had machetes to a standstill and then eluded them in the ocean!"

"There weren't that many," Braden said. "How did you know where to look for me?"

"They said you finally escaped into the brush. I guessed that when you came back you would not come by the beach, but would cut through the brush and come back overland. And I knew you would not want to use the main streets. So I looked for you along the edge of town until I spotted you."

As predictable as that, Braden thought sorely. He was fortunate not to have had the whole criminal element of Puerto Madero awaiting him upon his return. He glanced around him. "Who are they?"

"They are followers of Tobias, the brujo."

"Then it was he who set me up?"

"No, Senor, it was the other man who went to Tobias to recruit the men who attacked you."

"What other man? Where is he?"

"A gringo. A big man." Jorge said. "Bigger than you and very handsome, but with cold little eyes. He moves like a fighter. I think he would be very dangerous. I wanted to warn you about him."

Braden clamped down hard on the emotions which threatened to overwhelm him. Control, he thought, control. He made his voice sound calm. "Tell me about this man, Jorge."

Jorge shrugged, obviously sensing Braden's disquiet. "He came to the village maybe two days ago, I am not sure. He has been staying around the bars drinking heavily."

"Go on," Braden prodded the youth.

"He began making inquiries about another gringo who might be here and might be working for a church. When he learned of you, it is said he became very excited. Someone told him of what happened between you and Tobias, and he said he wanted to see the brujo. The two spent a long time together and then the men attacked you on the beach. I did not know all of this until afterwards, Senor. When I heard what had happened, I began to ask questions."

Braden's mind raced. "You are right, Jorge, this man is very dangerous. Do not try to fight him for any reason. You say he has been drinking?"

"Yes, Senor. But not so much since you escaped last night. They say he behaves as if he has some great pain inside him that will not let him rest."

"Perhaps he does," Braden said absently. The drinking did not sound like Chandler, but it could be no one else. "Where is he now?" he asked.

"I believe at a cantina." Jorge gave brief directions, then hesitated. "Senor..."

"Call me Eric. What is it?"

"I still want to talk to you, Eric, about the things you told me. But it can wait, for I can tell that you have serious business with this man."

"Yes, very serious," Braden said tightly. His mind was meshing with furious speed, but there were things that needed to be said to this youth. "Thank you for telling me this, Jorge. And we will be able to talk later, I hope. But Senor Dennison can answer your questions better than I can, I think. He is a good man, and when he was young, he too led a gang in the streets."

"Es verdad? Is that true? I did not know that about him."

"It is true, and I want you to do something for me."

"Anything, Sen— Eric."

"Go to the mission. Tell Senor Dennison and Cristina, his assistant, that you have seen me and that the man I told them about is in town. Tell them I think it would be wise for them to go the the mountains for a few days. Do you understand?"

Jorge's face was troubled. "Yes, I understand. But is that all you want for me to do? I could go with you to see this man."

"No. That is something I must do myself. And remember what I told you, be very careful of him."

Jorge attempted to hide his obvious disappointment. "Very well, I will do as you ask. And," he added, "I will stay with your friends to guard them."

"All right." Urgency was beginning to hammer at Braden. "Now go quickly!"

Braden watched him leave at a jogging run. He drew a deep breath. He had done all he could to protect Cristina and Dennison. Now it was between him and Chandler.

He found the bar without trouble and stood for a time unobtrusively in an alley across the road from it. A few shabby men lounged in front of it, but he did not recognize any of them. He saw nothing else to alarm him.

When he finally started across the road one of the men out front straightened suddenly and stared for a moment. Then he said something to one of his comrades before hurrying into the bar.

Braden kept walking. He did not know what to expect, but tension coiled in him. Were they waiting inside to ambush him? A dozen thugs with machetes? Or was Chandler even now drawing a bead on him with the big .357?

As he drew near, the loungers slunk away, disappearing inside or around the corners of the frame building. Though the door stood open, he could not see into the dim interior of the bar.

He paused a little to one side of the doorway, but sensed nothing. He went through the door in one swift, positive movement.

Inside was a sawdust floor and wooden bar complemented by flimsy tables and battered chairs. Flies buzzed desultorily about the room. A few hard-eyed men occupied the bar and a couple of the tables. They were pretending to ignore both him and the lone man stretched idly in a sagging chair at the table in the corner.

Chandler.

He had his back to the wall, and, as Braden approached, he could see the lines, the flaccid muscles in the once handsome face. His dark, curly hair was oily and unwashed, and stubble gave his face a ragged look. Chandler, indeed, looked like he was just coming off a binge.

He wore wrinkled slacks and a grubby sleeveless T-shirt that displayed his muscular arms and outlined his powerful chest. He wore the .357 openly on a slip-on holster at his waist. A heavy bottle of tequila and a bowl of salt were on the table in front of him.

The little eyes that were set too close together in that decaying handsome face watched Braden as he crossed the room. With seeming unconcern, Chandler took a pinch of salt, flicked it into his mouth, then swept up the bottle and pulled hard at it. His face never changed, but the impact of the bottle as he set it down made the table shake.

He lifted the bottle again in a mocking salute to Braden and gave a devil-may-care grin, as the latter stopped in front of him. Chandler's eyes were stone-cold sober.

"Chandler," Braden broke the silence, his voice toneless.

Chandler gestured with the heavy bottle, the movement making the muscles of his arm flex and roll. His voice was mocking. "Why, fancy meeting you here. My old instructor and amigo. Have a drink, buddy. On me."

"No thanks," Braden said.

"Hey, that's right. You don't drink anymore. A sin isn't it? Well, at least have a seat." He lifted one extended leg to shove a chair out from the table.

After a moment Braden shifted it so that he could detect movement in the rest of the room and sat down carefully. Chandler smirked at him. "I've got my back covered too. Just like you taught me."

"I taught you a lot of things."

"That's right, you did." Chandler set the bottle down with a resounding thud. The movement of his head indicated the shabby bar, though his eyes never left Braden. "A little different from that fancy bar where we drank last time, eh?"

"Not so different."

Chandler laughed without a trace of humor. "Maybe not at that. Do you know how long those police held me back in Oklahoma City?"

"They probably wanted to hold you longer, no matter how long it was."

"Ha! That's the truth. They held me all that night and until the next afternoon. Andruss had to pull some strings to get me released. He wasn't too happy about that, I'll tell you."

"I can imagine." Braden knew Chandler was playing another round in whatever obscure game he had begun back in Oklahoma City. And it was a game, Braden had no doubt, in which his death was the ultimate objective.

Chandler was grinning. Braden noticed the quick-release snap on the holster he wore. It was undone. Chandler saw the direction of his gaze. "I've got to admit that I like it down here, buddy. I mean, this is my kind of town. Laid back, wide-open, like the Old West."

Braden didn't respond. He had played the game long enough.

Chandler tilted his head and regarded him curiously for a moment. "Just what in the hell do you think you're doin' here, Eric?" he burst out then. "Playing at being a missionary?"

"I'm not playing."

Chandler snorted contemptuously. Briefly something twisted in his eyes. "I guess you're not," he said slowly. "They say you even preached a sermon. Led some kind of a revival." His voice held disbelief.

"That's right. I'm sorry you weren't there."

"I've heard enough of your little sermons," Chandler snapped. He uttered a single succinct noun.

"I'm sorry you feel that way."

Chandler's brief lapse of anger appeared to fade. "But you're still good. I saw part of that fight on the beach. You've still got all the old moves, but you're playing soft, just fighting to defend yourself. Oh, I'll grant that it worked against these poor slobs. But if you tried that on me, I'd take you apart." His lips curled.

"Why go to all that trouble of hiring them to kill me?"

Chandler grinned with genuine enjoyment. "You mean why not just a bullet in the back some dark night? Blam! and it's over? Well, you keep worrying about that, but when I saw the setup here, heard how mad that fool witch doctor was at you, and realized what kind of control he had over some of these spics, I just couldn't resist a little fun. Ol' Tobias was all for it, and I made it worth his boys' time. Hell, they'd carve up their own mothers for fifty bucks American. And I had fun directing the search after you went swimming. They all wanted to just give up, said that the current would get you. But I knew better. We almost had you, but when you got into that brush even those cutthroats wouldn't follow you very far—not for anything."

A fly settled on Chandler's cheek. He did not seem aware of it. When he moved his head it buzzed away. "And Tobias, when he found out you escaped, just disappeared. Like that." He snapped his fingers. "God, he stunk. I wasn't sorry to see him go." He paused. "Heard you got a pretty lady friend here too," he continued after a moment, "and a missionary pal."

"Leave them out of it." Braden said coldly.

"Ah, finally got a rise out of you, didn't I, buddy?" Chandler's glee was sadistic.

"I told you, I'm not playing at being a missionary. I'm doing mission work, the Lord's work. He wants me to be here doing this. He told His followers to go out into the world and spread the Gospel. That's what I'm doing. These people need God. So do you, if you'd just admit it."

"I don't need anything or anybody," Chandler said flatly.

Far back in those dark eyes, Braden saw something that writhed in hopeless agony.

"Why are you drinking then?" he demanded. "You never needed that kind of crutch before. Are the nights getting too long for you? Do the victims come back to haunt you when you close your eyes? I've been there, Bob, I know."

"You don't know anything," Chandler bit the words out. "You're crazy."

"Am I? Why did you send those poor villagers against me? Amateurs against a pro? Was it because you were scared to do it yourself, scared to face me, because you know what I say is right?"

He was getting through, Braden thought in a portion of his mind. He was making Chandler see, forcing him to understand. He would win; he could feel it. He would do this thing.

"Damn you!" Chandler's fist smashed down onto the table, splintering wood, the impact sending the tequila bottle flying. His face was livid and he had come half out of his chair, towering over Braden.

"I told you I don't need any more of your sermons! I remember all those things you said about your Lord providing for you and protecting you, and giving answers to questions you didn't even know existed. Well, I asked myself all those questions, and I found all the answers I'll ever need!"

Despite himself, despite the success he'd been having scant moments before, Braden felt a chill at the naked ferocity in Chandler's face. He found he could not speak.

Chandler seemed to sense his advantage. Slowly he settled back in his chair, but his eyes pierced Braden like twin blades. "And all that about the Lord providing for you. Well, He hasn't done too good a job so far, has He? You're broke and on the run and you can't escape. No matter where you go, we track you down. He can't even provide you with a hiding place!"

Something had happened. Somehow the tables had

turned. Braden groped for words, and found none. All his recently acquired skill at preaching had disappeared now, when he needed it most. Just as his dreams of safety and sanctuary had disappeared.

"Did you really think you could get away from us?" Chandler's tone was contemptuous, scornful. "Even coming down to this backwater to play holy man? Once I learned that you'd made yourself a forged passport, we started anticipating you. With all this religion that you'd gotten, it was easy to guess you'd go to a church, and when we checked and found a missionary from Mexico had been in the area and had left with a new volunteer assistant, we put it together real fast. Andruss put some subtle pressure on the Mexican government to look for you and—bingo!—there you were. Is that the way your God provides for you, by setting you up for your own execution?"

He was right, Braden thought numbly. Everything he had done since that moment of revelation during Dennison's sermon back in Oklahoma had been based on the premise that his future and his actions were in the Lord's hands, that with His protection and guidance in leading him to Puerto Madero, he would be safe.

But he had been wrong. There had been no divine intervention to protect and hide him from the Operation and its wolves. His worst fears had been realized. His executioner sat before him and taunted him. His dreams of a life with Cristina had been just that, dreams. Reality, as harsh and uncompromising as a slug from Chandler's .357, had destroyed those dreams, and whatever other illusions he had fostered.

Relying on blind faith, he had played an amateur's game against the pros, and, inevitably, he had lost.

This knowledge closed in upon him with a dismal crushing grip. What was he doing talking religion to the man who had come to kill him? Even if it was true—and how could he even believe it himself now—Chandler, ruthless professional that he was, would have no time for such tripe.

He, Braden, had told Cristina that himself. All that remained now was for Chandler to finish the job. Unarmed against Chandler's .357, he had no chance. And further effort seemed somehow pointless to him anyway. Let his life end here, now, amidst the ruins of his futile dreams and his foolish delusions.

He became aware of Chandler glaring at him with wicked satisfaction. The younger man seemed to read his expectation. "You don't think I'm going to kill you in front of these peons, do you?" he jeered. "Go on and run. I'll have you where I want you when I'm ready."

30

Where was Eric? Cristina wondered. She had sensed a coiling tension in him the night before when he had seen her to her door. He had been worried about something and he had chosen to conceal those worries behind the stony barrier he could at times erect between them. She questioned whether he would ever really be all hers. Had his past—the ruthless violent netherworld from which he had emerged into her life—left him so marked by scars, internal and external, that he could never completely give himself to another person?

But she could concern herself with that question when she located him.

She had arisen expecting to find him already at work on the dorm or having breakfast with Howard. But Howard himself seemed to have disappeared also. She had checked his house, even going into Eric's room, feeling a silly little thrill as she did so. But that feeling vanished as she realized that his bed did not appear to have been slept in.

Nor were either of the men at the mission, and they couldn't have gone far because the Scout was parked in its usual place. Baffled, she stood in the mission door staring out into the backyard. A few chickens scratched lethargically.

A sound behind her made her turn.

Dennison had halted just inside the room.

"Do you know where Eric is?" she asked quickly.

Dennison shook his head. "I was going to ask you the same thing. I thought he might have turned up by now. I've been looking for him down at a couple of the stores."

"And?" she prompted.

He shrugged. "No luck. No one's seen him."

"Where could he be?" Cristina knew she spoke their thoughts aloud.

Dennison came to stand beside her. As always, there was a comfort in his presence, and she needed his strength badly in that moment. "He didn't come in last night as far as I know," he told her. "At least he hadn't when I went to bed."

She recounted her own fruitless efforts to find him and told of the strain she had sensed in him the night before.

"He was worried about us, I think," Dennison said. "About our being in danger because of him."

Impulsively she caught his hand. "Howard, I'm scared. Pray with me. Please."

They knelt there and prayed, but the solace which prayer usually brought seemed to elude her. When they were finished, Dennison reached out and gently brushed a tear off her cheek. "You love him, don't you?" he asked softly.

Wordlessly she nodded and he drew her to him and hugged her. "He wouldn't have just left," she murmured. "Not without telling us."

"His things are still here." Dennison patted her shoulder reassuringly and released her. She was remotely grateful that he did not try to comfort her with empty platitudes. "I'll get Luis and some of the others and we'll look for him," he said instead. "You need to stay here so we can check back with you periodically to see if you've heard from him."

She wiped her eyes and nodded, suddenly angry at herself for behaving like a helpless woman.

Except that she felt so helpless, weighed down by a sense of impending doom. Something was wrong; she could feel it.

After a last affectionate squeeze of her shoulders,

Howard started back toward the main entrance when he came to an abrupt halt. She looked past him, and it took her a moment to recognize the figure who had appeared in the doorway.

"Jorge," Dennison voiced his own recognition.

"Si." The young man came further into the mission with a curious mixture of hesitancy and his usual arrogance. His glance flicked almost nervously about the room, came to rest on her, then returned to Howard as he stopped in front of the missionary. "I need to talk to you."

"What about, Jorge?" Cristina could sense the effort Dennison was making not to be abrupt.

Jorge hesitated. "I have seen Hermano Eric," he reported then. "He asked me to come and ... warn you."

"Where is he? Is he all right?" Cristina found herself at Dennison's side.

"He is fine...for now."

Her initial relief was replaced by a growing despair as she listened to Jorge speak. "He fought these men with machetes and he wasn't hurt? You're sure?" she demanded when he paused.

Jorge's chin lifted. "He was not hurt, Senorita," he said proudly. "He is too good to be defeated by such as those."

"Go on," Howard's voice was terse, but this time it was he who interrupted as Jorge continued the saga. "You say this man Chandler is here? in Puerto Madero?"

"I do not know his name, but he is a dangerous man. This I can tell from seeing him," Jorge asserted.

"Where is Eric? We must go to him now!" Cristina could contain herself no longer.

"No, Senorita. You must not. Eric said that you should both go to the mountains for a few days to be safe."

"No!" Cristina exclaimed. "I'm not going to leave him here alone!"

"What else did he say?" Dennison wanted to know. "Did he tell you what he was going to do?"

"No, Senor, but I think he was going to see this man."

Cristina grabbed Dennison's arm so tightly it must have hurt. "Howard..."

"I know," he cut her off. "But wait a minute." His brow furrowed in thought. "If we try to look for him or to help him, we'll just get in his way," he said then. "He's a professional, or he used to be. I don't think we can help him. In fact I think we would just be a burden to him because he would be worried about us being in danger."

Cristina felt her shoulders sag. "But we can't just leave him here alone," she protested again.

"No, you're right," Dennison agreed. "We're going to stay here at the mission."

"I told Eric I would stay here with you to protect you!" Jorge interjected.

Surprisingly, Dennison did not object. He studied Jorge for a brief, gauging moment. "Okay," he responded, accepting the offer. He turned to Cristina and her face must have revealed her unspoken doubts. "We've got to trust Eric's judgment on this one. At least," he added, "for the time being." He appeared to think a moment longer. "If we haven't learned anything in a couple of hours, we'll go see if we can find him. In the meantime, we stay here and wait. Okay?"

Reluctantly Cristina nodded. She did not know if he was right; she only knew that to sit helplessly here and wait was all but unbearable. Lord, she thought, please protect him. Send your angels to guard and keep him.

She forced herself to help as Howard and Jorge closed and locked the doors. She recalled Eric's description of Chandler—of his ruthlessness, his deadly skills—and the precautions Howard was taking did not seem foolish at all. She knew, instinctively, that Eric would stay away from the mission rather than subject them to possible danger. There was no comfort in the thought. If Eric was in danger, she wanted, irrationally, to share it with him.

With the door closed, the circulation of air which served to cool the building was restricted. the heat seemed to hang as heavily as the passing minutes. She made an effort at occupying herself with menial tasks, but it was as if her mind and hands were no longer connected. At last she settled in a pew near the back, her legs tucked up under her, her eyes sightlessly scanning the Bible she tried to read. At the front of the sanctuary Dennison was engaged in earnest conversation with Jorge. What about? she wondered dully.

The crash of the double doors being kicked in seemed to hit her like a physical blow. Instantly she was on her feet, staring in shock and dawning horror at the wild-eyed man with the muscular body, dark curly hair, and handsome features who was framed there in the doorway.

Then she staggered as Jorge brushed past her to fling himself at the intruder.

31

Braden spotted a dirt track leading off the blacktop road into Tapachula and hauled the dilapidated old Chevy onto it, its ancient transmission groaning in protest as he shifted. He barely felt the jolts of the bald tires bouncing over the rough terrain. In his ears rasped Chandler's harsh mocking laughter which had followed him as he all but fled the cantina.

The old Chevy had been parked near the bar. It had been rewired for a pushbutton start and had turned over reluctantly when, on impulse, he had yanked the door and tried the button. He did not know whose car it was; he did not particularly care. It was enough that it ran and could carry him away from Puerto Madero and his relentless nemesis.

The track meandered. He drove over a primitive wooden cattleguard set in a gap in a jury-rigged barbed-wire fence. Skeletal cattle watched dumbly as the vehicle passed.

He drove almost blindly, despair and depression weighing on both his body and his mind. When the Chevy bottomed out in a rut and the engine died, he made no immediate attempt to restart it. The effort seemed too great. He crossed his arms on the steering wheel and rested his head on them. He felt lost and alone and scared, his mind revolving sluggishly in impotent circles of despair.

He did not know when he began to pray. Words came together in his mind and formed phrases, incoherent fragments of sentences that slowly evolved into heartleft pleas for guidance and understanding. With nowhere else to turn, he turned once again to the Lord.

Lord, I don't know what to do or where to go. Stay with me. Show me.

He recalled Chandler's cryptic parting words. What had he meant? How could he manipulate Braden as he had implied? He, Braden, would not go back to Puerto Madero; Chandler would have no way of tracking him this time. He would leave no trail, no betraying clues. He would not go back and place Cristina and Dennison in danger.

Cristina.

Chandler had known about her and Dennison. Then they were already in mortal danger, for Chandler would never believe that they did not know his whereabouts. Further, with the knowledge of Braden and the Operation which Chandler would assume Braden had imparted to them, they would be a liability, a potential danger which Chandler could not afford to leave behind him.

The Chevy started with a grinding sound when he hit the button. He threw it into a tight turn and kept the pedal on the the floor as he ripped up through the gears. The distance back to the blacktop road seemed endless, and he feared that at any moment the vehicle would quit on him altogether.

But it did not. Once he reached the blacktop, he coaxed a fraction more speed out of it. Behind him he could see the cloud of black exhaust fumes being emitted by the ancient overburdened engine. Grimly he kept driving.

It was sometime past noon, he noted absently. How long since he had fled Chandler's presence in the bar? He did not know. Time had been distorted for him. What would Chandler have done? Gone directly to the mission? Or sat with his tequila and gloated over his victory? Braden didn't know. For all his taunting of Braden, Chandler had not been behaving much like a professional himself. Therefore his actions were difficult to predict.

Braden recalled the pain in Chandler's eyes. Jorge's diagnosis of some intense inner agony might be correct. In any case, in his present twisted mood, Chandler would be extremely dangerous and unpredictable.

The people on the streets hurried out of his way as he sent the old car lumbering through the village, dust billowing behind him. He had no time for their uncomprehending stares. Urgency had become a pounding beat within him.

He barely saw from the corner of his eye the hobbling figure who waved him down from beside a sagging shack not far from the mission. He hit the brakes, and the engine sputtered and died as the vehicle rocked to a stop. He was out of it even as the dust began to settle.

"Jorge!" he could hear the surprise and pain in his own voice as he recognized the youth. For this was a Jorge far different from the cocky, partially reformed juvenile delinquent he had faced just hours before. The youth moved with a decided limp, and one arm hung at an awkward angle. His lower lip was swollen, one eye blackened almost shut.

"Eric!" he gasped past his swollen lip. "He is waiting for you. In the mission."

A steel band had tightened around Braden's ribs. "Cristina?" he bit out. "Dennison? Are they all right?" He could taste the settling dust.

Jorge gestured with his good arm. "I don't know. I—I think so. Senor Dennison and I tried to stop him." Jorge shook his head in disbelief. "He beat us both, with his bare hands. In seconds."

For the first time Braden saw the sweat beaded on Jorge's forehead. The youth was obviously in extreme pain. His arm was broken or dislocated or both; his leg was also badly damaged.

Jorge saw the direction of his gaze. "Senor Dennison is not so badly hurt as I am, I think. I would not stop fighting."

He swayed and Braden reached out to catch him. But Jorge straightened proudly.

"Thank the Lord you're alive," Braden told him. "And don't worry about it. Chandler is good. I trained him."

Jorge stared at him with wide eyes.

"What happened next?" Braden demanded.

With his opposition disposed of, Chandler had produced a gun. Braden recognized the description of the .357. He had herded Cristina and Dennison out into the yard behind the mission, and released Jorge with a message for Braden.

"He told me to look for you; that he knew you would be coming back to protect your—the Senorita. He said if I saw you, to tell you that he was waiting and that there would be no more sermons this time. He said you would understand."

"I do." Braden's face felt tight as if the skin were stretched tautly across his skull. "Listen to me, Jorge," his voice echoed hollowly in his ears. "Go to a doctor. Do you know one?"

"Si."

"You may need a hospital. I think you will. Thank you for waiting for me. It is a very brave thing you have done. You are mucho hombre—very much a man."

Jorge's face was troubled now in addition to the pain. "Do not go after him, Eric. I have seen him fight. He waits to kill you. I could get help—"

"No." Braden cut him off firmly. "This is between him and me and maybe Someone Else now. I'll handle it. You do like I said."

As Jorge limped off, casting one last disturbed glance over his shoulder, Braden looked down the road to the familiar front of the mission.

Chandler was there waiting for him. No more sermons, he had said. And no more games, Braden thought. Chandler was there to kill him, with Cristina and Dennison as hostages.

There were procedures for such a situation. Tactics and strategies to outmaneuver and outwit a man with hostages in a known position. But Chandler knew all the moves and countermoves, and he would be perfectly willing to kill either of his hostages at the slightest provocation.

There were really no choices at all, Braden thought with an odd kind of relief. He had spent long enough relying partly on himself and his acquired wisdom. Time now, at last and in all things, to finally trust fully in the Lord.

He strode openly down the dirt street to the mission.

The sanctuary was deserted, and Braden walked down the aisle to the front. A profession of faith, he thought. A rededication. He stepped out into the yard where he and the others had shared soft drinks and coconuts only the day before. Almost immediately he saw Cristina and Dennison seated at the old wooden table. They were secured to it somehow, he was certain. Handcuffed perhaps. A sense of gratitude welled from deep within him. They were still alive.

"Eric! Over there!" Cristina cried, trying to rise, but prevented by her restraints.

Braden turned slowly in the direction she had indicated, toward the half-completed dormitory wing. Chandler stepped into the view in the doorway. He still wore the same wrinkled clothing; the .357 dangled now at his side in one big hand. He had a look of baffled surprise on his haggard features, and Braden realized that the assassin had been concealed in the dorm, using an unfinished window to cover the yard area. He had expected Braden's approach to be covert, by the back, and he had been waiting for him.

For a moment Braden stared into his eyes across the twenty feet separating them.

"What are you doing?" Chandler burst out at last. "Are you crazy coming in here like that?"

"No, Bob," Braden said softly, "I'm not crazy."

The big gun came up smoothly then, centered between Braden's eyes. He stared into the hole of the bore, saw the lead tips of the slugs in the cylinder.

"Bang!" Chandler snapped savagely. "You're dead!"

"That's in God's hands," Braden said gently. "It really always has been, Bob, even when you tracked me down here. I just didn't want to let loose of the controls, too used to making my own decisions, I guess. But the Lord wanted me to learn a few things. I think He wants you to learn them too."

"I'm going to kill you! Don't you know that?"

"That's not up to you."

"Damn you! It is too! Nobody walks away from the Operation and lives!"

"I did."

Chandler's features twisted and for a moment Braden thought he would pull the trigger. The bore of the gun looked huge. "Why did you come back here?" Chandler demanded then.

"You knew I'd be back," Braden told him. "You set it up like that."

"But not like this! Not walking in here unarmed so I can kill you! That doesn't make any sense!"

"Lots of things don't make sense. What's happened to me is one of them. Like I said, all of this has been in the Lord's hands from the very beginning."

"God deserted you!" Chandler cried. "I proved that back at the bar. I tracked you down. Your precious God couldn't protect you from me!"

"But He has. And He let you track me down so I could learn a few things. You, see I committed my life to Him, but I didn't want to quite give up making the decisions. When I felt led to come down here, I didn't rely on the Lord to provide me with a way. Instead, the first thing I did was go out and get an illegal passport in a false name. Lies, all of it. That's no way to serve God. And He used that mistake to let you find me here. But I still wasn't ready to let go. Cristina told me once up in the mountains that things are always beyond our control; that's why in the end we have to rely on Christ."

Chandler's expression was tormented, but the gun never wavered. Braden kept talking, verbalizing the things that had come clear to him, speaking to himself almost as much as to Chandler. "In that bar, I got cocky. I was trying to win you over to the right side all by myself, leaving the Lord out of it, just like I left Him out of so many decisions. He let me see all that after I left the bar, after I ran. I had just been fooling myself in thinking I had turned everything over to Him. I was finally at the end of my own resources, and I didn't have anywhere else to turn." He paused. "I think you're about at that place now."

"I told you I don't need anybody," Chandler retorted, but the gun slowly lowered until he held it at waist level, still directed at Braden.

"The Lord's been working on you from the very beginning of this," Braden went on. "That's why you've played amateur games with me, passing up opportunities to kill me and instead forcing confrontations. You kept saying you didn't want to hear what I had to say, but you kept coming back."

"No," Chandler's mouth twitched as he spoke. "I've outmaneuvered you, proved that I was better than you. Admit that I have. Admit it!"

"You haven't proved anything," Braden's voice was low. "They say there are no atheists in foxholes, and you're in a foxhole now, Bob. You have been for a long, long time. Like I told you, I know, I've been there."

"You couldn't handle it!" Chandler exclaimed. "That was your problem. You couldn't take the pressure. You were too weak!"

"Was I? You told me once yourself that I seemed stronger somehow since my 'religious experience.' Well, I am stronger, but it's not my strength. It's the Lord's."

"I don't need your phony religion! I told you that!" The hand that held the .357 was trembling now, and Chandler's face wore the agonized snarl of a wolf with its leg in a steel-jaw trap.

Braden was relentless. "I didn't think you could possibly

be under conviction, but I was wrong. Anybody can come to the realization that he is a sinner. Even you."

"No!" Chandler's denial was a vehement shout. He took two steps closer to Braden, and the gun never wavered. "You sound like your stinking missionary buddy and that slut!" He indicated the captives with a vicious jerk of his head. "They kept talking to me, trying to feed me that garbage! But I told them what I'll tell you, I'm gonna kill you all! Do you hear me?"

"That won't change things," Dennison spoke up for the first time from where he sat. "The truth of what we say will still be with you even if you kill us."

Braden envied Dennison, the calmness in his voice.

"That's not the truth!" Chandler's head snapped around toward the missionary. "You're lying! All of you."

"Listen to us, Bob, please," it was Cristina. Her face was strained, but her voice held the same calm assurance as Dennison's had. "You can't keep living like you are. Ask Eric, he knows. It's a dead end. The Bible says that everyone has sinned, and that the consequence of that sin is death, a spiritual death. You don't want that for yourself. You can't want it."

"She's right," Dennison joined in. "The only way to escape that spiritual death is to turn your life over to Christ. He died for your sins. You've been serving the Operation. You've made it your god. But it can't save you. It can't keep you out of Hell. Only Christ can do that, but you have to commit youself to serve him rather than the Operation or anything else in this world."

Chandler's body was shaking as if charged by an electric current. But when he moved it was like a stalking cat. He crossed the remaining distance between him and Braden and faced him. Braden saw pain and fear, hatred and savagery in the close-set eyes. And he saw something else, something too full of old meanings for him to mistake.

Under conviction or no, Chandler was primed to kill.

There was no way to try for the gun, Braden thought, but he knew he would do it anyway. Because with him dead, Chandler would turn on Christina and Dennison vent his murderous wrath on them. Braden would have to try to take him now, for better or worse, because there was really no other choice.

But, Braden thought, was that his decision to make? He stood immobile.

"You're first, buddy," Chandler snarled with evil savagery. The trembling had vanished. His knuckles whitened as he began to pull the trigger.

Help us, Lord, Braden thought, prayed.

"Bob, don't!" Cristina cried, and Chandler wheeled toward the sound, the gun swinging with him. For the first time Braden was clear of its threat, and he struck fast with the edge of his palm at Chandler's wrist. The big .357 fell to the dirt unfired.

Immediately Braden kicked it away, anticipating Chandler's grab for it. But Chandler ignored it. He spun to his left, coming all the way around to deliver a backfisted strike to the temple that Braden, intent on kicking the gun clear, could not completely avoid. Had the blow landed squarely, it could have fractured Braden's skull. But it hit high as Braden moved, staggering him sidewise.

Braden got his hands up as Chandler came after him. There was no hesitation on Chandler's part. Gone was the indecision. His moves were fast and hard and very competent. He had become a professional killer intent on doing his job, and going about it with every factor of skill he possessed.

Chandler's hands blurred in a flurry of strikes, slashing, hooking, punching, looping in from the outside. Braden had room and he went backwards before the attack, accepting the rush, gauging the rhythm of that onslaught of blows. And his parries and blocks and deflections turned the blows, baffled them, struck them aside. He came up against one of the palms, slipped deftly away from it to avoid Chandler's strike.

Chandler drew back, still poised, still on balance, but with anger twisting his handsome features. Braden had not struck a single offensive blow.

"I told you what would happen if you tried to fight like that with me," he spat the words from between gritted teeth.

"Give it up, Bob," Braden said.

Chandler leapt, spinning, and the heel of his right foot came at Braden's skull like the whirling rotor of a helicopter.

Braden evaded it with a brief duck of his head, and snapped his left arm up to block the left roundhouse kick that Chandler ripped next out of the whirling sequence. He had kicked twice high, and he let his left foot meet the ground, then used it again to fire a side-thrust kick low at Braden's middle, an unorthodox move that struck home.

Chandler's driving foot rammed the air out of Braden's lungs, doubled him slightly. Chandler swiveled up on his toes, his flattened left hand going back across his chest in preparation for a slashing chop to the back of Braden's offered neck. Even as the blow swept down, Braden bent further over and lunged, throwing his shoulder into Chandler's midriff, wrapping an arm around him, twisting to get his hips out and heave Chandler over him in body throw.

Chandler hit the ground hard, lashing out with his feet. Braden skipped back to evade the kicks. He had only a moment to regain his breath. Chandler came back erect, even as the knowledge grew in Braden that he played a dangerous game with the man, in a sense even more deadly than the defensive fight he had waged against the machete-wielding thugs on the beach. For Chandler was trained, an expert in the killing arts just as he himself was. Chandler's hands alone could be every bit as devastating as the heavy blades of the machetes.

Chandler was breathing heavily too now, but more from rage and frustration than exertion. He circled Braden and deliberately left an opening. "Come on," he snarled. "You can't take me and you know it."

Braden pivoted to match the relentless circling. Abruptly Chandler's right foot kicked high at Braden's jaw. Braden dropped, scything his leg around at Chandler's anchor leg. But the kick had been a feint, and Chandler hopped over the sweeping leg, switched feet as deftly as a ballet dancer and snapped his left foot into Braden's face.

The impact lifted Braden or he might have gone down. He staggered back; his face had gone frighteningly numb. Chandler snarled his triumph, and lunged with stiffened fingers at his solar plexus. Desperately Braden twisted aside, felt the spear-hand blow glance from his ribs. He caught Chandler's extended arm with both hands and heaved to pull him on past.

It didn't work on Chandler—his stance was too good, his balance too perfect. But it allowed Braden to slip behind him, to clamp his right arm around his throat from behind. Fast, then, before Chandler could counter, he bent the younger man back over his extended leg and dumped him hard on the ground.

Again Chandler lashed at him with both feet as he went down. Braden batted one flailing leg aside hard enough, he knew, to hurt as he dodged back and clear. Chandler bridged and flipped back up onto his feet like an acrobat. His big shoulders heaved, and his curse was foul.

"I taught you everything *you* know," Braden told him grimly. "What made you think it was everything *I* know?"

Chandler shook his head in mute denial. He edged closer, cautious now, but the frustration and rage still flared in his eyes. He flicked out a backfisted blow in a feint, then launched another side-thrust kick, following it with the real backfist strike that snapped through the air. Braden chopped down, diverting the kick past his hip as he leaned back out of range of the back-fisted follow-up.

Chandler dropped his kicking foot to the ground, planted it and spun, hooking his other leg back and around at Braden's groin. Braden dropped crossed arms to smother the kick, hunching to avoid the spinning axe-hand strike that would follow it. The force of the kick shoved his arms against his body, but he got a grip on Chandler's calf and lunged with it like he was using a battering ram, sending Chandler stumbling awkwardly forward.

Chandler recovered his balance and whirled. The trembling washed over him again like a wave; his face twitched spasmodically. But he wasn't done yet, and he was still very, very dangerous.

He came back in with a front snap kick, waiting until Braden's block had already started before he folded his leg and converted the move into a high roundhouse kick. But Braden's hands didn't have as far to travel as Chandler's foot, and he was able to block the kick using both hands, catching the foot in mid-air inches from his skull.

There was a counter for this, but it required a superb athlete to accomplish it. Chandler was superb. He flexed his anchor leg, then leaped to kick Braden in the face with his free foot. Braden released his hold with one hand and caught that second foot too. He yanked up and back with both arms. Chandler, with no way to break his fall, slammed to the ground on his shoulders and back.

Braden moved away from Chandler. Each breath sent a stab of pain through him. His face hurt, and his head throbbed. He was dimly aware of the strained faces of Cristina and Dennison. He watched Chandler climb to his feet.

The younger man straightened. His breath came in panting gasps. His face was a mask of mingled rage and consternation. Braden opened his mouth to speak, and Chandler let out a despairing cry from the anguished depths of his soul and flung himself forward. He came with all the abandon of one of the machete-men, uplifted fist smashing down and around in a terrible hammer blow.

Braden stepped to the side, not even bothering to counter. Chandler's momentum sent him stumbling past to sprawl on his face in the dirt. Braden stepped in, put his foot between Chandler's shoulderblades and bore down hard.

For a moment Chandler pressed his palms against the dirt and strained trembling up against the pressure. Braden's face hardened and he thrust him back flat.

"Give it up, Bob," he panted. "I don't want to hurt you anymore. I've beaten you. Admit it."

After a moment Braden lifted his foot and turned his back on Chandler to cross to Cristina and Dennison. They had been bound in wire, not cuffs as he had first supposed. He released them, unwinding the wire from their wrists and hugged Cristina to him, accepting the firm clasp of Dennison's hand.

With his arm around Cristina's shoulders, he turned back to Chandler. The younger man was on his feet, swaying, his features contorted, his shoulder slumped.

"Go on, Bob," Braden told him sorrowfully. "Get out. Leave us alone."

Chandler's mouth worked. "You're not going to kill me?" he managed in disbelief. "You're letting me go?"

Braden felt a great tiredness settle on him. "I don't want to kill you, Bob. I'm not even sure I could."

"I'll follow you," Chandler said. "You know I will. I won't give up till I've killed you."

"My God will protect me," Braden answered.

The words might have been one of the blows Braden had refused to strike. Chandler staggered. "You mean it—" he started, then broke off. "I never believed—"

He took two steps backwards, then his legs buckled. He dropped to his knees, buried his face in his hands, and wept convulsively.

32

Andruss looked up from behind that barren metallic desk as they entered his office, and for just a moment a trace of shock disturbed his austere features. One shoulder dipped slightly.

"Cool it." Chandler had the .357 in his hand. "No alarms. Push back from your desk." His grin was tight. "You know the routine."

For a long, gauging moment, Andruss stared at Chandler, and Braden remembered the dissecting power of that gaze. Chandler's grin never faltered. They had separated upon entering, one of them moving to either side of the door. Braden's own .38 was undrawn.

At last Andruss exhaled almost inaudibly and pushed his chair back from his desk. Braden had an eerie feeling of deja vu. For the first time Andruss directed his gaze toward him. "I told you not to send him after me," Braden said.

That expression of subtle distaste lifted one corner of Andruss' thin lips. "I suppose I should have anticipated this," he addressed Braden. "You have managed to infect him as well."

"Ain't that the truth," Chandler answered him. "I'm a born-again child of God." His grin was irrepressible.

Now Andruss looked pained.

"I did not think he could get to you like this, Robert."

"He didn't," Chandler said flatly, some of his levity fading. "Jesus Christ did. Eric just showed me the way."

The office looked the same, Braden thought. As barren and sterile as ever. Yet now neither it nor its occupant held any fears for him. He kept his eyes on Andruss, but watched Chandler from the edge of his vision and remembered the aftermath of their duel in Puerto Madero.

"You're making a mistake," Andruss' voice was level. He was concentrating on Chandler.

"No mistake," Chandler was firm. "And didn't you use that line on Eric? Just like old times, isn't it?"

Andruss' hands, where they rested on the arms of his swivel chair, rose upon their fingertips like great pale spiders poised for attack. "You, better than anyone, Robert, should realize the foolishness of this, the futility of it. You can still change your mind." He leaned forward slightly. "It is not too late. Don't give up your career by listening to a fool, a neurotic who buckled under pressure. You have your gun, use it on him. Now! I'll forget all this. Do you understand?"

Chandler's laughter was mocking. " My 'career,' you said? As what? Your private hit man? Your pet mercenary? And you don't seem to understand. I'm not following Eric, or obeying him. I've answered a calling from One higher than you or the Operation or anything in this world. You're wasting your breath."

The arachnoid hands relaxed slightly. "And so you've joined forces."

"That's right," Chandler agreed. "And we work pretty good together. Right, buddy?"

"Listen to him, Andruss," Braden said. "God loves you too."

"This discussion is pointless!" Andruss snapped abruptly. "I assume you have come to tender your resignation too, Robert."

"Yeah, I guess you could say that," Chandler said facetiously.

"Very well." Abruptly Andruss rose to his feet, an ominous towering presence in the room. His dark enigmatic eyes were harsh. "I shall have the proper paperwork prepared. There is no place for either of you in this organization, and, believe me, I want you out. There will be no repercussions, no attempts to eliminate either of you. The sooner all ties between you and the Operation are severed the more satisfied I will be."

"Tell us another one," Chandler jeered.

Braden took a step forward, his face hard, and Andruss actually retreated a bit before him. "You listen to me, Andruss," Braden's voice had gone as hard as his face. "I've had this discussion with you before, and you didn't pay any attention. This time maybe you will. Don't ever think, even for a second, that finding the Lord has made us fools. You'd have hit men after us before we made it out of the building. But you remember a few things. We're the best you had. We made it into this country and through your little defenses and even into your office before you knew we were coming. We know this organization inside and out. Don't you even dream of coming after us, or you personally and your whole organization will be sorry."

"Such melodramatics are hardly necessary." There was a barely perceptible undertone of strain in Andruss' voice.

"No melodramatics," Braden said coldly. "No bluffs. But you hear what I have to say. We have joined forces. And like Bob said, we make a good team. We've already proven that down in Central America two days ago."

Something in Braden's voice caught Andruss' attention, made him try to vivisect Braden with those razor eyes. He failed. "What do you mean?" he asked tightly.

"I mean that Bob and I swung down and made a stopover in Central America before we came up here," Braden told him. "And if you're expecting to hear from Hansen and the hit squad you sent down there to take out Preston Gates, don't hold your breath." Braden waited and let the understanding dawn slowly in Andruss' eyes. "That's right," he went on then. "Like I said, we're the best you had. It wasn't hard at all for us to foil the assasination attempt and arrange to have your goons taken into custody."

For the first time Braden saw an emotion register in Andruss' eyes. Could it actually be fear?

"Since they were U.S. citizens, Gates pulled a few strings and had them turned over to the American Embassy security force down there. He gave them a choice. They could either agree to testify to his Committee or be released to the local officials and be tried as terrorists." Braden's grin was cold and hard. "They broke, Andruss. Hansen himself is down there right now giving sworn depositions on everything he knows about you and the Operation."

"Which means you've had it, buddy," Chandler broke in cheerfully. "Your days are numbered. The good Senator is going to come down on you and yours with both feet."

Andruss looked wordlessly from one to the other of them. His features had become pinched and strained and he had actually gone a little pale, Braden noticed.

"The last we heard, the Senator was enjoying hearing all about your scheme to kill him," Braden went on relentlessly. "I warned you not to come after us before, but truthfully, we're really not too worried about that. By the time Gates and his commission get through cleaning up the Operation's illegal covert activities, you won't be in any position to order a hit on a mosquito, much less pose any threat to either of us. Funny how the Lord works things out, isn't it?"

He looked at Andruss one last time, staring into those hitherto unfathomable eyes. He saw their owner's baffled defeat and impotence mirrored there.

He moved to the door and opened it a crack. Chandler kept the .357 pointed at Andruss. "Clear," Braden reported after a moment. Chandler nodded and backed to the door. The brief glance exchanged there with Braden said he, too, had read their victory in Andruss' eyes.

"Let's get out of here," Chandler said aloud.

*   *   *

The completed dormitory wing of the mission, with bunk beds installed, would house a half dozen youngsters of each sex. The beds were hand-made, as were the other crude furnishings. Much had been accomplished, Braden thought, during his and Chandler's absence.

"Impressive, isn't it?" Dennison, standing in the boys' section, included the whole structure with an expansive sweep of his arm. "They've really worked hard while you were gone. Even Pablo, Rosa's husband, got in on it. He's quite industrious when he wants to be. And we've already got kids ready to move in."

Cristina tossed her head toward Braden and grinned at Dennison's obvious enthusiasm. Braden reached out, put his arm around her shoulders, and drew her to him.

"Senor Santego and his wife have agreed to act as house parents," Dennison was continuing. "They will move into Cristina's apartment when you two leave." A note of sadness crept into Dennison's voice. "I know we need to get a mission started up in the mountains, but I sure am going to miss you both."

"Oh, we'll come visit," Cristina was quick to reassure him. "The mountains aren't that far away. And we can take any overflow of kids you have up there with us. We've already planned it."

"The wedding will need to be soon so that Bob can move on," Braden reminded them. "It's not a good idea for him and me to be together for very long at any one time until we're sure the Operation's illegal activities have really ceased."

Cristina bumped him with her hip. "I love it when he's romantic," she confided in Dennison.

"Day after tomorrow soon enough?" Dennison wanted to know. "We'll need a little time to get ready for the crowd.

You two are a hot item. We'll have nearly all the church members here, plus a good turnout from your potential congregation in the mountains. Your wedding's going to be a real social event in this area."

"Couldn't you just do it now and get it over with?" Braden asked. Cristina bumped him again.

Dennison grinned. "Come on. Let's check with your best man."

He led the way out into the yard. The sky was a brilliant azure, the sun overhead casting an emerald glow through the coconut palms.

Cristina was wearing her habitual jeans and loose lightweight blouse. Braden liked the feel of her nearness. He found himself unwilling for her to be away from him for any length of time, or even out of his arm's reach.

"And this was where you fought?" came the unmistakable voice of Jorge as they neared the two figures seated at the rough-hewn wooden table.

"That's right," Chandler told him, pausing to slice a piece of meat from the split coconut on the table. "You see," he went on then, "I was taking it easy on Eric cause he's an old man and I didn't want to hurt him." He glanced around and feigned surprise at seeing them. "Oh, hi, Eric." He gave an unabashed grin. "Say, I've been meaning to ask you—is there any payment involved for my acting as your best man? My paychecks seem to have stopped." He swatted at a gnat.

"We'll take a love offering at the wedding to help you out," Braden told him drily.

Jorge, Braden noticed, as the others talked, had largely recovered from his struggle with Chandler. The former street fighter, Dennison had told him, had accepted the Lord during Braden's and Chandler's absence. "He's turning out to be a pretty good assistant," Dennison had said. "He's talking about going into the ministry full time."

"Incidentally,"— Dennison was addressing Braden now — "I made one trip to the mountains to look for a site for your mission. I might have found one."

"Subject to Cristina's approval of course," Braden added. She smiled at him.

His mission. The words still sounded odd to Braden. But the concept of him and Cristina running a mission in the remote jungle area of the mountains was becoming more and more real to him now that he had made that decision.

There was much he didn't know about this new calling, but he had two good teachers in Dennison and Cristina. And, of course, the One who had given him this calling would always be with him.

He recalled the people of the mountain villages—the snakebitten youth, the earthquake victim he and Cristina had revived, Jose, and all the others. There was a need among those people as Dennison himself had said. And it was likely that Tobias still lurked in the jungle, waiting to spread his evil. But God loved Tobias too. Yes, Braden reflected, there was much work to be done.

And what else was it Dennison had said during his sermon back in Oklahoma? A covenant with death. He, Braden, had had such a covenant. But, he thought now, the Lord had voided it and replaced it with a different kind of covenant. A covenant with life.